Escape to the North

Escape to the North

Carlos Hugo Rojas

PIÑATA BOOKS
ARTE PÚBLICO PRESS
HOUSTON, TEXAS

Escape to the North is funded in part by grants from the Texas Commission on the Arts. We are thankful for its support.

Piñata Books are full of surprises!

Piñata Books

An imprint of
Arte Público Press
University of Houston
4902 Gulf Fwy, Bldg 19, Rm 100
Houston, Texas 77204-2004

Cover design by Ryan Hoston
Credit photo by Debbie Christoforatos

Library of Congress Control Number: 2025946429

∞ The paper used in this publication meets the requirements of the American National Standard for Information Sciences—Permanence of Paper for Printed Library Materials, ANSI Z39.48-1984.

Escape to the North © 2025 by Carlos Hugo Rojas

Printed in the United States of America

October 2025–November 2025
5 4 3 2 1

This book is dedicated to all women, especially the single mothers whose strength, courage and love carry generations forward. I also dedicate this book to my mother, whose resilience continues to inspire me. She is no longer here to see it completed, but her memory threads itself through every page.

The Omen

Santa Rosa de Copán, Honduras, April 2014

Mamá came through the bead curtain, leaving it rattling behind her. "Get up, girls. And get Juanito up, so he can go out to the henhouse. I need eggs to make breakfast."

That was our *mamá*, María, getting us up in her usual manner. Her strict, yet tender voice, had a gentle way of waking us up on school mornings. Behind her call came the smell of bacon. It awakened my hunger before I could even open my eyes. I was not fully awake when I heard wings flapping on our windowsill.

"Oh, no." I covered my head in an attempt to muffle the loud noise.

The rooster puffed up his chest and let out his irritating, morning crow. My little brother had named him Wally after our dog that had died a year ago. Juanito always bothered Mamá to let him have another dog, but she refused.

"Why does that stupid rooster have to stand on our windowsill and crow every morning?" I asked my sister, Julia, who lay next to me. I pulled the blankets off my face, wishing I had more time to sleep.

Wally flapped his wings and crowed again. Julia and I stared at the rooster who looked back at us proudly.

"Look at the way he stares at you," Julia said.

We propped ourselves up on our elbows, wondering how to deal with this stubborn rooster. I made eye contact with Wally, and he stared back at me, tilting his head slightly. I got out of bed and went toward the window.

"Shoo! Shoo!" I yelled.

He flew away before I could reach him. A smile drew across my face when I saw Wally clucking away.

"I wish Mamá would make soup out of him. That would be delicious revenge ... literally."

I went to the window and took a deep breath. It was a beautiful spring morning. The mountains slowly came into view as the fog lifted. The scent of the jungle brought me fully awake, energizing my inner being. I stretched my arms up and yawned.

Julia came in carrying a basin filled with cold water. "Wash your face. When you're finished, dump it and get fresh water for Juanito."

I splashed the cold water on my face. It stung my skin, but it cleared my mind from my earlier frustrations with Wally.

Julia was looking through her clothes. I admired her so much. She was eighteen years old. Her light-brown hair cascaded in light curls below her shoulders. Her big, brown eyes always seemed full of wonder. She had a small, pointed nose that gave her a conceited look, yet her smile reassured every one of her good nature. She loved to play sports in school and had the body to show for it. Many good-hearted boys liked Julia, but she was in love with her boyfriend.

Mamá said that I was just as beautiful as Julia, only more of a tomboy. That was the reason boys hardly noticed me. I thought that was a good thing. I would be turning fifteen tomorrow. Although my body began to look more and more like Julia's, I was not yet interested in boys. My hopes were to become an elementary school teacher someday. That day was not far off. Plans were already in place to build a school in Santa Rosa.

I went to the next room where Juanito shared the bed with Mamá. At ten years old, he dreamed of becoming a fisherman like Papá. He didn't have our skin tone or hair color. His dark skin and straight black hair were the young image of our father. Mamá had put him in charge of the chickens to teach him responsibility. That included feeding them, gathering the eggs in the morning and keeping the henhouse clean. I glanced at the alarm clock. It read 6:00 a.m. Juanito slept soundly beneath a bundle of blankets.

I sat down on the edge of the bed and shook him. "Juanito, Mamá needs you to get up and gather the eggs."

"No," he said, rolling away from my hand. He pulled the blankets tight around his head. "Go away."

"If you don't get up by the count of three, I'm going to tickle you." I walked my fingers firmly over the blankets, threatening his small ribs and leaned into his ear. "And you know that I can turn into the evil tickle monster if you don't get up."

Juanito ignored me. I dug my fingers into the blankets.

"Okay! Okay!" he shouted, wiggling away. "I'm up already." He came out from under the blankets. "Why isn't Wally crowing? He always crows until I wake up."

"I shooed him away because he's too annoying."

"No, he isn't. He's just doing his job. That's what roosters do."

"I'll go get you some fresh water, so you can wash your face."

When I returned, he was looking through his clothes. I set the basin down on the small wooden table that Mamá kept in her room for Juanito to do his homework. Papá had built it for Julia when she was a child, emphasizing the importance of school.

Juanito walked to the fireplace, where Mamá stood and gave her his usual morning kiss. Then he grabbed the basket from the table and headed outside. He returned shortly and set the basket full of eggs next to the fireplace.

Mamá began cracking eggs onto a skillet. She sold whatever eggs were left over to Doña Marta. She and her husband, Don Manuel, owned the village fish market. It was our responsibility to drop off the eggs on our way to school. Mamá would collect the money later during the day. Doña Marta and her family were close friends of my family. After Papá died, they were always willing to help. They treated us like family, and in many ways we were.

Papá had worked as a fisherman his entire life. When he was alive, there was always plenty of fish to eat. He always made sure that the family wore decent clothes. Two winters ago, he had come down with a severe flu. Mamá tried her best to heal him, but he never recovered. What small savings we had were spent on a wooden coffin and a plot at the cemetery big enough for two. Mamá did not have enough money for a gravestone. On his grave, we were only able to place a rock that Juanito struggled to bring up from the riverbank. Mamá assured us that it was temporary until she could earn enough money to buy a proper marker. She never tired of going by every day to place fresh wildflowers at the head of his grave. We somehow felt Papá was content with that.

From then on, Mamá was our sole provider. She managed by washing clothes for the fishermen and selling them freshly baked bread. Julia and I helped her after school.

Mamá was a tall, beautiful woman in her mid-forties. She had a thin, yet strong figure. Her skin was light, and she had light hair that fell halfway down her back. She had a complexion that required no make-up, and now, crow's feet surrounded her eyes. She usually wore a tan dress with a white headscarf and an apron tied around her waist. Her leather sandals were made by the local villagers.

Even after Papá's death, we lived happy lives in the small village called Santa Rosa de Copán. Papá, Mamá and baby Julia moved here when Mamá was pregnant with me. Papá wanted to try his luck fishing in a bigger river. That's where I got my name, after the village that, according to Papá, would bring us good fortune.

"I think I'll wear the pink dress Kike bought me," Julia said, pressing the dress against her figure and contemplating her image in the long, thin mirror that hung in our room. "I'm meeting him after school." She spun around in a dance. "I want to look pretty for him."

I put on my school uniform: a white blouse with a dark-blue dress that went below the knees. It had two pockets at the waist. Julia put on a pair of sandals like Mamá's. I put on my mountain shoes. Aunt Teresa had sent them from Houston. I loved my shoes. I wore them with long white socks. Some of the kids at school made fun of me because I didn't wear shoes or sandals like other girls. They said that they looked like boys' shoes. I didn't care. My mountain shoes were perfect.

Julia and I finished doing each other's hair and went to sit at the table facing the fireplace. Mamá was serving breakfast.

Papá had made the table with the wood that was left over after he built our hut. Our house had two bedrooms and a kitchen-living area. Compared to other huts in the village, ours was the best. There was only one home and business made of brick in Santa Rosa. It belonged to Doña Marta and her family. We loved our home, our kitchen table, our way of life.

Breakfast smelt delicious. Mamá served us scrambled eggs, bacon and fried bananas. My mouth watered before I sat down.

Mamá took one look at Julia and shook her head, clearly reading her after-school intentions. "I wish you would find a more suitable companion. One who is your age and not a gang member," Mamá said. "I don't approve of Kike. He doesn't work. I don't know where he gets the money to buy you all those nice things. All I know is it can't be good."

"He's not a bad person, Mamá. He loves me and he treats me well."

"He's a Mara, Julia. All he does is drink and smoke with his gang in the plaza," Mamá disagreed.

The Mara, short for Mara Salvatrucha, otherwise known as the MS-13, were a notorious international gang that originated in a faraway place called Los Angeles. I remember Papá asking why they called that place Los Angeles when they were sending us nothing but demons. "They should call it Los Demonios," he'd say.

Many kids from Central America who had gone to the United States looking for work ended up in jail or deported for breaking the law. Some of them joined gangs while on the streets or during their time in prison. When they were sent back to their home countries, they brought with them a criminal mentality and a deep hostility toward society. Their violent behavior caused serious problems for the peasants, who had previously lived in relative peace.

Papá said that the Maras were scattered across all Central America, Mexico, the United States and even as far north as Canada. For a long time, the Maras stole from the peasants, murdering anyone who might report them or stand in their way. The peasants grew tired of the senseless killings and soon armed themselves. War broke out. The peasants began targeting anyone associated with the Maras.

The military stepped in and detained as many Maras as they could. Although a peace treaty was brokered, the violence soon reignited. Occasionally, someone was severely beaten and robbed. Before long, unsolved murders reappeared in different regions, causing new tensions.

One of the main reasons that Mamá didn't approve of Kike was his age. He was ten years older than Julia and had a reputation for violence. It was rumored that he had been deported from the United States for nearly killing a man with a tire iron. Kike's chest, back and upper arms were covered with tattoos. He didn't have any on his face or neck, like other Maras often did. Most of their tattoos consisted of numbers and symbols that made sense only to them. Most Maras dressed in California street-gang garb, such as a white muscle shirt, baggy khaki pants with sharp creases and Nike sneakers.

What worried Mamá the most about Kike was his cold stare. It never let her peek past his eyes. Julia didn't see that. She seemed to love all the nice gifts he brought her. He even promised her a life free from poverty for her and our family.

"Mamá, Rosa thinks you should cook that rooster," Julia said, changing the subject.

"What rooster?" Juanito asked.

"The one that crows on our windowsill," Julia said.

"You mean Wally? I won't ever catch him for that. He's my favorite rooster." Juanito smiled to himself when he figured that only he could catch Wally.

"I like him, too," Mamá said. "Without Wally, none of you would get up in the morning."

"I just don't understand why he has to crow on our windowsill," I said through a mouthful. "There are so many trees out there, but no, he has to stand on our window, flap his wings and crow his head off in our ears. What's that chicken's problem?"

"It's not a chicken," Juanito said. "Don't you know the difference between a hen and a rooster? Wally's a rooster, dummy."

"Don't call your sister names," Mamá scolded.

"Sorry."

"Well, it just might be a good omen that Wally wants all of you to be awake and alert every day." Mamá winked at Juanito.

"Can we get another dog?" Juanito asked, taking Mamá's wink as a sign to push his luck. "One of my friends at school has puppies."

"What kind of dogs are they?"

"Pit bulls. They're really cool."

"Oh no. Those beasts can devour more food than all of us put together. When you grow up and find yourself a good job, if you still want to raise one of those things, get it. That's up to you, but not here, and not now," Mamá said.

"So much for that," Juanito mumbled and went back to eating.

"I need all of you to come straight home after school," Mamá said, looking straight at Julia.

Julia looked down at her food with a slight nod.

"We're expecting a large package from your aunt Teresa. It's scheduled to arrive on the evening bus. I want all of us to walk together to pick it up. We're going to have lots of stuff to sell, so we can have a birthday party for Rosita tomorrow. Julia and I will make the cake. Doña Marta's making Rosita's favorite chicken and rice *pastelitos*."

I looked up at Mamá and smiled when she winked. I felt so special.

Aunt Teresa was Mamá's younger sister. She left Honduras to work in a place called Houston, but she never forgot us. Every month she sent a big package filled with new clothes, canned foods, shoes, toys and cheap jewelry. She always tried to send us our sizes. We kept whatever we liked and sold the rest to buy things we needed.

She often wrote about her job as a maid for some rich people she called "Gringos." Mamá said that our ancestors were also *gringos* and described them as light-skinned people. According to Mamá, her ancestors came from Spain. They colonized Honduras hundreds of years ago. That's why our skin tone is much lighter than other natives. The only one in our family who resembled the Native Americans was Juanito. He took after Papá's side of the family. They had straight black hair with milk-chocolate skin. They lived in the southeast regions of the country, fishing the Atlantic.

When we finished our breakfast, we stood before Mamá for our blessing. She always did this as we left for school.

Julia grabbed the egg basket, and we headed out to the fish market, which was down the road from our home. The school was in the next village called Los Pescadores, named after the local fishing trade. It was a half mile walk through a path in the jungle that had been made over the years by students and villagers. This was our usual route since walking along the main highway was dangerous and took twice as long.

When we arrived at the market, Doña Marta was busy wrapping homemade milk candies. She was a strong woman in her mid-forties. Her salt-and-pepper hair was held back with a pink hair band. She wore the traditional dresses made by local women. Her facial characteristics displayed her Native American beauty.

"Good morning, Doña Marta," we greeted her, as Julia placed the basket on the counter.

"Good morning, children. Here, have a piece of candy for the road. And hurry. You kids are running late this morning."

"Thank you," we said and headed across the fish market to enter the path in the jungle.

"Wait for me," called Herman. He was short and Julia's age. What he lacked in height, he made up with his athletic ability. He was considered the class clown, yet everyone loved his sense of humor. Herman claimed to be in love with Julia. He was good at making goofy faces to get her laughing and often tried to impress her. He never tired of hearing "No" every time he asked her to be his girlfriend. But she only saw him as a friend.

This morning, he overstepped his boundaries when he unexpectedly took Julia in his arms and kissed her on the lips.

"Stop it!" Julia yelled and pushed him away. "Don't ever do that again, Herman. I've told you plenty of times that I have a boyfriend."

Herman cocked his head back and laughed. "I had to kiss you. You look too beautiful in that dress. I couldn't resist. You're more beautiful than all the wild orchids in the jungle."

He gave Julia a chivalrous bow, that made her blush and giggle. Filled with courage from the kiss he stole, he led the way into the jungle.

One of Kike's gang members had seen us from a distance. They called him Zapato, because of the way his large jawbone resembled a shoe. He was 5'10" with a heavy build. His face was covered with tattoos. He wore khaki shorts and sneakers, but no shirt, revealing the tattoos on his upper body.

When he saw Herman kiss Julia, he ran toward the back of an abandoned hut, where Kike sat with Gato smoking a cigarette. He wasted no time in reporting what he had witnessed.

Fury overwhelmed Kike. He stood up, flicked his cigarette and said, "Gato, cut them off before they come out on the other side. Zapato and I will come in from behind."

Of all Kike's gang members, Gato was by far the most violent. He earned his nickname for the predatory way in which he hunted his victims through the jungle with rapid speed. Gato wasted no time disappearing into the jungle.

Suddenly, Gato appeared in our path, breathing heavily.

Goosebumps erupted all over my skin.

Julia stopped a few feet from him. "Get out of our way, or I'll tell Kike you're bothering us."

"Why don't you explain why you cheat on me with this piece of shit?" Kike said from behind.

Just then, Gato grabbed Herman from behind in a choke hold, and Kike moved in close to him. Looking at Julia, he said, "You stab me in the back with this clown? After I give you everything?"

Herman struggled with fear-stricken eyes, but it was no use. Gato's hold was too tight. Kike slowly withdrew his knife and put it close to Herman's face.

"Stop, Kike! Stop! He was only playing!" Julia pleaded.

"I wanna play too," Kike said. "I'll be the jealous boyfriend who killed his girlfriend and her midget lover."

His eyes locked into Herman's fear. Zapato, who had appeared out of nowhere, grabbed Julia from behind, holding her arms to her waist. She tried to wiggle free, but he was too strong. She dug her nails into his sides, but he only squeezed tighter, constricting her breath.

"Let me go!" screamed Julia.

Kike plunged the dagger into Herman's chest. Herman's mouth fell open as if trying to let out a cry for help. No words followed his last breaths. Kike twisted the dagger, withdrew it and plunged it into Herman's stomach.

Juanito and I were horrified and didn't know what to do.

After Herman's body fell to the ground, Kike turned his attention to Julia. He moved close to her, his eyes fixed on hers. Juanito and I stood frozen, we knew we needed to make a run for it.

"No, Kike, please!" Julia whimpered. "I love you."

Kike embraced Julia and put his lips to hers. Sobbing, she tried to kiss him back. Her eyes grew wide and desperately motioned for Juanito and me to run.

Kike kissed her neck as he plunged the dagger into her. He twisted the dagger, bleeding the life from her. Julia's head fell on Kike's shoulder. He loosened his hold and watched her slide down from his body until she crumbled to the ground. Kike and Gato stared at her with disregard.

Juanito and I sprinted back the way we came. We ran for our lives as fast as our legs could carry us. Juanito took the lead. I followed behind, barely able to keep up. We heard them coming but didn't dare look back for fear of stumbling. My only concern was that my little brother would get away, even if I didn't.

As Juanito cleared the jungle, I felt the heavy breathing of one of them close behind me. A hand caught a lock of my hair and jerked my head back. I shook his hand free and followed Juanito into the fish market. Juanito ran past Doña Marta and hid behind a stack of boxes near the back door. I ran to the register, breathing hard, unable to speak. I looked back, my eyes wide with terror, expecting them to come rushing in at any second.

Doña Marta turned her attention toward me. "Rosita, why are you and Juanito not in school? And why are you breathing so hard? What's wrong?" she asked, making her way around the counter to take hold of my arms. "Rosa, talk to me. What's the matter with you two?"

I could not speak. My heavy breathing combined with the intense fear held me in shock. My heart pounded fiercely, pushing retched lumps of terror up my throat.

Doña Marta shook me. "Why is your brother hiding in the back? Rosa, answer me!"

I ran back to the screen door to look toward the path. I needed to see if they were outside, but they were nowhere to be seen. Still, I felt them there, in the jungle, lurking, watching me.

Doña Marta came up behind me, curious to see what I was looking for. When she saw that no one was there, she turned me around and hugged me in her bosom. She held me long enough to feel my heart pound against her chest. Then she withdrew and looked into my terrified eyes.

I choked on my sobs, trying to explain the horror that had just taken place.

"What are you saying, child? I can't understand you."

"It's Julia," I managed to cry out.

Doña Marta turned my face toward her. "What about Julia?"

"Julia's hurt!" I cried. "Kike hurt her and Herman with his knife." Agony choking my voice, I turned to look outside and pointed toward the path. "There."

"Oh my God! Manuel!" Doña Marta yelled.

Don Manuel was working out back with his twenty-two-year-old son, Pepe, gutting fish.

"Manuel! Come quickly!"

"What's all the fuss about?" Don Manuel asked from out back.

The rear door flew open, and Don Manuel came into the fish market with a knife in his hand. He was a tall, muscular man in his fifties, his brown skin wrinkled and rough from the years of fishing the river under the scorching sun. He was wearing a black rubber apron with his jeans tucked into black rubber boots.

"Come out from behind them boxes, boy," Don Manuel said when he saw Juanito hiding. "What's wrong with you?" Pepe walked in after his father. He was dressed the same. A younger version of Don Manuel, he stood next to him, studying Juanito. My little brother looked up in horror and let out a burst of air and cried. Hearing Juanito made me cry louder.

"What's going on?" Don Manuel asked.

I pointed outside. "There," I cried. "In the path. Kike hurt Julia and Herman with his knife."

Don Manuel and Pepe threw off their aprons, ran outside and disappeared into the jungle.

Juanito ran to hug me. Doña Marta hugged the two of us tightly. We dug our faces into her and waited with uncertainty.

Manuel was the first to surface, carrying Herman's body. Pepe followed, carrying Julia. The bodies hung loosely from the arms of the father and son, whose torsos were covered in blood. Herman and Julia's necks and limbs swayed in a lifeless rhythm with each step. Don Manuel and Pepe laid the bodies down a few feet from each other on a patch of grass. They were dead.

Juanito and I peeked, then buried our faces back into Doña Marta.

"Oh no," Doña Marta whispered, her eyes wide with horror. She crossed herself religiously, pulled away from us and rushed outside toward her husband and son.

"Pepe, quickly, go get María. Manuel, go get Herman's father."

The men ran off in different directions. The villagers came out of their huts and gathered around the bodies. News of the double murder spread throughout Santa Rosa rapidly. The villagers didn't need anyone to tell them who was responsible for such butchery.

Juanito and I saw Mamá approach, running alongside Pepe. We ran out of the fish market to meet her embrace. She knelt to hug us and kiss our faces with dreadful confusion.

"Kike hurt Julia and Herman with his knife," I cried. Mamá's eyes grew wide. She looked past us toward the large crowd across from the fish market. "Oh, no," she whispered and then cried out, "God, no. Not my Julia! Not my Julia!"

She rose quickly and pulled us fast toward the crowd. The villagers saw us coming and made a gap to let Mamá through. Mamá let go of our hands and covered her mouth when she saw Julia and Herman lying in the ground.

"Julia!" she kept repeating as she knelt beside our sister. She lifted Julia's lifeless head to her bosom and whispered loving words as she caressed her hair, pausing momentarily for a reaction. Julia's eyes were closed. Her face was pale gray. Her pink dress was covered in blood.

Mamá cried hopelessly with Julia in her arms. "Why, my God?" She cried looking up to the heavens for a divine response, but none came.

Juanito and I stood behind Mamá, watching her kiss Julia's face over and over.

Herman's parents arrived soon, crying loudly for their slain son. At times, they looked at Mamá and Julia in confusion. The cries from our parents mixed into a chorus of agony and sorrow. Village women and some of our classmates joined in crying. Soon the entire village was in mourning.

Doña Marta knelt next to Mamá to try and persuade her to stand. She refused to let go of Julia. She finally stood up when she realized that Julia was gone. She and Doña Marta hugged each other and continued crying in bewilderment as they looked down at Julia and Herman.

"María, we need to talk," Doña Marta said, trying to get Mamá's attention.

"Pepe, come here," Doña Marta called. "Take Julia's body to María's home."

Pepe picked up Julia's body with gentle care, tears rolling from his eyes.

Mamá caressed Julia's face one more time before Pepe led the way back to our home.

Herman's father picked up his son, and his parents headed home with their son's body.

The morning sun cast its bright rays over the mountains and into our eyes. Mamá held our hands, taking us in tow behind Pepe. Don Manuel and Doña Marta walked behind us along with some of the villagers.

When Mamá opened the front door for Pepe, she gasped at the sight of her dead daughter being carried into our home. Doña Marta cleared the kitchen table, where only moments ago we had eaten breakfast. She covered it with a clean sheet, then instructed Pepe to lay Julia's body over it. Pepe did as he was told, then excused himself to join the village men, who were gathered outside our home.

Mamá, Juanito and I sat a few feet from the table feeling devastated, staring at what had become of Julia. Doña Marta walked up to Mamá and took her hands to get her to stand. Mamá stood up weakly. We followed her up with puffy eyes.

"Listen to me, María," whispered Doña Marta. "You have to protect Rosa and Juanito from the Maras. Manuel has sent for the military police. The men from the village are ready to protect your children."

Mamá said nothing, her mind lost in thought.

"The military will come and arrest whoever's responsible for this, but they'll need the testimony of the witnesses. It's for that very reason that the Maras may come back tonight to try and kill them." She paused momentarily to look into Mamá's teary eyes for a response.

Mamá's eyes grew wide.

"You have to send Rosa and Juanito away as soon as possible," Doña Marta continued. "The Maras outnumber the village men. If they decide to attack, the men will have a hard time protecting your children." Doña Marta went silent, letting her words sink in. She looked down at her watch. "The morning bus will be coming through here soon. You have to send them away. For their own safety ... until it's safe for them to return."

Some of the village women took the liberty of cleaning Julia's body while reciting prayers. They changed her into a clean dress while we sat grieving.

Mamá faced Juanito and me. "Get up. Both of you," she snapped, wiping her tears with the backs of her hands. "You're leaving Santa Rosa."

Juanito and I looked at one another. "But where will we go?" I mumbled.

"Go where, Mamá?" Juanito asked. "Why?"

"To Aunt Hilda in Guatemala." She wiped away new tears. "I'll come get you as soon as this is all over."

"But I don't want to go," Juanito pouted.

I thought about pleading with Mamá but saw the strict look on her face. It was pointless to argue with her once her mind was made up. She took us by the hand and led us to her room. She pulled two small suitcases from beneath her bed and began packing our clothes.

Doña Marta came in soon with a lunch bag and some Guatemalan money. "Here, put this money in your front pocket. Use it for the taxi. Hide the rest of this in your shoe. That's in case of an emergency. Only take it out if you need to. Be careful that no one sees you. I filled this bag with the chicken and rice *pastelitos* that you and Juanito love so much." She handed the bag to me tearfully and gave us a tight hug.

Mamá wrote on a piece of paper and handed it to me. "This is your aunt Hilda's address."

I put the paper in my front pocket and followed Doña Marta's instructions for the money. Mamá pulled us into a tight embrace and kissed our faces. She then took Juanito's face in her hands tenderly, "Listen to me, son. I need you to take good care of your sister, but I also need you to listen to her." She looked compassionately into his eyes. "Do you understand?"

Juanito nodded, his face tight between Mamá's hands. He let out a burst of despair with a choked sob. Tears trickled down his cheeks.

Mamá let go of his face, took my hands and looked deep into my eyes. "I promise to come get you as soon as this is over. You heard Doña Marta. I must send you away for your own protection. Take good care of each other. If you feel that you might be in danger, run," she said firmly, looking from Juanito to me. "The both of you, run. Run like you ran out of the jungle. Run like you've never run before."

We nodded, obediently submitting to her instructions.

Mamá gave me another hug with a kiss on the cheek. Then we cried together for the last time.

Doña Marta called Pepe and a couple of the men to escort us to the bus stop. It suddenly dawned on me that we were not going to school like we were supposed to. Time went by so fast that before we knew it, we were on our way to Guatemala City. We heard the diesel engine of the bus approaching, making our dire situation real.

"Don't make conversation with anybody unless you need to. Do you understand?" Doña Marta asked.

We nodded.

"Once all of this is over, your mother will go get you like she promised. Don't worry about her. The village will protect her. I promise that nothing will happen to her while you're away," Doña Marta said.

The bus came into view and finally rolled to a stop beside us. The driver stepped off in a cheery mood that changed quickly when he noticed the frowns on our faces. He was a short man with a larger than average belly and a thick mustache.

Pepe walked up to him and shook his hand. He explained our situation to the driver, who then looked us over and nodded. Pepe paid him for our tickets and motioned for us to get on. We boarded and took the first seat opposite the driver and placed our suitcases behind our feet. The driver took his seat, pulled the door handle firmly and gave us another once-over through the rearview mirror.

We looked out the window and waved goodbye to Pepe. He waved back. The bus let out a burst of air pressure as the driver put the bus in gear and drove slowly away from our village and onto the main highway. There were people of all ages on board. Some had brought their chickens and small pigs.

Juanito turned to look at me with the same sad face he'd worn all morning. "Why are we leaving?" he asked in a frightened whisper, hoping we could get off before it was too late. "We've never even been to Aunt Hilda's house. I'm scared."

"Me too," I whispered.

He placed his head on my shoulder, and I leaned my chin on top of his head. We cried silently. All I could think about was leaving Mamá alone to bury Julia. Surely, Mamá would bury her next to Papá.

I'm sure Papá will take good care of her, I thought to myself. Then they'll both enjoy the fresh wildflowers that Mamá, Juanito and I will take to their graves every morning.

The Maras

Gato stood at the end of the path, cloaked by the jungle's greenery. He breathed hard, inhaling a fistful of Rosa's hair pressed against his nose and mouth. He had missed grabbing her by the collar although he managed to snatch her hair flowing behind her. Kike and Zapato arrived behind Gato, breathing heavily. Zapato nearly ran into them.

"You let them get away," Kike said, hardly able to speak, his hands on his knees.

Gato ignored him as he filled himself with the scent of Rosa's hair.

"You're getting slow," Kike said, then looked back at Zapato, who was bent over trying to catch his breath. "You all right?"

Zapato nodded and straightened up. He put his hands on his waist and looked at Kike. His nostrils flared as he took deep breaths.

"Let's go to the hideout and change," Kike said. "Then, we'll head east toward San Pedro. We'll have to cut through the jungle and stay off the main roads. We'll hide there until it's safe to go back to Los Angeles."

Zapato turned around and began a slow jog, Kike followed behind him. Kike noticed that Gato was not coming and went back to get him. He found him still smelling the hair in his fist and staring at the fish market. Kike jerked him by the arm, bringing him back to his senses.

"Let's go," he urged. "They're going to bring the soldiers." Gato turned around without saying a word and sprinted toward their hideout. Kike took one last look at the fish market. He caught a glimpse of Rosa standing behind the screen door in front of Doña Marta. He cursed himself for letting them get away. He turned around and sprinted back along the path, passing Zapato, the slowest of the three.

The three of them ran into the brush. They deviated to the left on a path leading to the abandoned hut they had taken over. They reached it in a matter of minutes and changed out of their bloodstained clothes. They filled three backpacks with goods they had previously stolen.

In the distance, they heard a helicopter. It seemed to be approaching. The three looked at each other expectantly.

"Hurry," Kike said. "If we get separated, stay in the thickest parts of the jungle. We'll meet up in San Pedro, sell this stuff and lay low."

The helicopter sounded closer. They stood still, listening, trying to determine how much time they had to get away. Kike stepped out of the hut and looked up, straining to listen. He hoped the helicopter was only on a flyby routine, but his gut instinct told him otherwise.

Zapato came out of the hut with his backpack on and tossed a backpack to Kike. They suddenly heard male voices coming from the jungle, and the three Maras took off running. Gato took the lead with the helicopter thundering high above. Kike ran behind him, putting his backpack on at full speed. Zapato fell behind.

"There they go!" a soldier yelled.

Kike and Gato knew that Zapato had been spotted. They picked up speed, hoping he would keep the soldiers busy long enough for them to get deeper into the jungle.

"Freeze!" a soldier yelled at Zapato. "I command you in the name of the Honduran military."

There was no use running. Zapato's legs could carry him no further. He came to a stop when he heard a weapon lock and load behind him. Zapato bent over with his hands on his knees, trying to catch his breath.

"Put your hands on top of your head and turn around slowly. Do as I say and don't try anything stupid!" the soldier ordered.

Zapato knew he was finished, but he could not let himself be taken alive. The Maras knew the countless stories of how the military tortured them for information about unsolved crimes. They knew that to be taken alive only meant days of torment, most often resulting in a slow, agonizing death.

Zapato straightened himself, letting his backpack slide off and hit the ground. Ignoring the orders, he pulled the dagger from his waist, hoping that the soldier was close enough to stab him in the neck. He took a deep breath, spun around and lunged at the soldier.

The soldier was down on one knee in a shooter's position. Zapato came at him with the raised dagger tightly fisted in his right hand. The soldier pulled the trigger. A tri-burst of bullets hit the center of Zapato's chest, throwing him on his back. The soldier walked toward him carefully, keeping his weapon pointed at the dead Mara. Zapato lay with his eyes open. The look of anger was now a frightful expression.

Gato heard the rapid fire and tightened his lips with frustration. In the chaos, he and Kike were separated. Kike forced one way through the dense jungle, while Gato was pushed to the other, their shouts swallowed by the gunfire. He hoped

Kike would get away. The river and its banks were filled with boats and fishermen when Gato cleared the jungle. He got rid of his backpack and dove into the river. He hated the thought of leaving Kike behind. Gato swam deep and for as long as he could. When he felt he could no longer hold his breath, he began his ascent. The sun shone over the surface, outlining the boats. He swam for the largest boat, one that had tires around it, and came out of the water. Gato grabbed onto one of the tires that faced the jungle and peeked from behind it to see if he could spot his friend.

He saw Kike run out of the jungle and bump into a fisherman with a load of nets. Both fell to the ground. Kike was on his feet instantly and about to dive into the water, when a soldier cleared the jungle behind him.

"Freeze!" a soldier yelled and knelt to a shooter's position.

Kike froze when he saw the soldier pointing his machine gun.

"In the name of the Honduran military, I order you to put your hands on top of your head."

Kike made a grab for a fisherman on shore, but he got away quickly. Kike gave the soldier a cold-hearted stare, sighed and let his backpack slide off his back. Then he smiled wickedly and pulled a dagger from his waist. The soldier tilted his head and took aim. Kike charged toward his death. The soldier pulled the trigger and fired. Kike tumbled back, looking down at his chest, and fell into the river.

Gato hid behind the boat's tire, letting himself be towed upstream. He held on for almost an hour without the knowledge of the boat's pilot. When the boat entered another congested riverbank, Gato let go.

→→→

The village by the river was heavily populated with fishermen and people coming to buy fish. Gato swam to the riverbank, climbed ashore and looked around cautiously, making sure there were no soldiers. He tried to remain calm and blend in. No one seemed to notice him. He felt his waist for his dagger. It was gone. The Mara exhaled with frustration. He needed his dagger to survive the long journey to Los Angeles. He needed it to defend himself and for the robberies he would commit along the way. He waved to a boy selling his morning's catch. The boy hesitated but made his way over. Gato reached into his pocket for some wet bills and quickly paid the boy for his entire catch. The boy went away, happy to have sold his fish so quickly.

Gato made his way east of the village toward the jungle, walking casually, making as if to sell his fish. And he did manage to sell them for half of what he paid. When a bus pulled into the village, he developed a different escape plan. Gato approached the bus stop and paid the driver for a ticket to Ciudad Tecún Umán, a small town on the Guatemalan side of the Suchiate River.

He waited impatiently, hidden in the bustle of the village crowds, trapped in time between the bus' departure and the arrival of the military. If the soldiers came first, he was close enough to the edge of the jungle to sneak away. The bus did not delay. After a few packages were unloaded and new passengers boarded, the bus left for the road north to Guatemala.

Feeling relieved, Gato smiled at the thought of the stops the bus would make in small villages along the way. He sat at the rear after making sure that the windows on both sides were open, in case he needed an emergency exit. Two military trucks came from the opposite direction. He ducked out of sight as they went by and peeked out the back window until they disappeared. Then he sat back and smiled again. They were too late. Gato was getting away again. He let out a deep breath and relaxed. He needed to rest after the intense morning.

Gato thought about the long journey that awaited him. He had traveled this road to the United States before, as a young adventurer. It was a hard voyage, but for a confident Gato, it was a walk across a different type of jungle, a jungle where the beasts were men, cold-blooded and heartless. This was the jungle that molded him into the predator that he had become.

Angélica

The cellphone rang, interrupting Angélica. She was busy putting her one-year-old son, Pablo Jr., to sleep for his afternoon nap. Wendy, her eleven-year-old daughter, attended school close by. She would not be out for a few more hours. Pablo Jr. usually woke by two o'clock. Angélica would then place him in his stroller and give him a bottle. They would stroll a few blocks to meet Wendy walking home from school and listen to her talk about the day's activities. Until today, that was their daily routine.

Her cellphone buzzed. It was an unknown number.

"Hello?"

"Angélica, it's me." Her husband sounded distressed. "I need you to act fast and get out of the house."

"Pablo, what's wrong? You're scaring me."

"My cover's been blown. Hurry! You don't have much time."

"But ..."

"Angélica, go now! I'll meet you there!"

"Pablo, wait!" A dial tone came over the line. "Pablo?"

Pablo worked undercover for the Guatemalan government and the United States Drug Enforcement Agency, the DEA. He was in an operation to expose corrupt government officials in

Guatemala, Honduras, El Salvador and Mexico. Now he was in trouble, and the family had to abandon their home or face the consequences.

Pablo and Angélica had a well-planned exit strategy in case they were suddenly forced to flee. All that they needed to do was stick to the plan. Three backpacks with supplies were stored a few towns north. They were to meet at a small cafe and from there blend in with a caravan of migrants headed north. They planned to ride the bus to Ciudad Tecún Umán and cross the Suchiate River into Mexico. Then they would board the Mexican train known as La Bestia. Many migrants crossed through Mexico in this way. It was the perfect cloak. They would ride La Bestia north until it was safe enough to travel a different way.

Angélica immediately called the school to have Wendy ready to go as soon as she arrived. She ended the call and placed her purse and diaper bag around her neck and shoulders. Then she bundled Pablo Jr. in a carrier and headed for the door. She tossed her cell phone into the trash on her way out. Then, she rushed with the baby in her arms to the busy intersection a half block from her home and waved down the first taxi she saw. She climbed into the back seat and gave the driver directions to the school. Wendy was being escorted into the front office when Angélica rushed in nervously.

"Where are we going?" Wendy asked, sensing her mother's worry.

"We're going to meet your father, then were going on a trip."

Wendy climbed into the back seat of the taxi. She had a million questions on her mind, yet remained silent, confused by her mother's demeanor.

"Driver, please take us back to where you picked us up." Angélica wanted to see if she noticed anything strange by her home.

The driver pulled over, as instructed, giving her a clear view down the street. Their home was surrounded by large SUVs and armed men. Some wore military uniforms. The others wore colorful silk shirts. Angélica turned away to avoid the driver's curiosity. She instructed him to take them downtown. When they arrived, Angelica and her two children switched taxis and headed to the next town, where they would rendezvous with her husband.

When they arrived, they entered the cafe, which was busy with clients. Angélica sat down and waited with her children. She ordered some food to keep them busy, hoping that Pablo would arrive soon, and they would move on to the next step of their plan. They waited for a couple of hours, Angélica worrying the whole time. Wendy fell asleep with her head on the table. Pablo Jr. became uneasy.

"Can I get you anything else?" the manager asked.

"No, thank you," Angélica said, smiling kindly. "We're waiting for my husband. He's just running a little behind."

"I'm sorry to have to tell you, ma'am, but you can't sit here taking up space from potential customers." He looked down at Wendy. "I'm going to have to ask you to leave."

The manager was tired of the excuses made by migrants to use the cafe as a rest area. Many of them showed no consideration for his business. They dirtied the restrooms or simply sat there looking homeless and begged for whatever food they could get. They were bad for business.

Angélica looked up at him with despair, a despair he knew too well. The manager felt no remorse but waited next to the table for Angélica to gather her children and leave.

"Well, I'd like to order a sandwich combo to go," Angélica said, trying to buy more time. She looked worriedly at her watch. "I'm sure he'll be here by the time the order is ready." The manager gave her a frustrated look and walked away to place the order.

The sandwich combo came. Pablo did not. Angélica looked at her watch nervously, hoping her husband was okay.

"When's Daddy coming?" Wendy whined.

"He's on his way, honey. He's just running late."

The manager returned after giving her an extra ten minutes, a look of determination on his face.

"Ma'am, it's time for you and your children to leave."

"I promise you my husband will be here soon."

"Look, lady, I'm really sorry, but if you don't leave, I'll be forced to call the police."

Fear overcame Angélica. She knew the drug cartel would have every crooked cop in Guatemala looking for them. She could not allow the problem to worsen. The next part of the plan, if Pablo did not make the rendezvous, was for her and the children to go to Ciudad Tecún Umán. They would meet there before crossing into Mexico. She felt like she was distancing the children and herself from Pablo, but there was no other choice. She had to trust the plan. She gathered the children and her things quickly, heading to the street.

Angélica stood hesitantly on the sidewalk, knowing she had to take the next step without Pablo. She could not deviate from the plan. Airports were out of the question. The bus stations in the cities were dangerous. The cartel had eyes everywhere. She had to maintain a low profile. Keeping her children safe was her priority.

Angélica waved down the first taxi she saw. She intended to place the children in it, then retrieve the backpacks Pablo stored in the storage unit next to the cafe. When the taxi pulled over, Pablo jumped out from the back seat. Tears of relief rolled from Angélica's eyes.

"Daddy!" Wendy yelled. She threw herself into his arms, the sandwich combo gripped tightly in her hand.

Pablo kissed his daughter's forehead. "It's okay, honey. Daddy's here now." He withdrew from her and looked at his wife.

"Pablo," Angélica whispered, her eyes teary with disbelief as she stood on the sidewalk with their baby.

Her purse and diaper bag hung from her neck and shoulders, crisscrossing her chest like the bandoliers of a revolutionary. She had ignored thoughts of him being captured and tortured for fear of losing strength. Now, Pablo was back from the dead. She cried solemnly, realizing that she thought she had lost him.

Pablo took her in his arms and kissed the tears from her face, reading her thoughts, reassuring her that everything was going to be all right. He looked down at his son and kissed his forehead. The child giggled, happy to see his father.

"Sorry I'm late," he whispered as he wiped away fresh tears from her eyes.

"It's okay," she said, drying her tears. "You're here now, and that's all that matters."

"Get in the taxi with the kids. I'll get the backpacks." Pablo placed Wendy in the back seat and buckled her seatbelt. Angélica sat next to her with the baby.

"I'll be right back."

Pablo hurried to the storage unit and returned a few minutes later with the backpacks. The driver got out and opened the trunk. They drove a few miles to a small village, Pablo eating his sandwich on the way. No one said a word. They did not want to mention the situation in earshot of the driver, or their daughter. He finished the sandwich minutes before they arrived at the next step in their journey.

The taxi dropped the family off at a bus stop at the edge of the small village and drove off, leaving them in the dust. They had not missed the bus, and everything was going as planned. The bus soon arrived and stopped next to them, bringing more dust. They boarded and took the first two seats directly behind the driver. Wendy took the seat in front of her parents, where she could stretch out and sleep in their sight. Pablo took his son from Angélica.

Pablo had chosen to travel by bus because of its frequent use by migrants heading north. It would provide the perfect cover. The bus would take them through Guatemala City. This route would not require them to change buses. They would not have to get off for anything. The bus would only drop off, pick up and be on its way to the next step in their plan: Ciudad Tecún Umán.

Pablo and Angélica felt relief when the bus was on the highway. They were sure that everything would go smoothly from there. They were finally able to relax.

"What happened?" Angélica asked her husband.

"My partner, Santiago, was picked up by the Medellín cartel," Pablo whispered. "I couldn't take any chances. I called you to get out of the house as soon as I found out. I knew he would be tortured and forced to give up my name. It wouldn't be long before they extracted all that information from him. The hunt for us would begin immediately."

Angélica shook her head, saddened by Santiago's misfortune, but she was relieved that it had not been her husband who had been picked up.

Aunt Hilda

Juanito and I dozed off and on, leaning against each other, as the bus made its way north. It stopped in remote villages for a few minutes, then continued its journey. The driver was quick about his business, loading and unloading passengers. We didn't dare get off at any of the villages, we were still shaken by our sister's murder.

We woke up when the bus came to a stop at the Guatemalan checkpoint. Two soldiers boarded the bus. One of them waited in the front while the other made his way to the rear, asking passengers for their passports. When it was our turn, my brother and I handed over our school IDs. The soldier gave us a puzzled look. The driver noticed his confusion and quickly moved to whisper in his ear. The soldier listened intently, looking down at us with pity. There was trust between them. I remembered Pepe talking to the driver and realized that those were his words being spoken to the soldier. I felt grateful for Pepe and the driver.

We arrived in Guatemala City in the late afternoon. There were people everywhere. Giant buildings surrounded us like the mountains in Santa Rosa. Everyone seemed to be headed somewhere urgently.

"This has to be the biggest village in the world," exclaimed Juanito.

"This isn't a village," I explained. "It's a city like the ones they teach us about in school."

"I've never been to a city before."

"Actually, you have," I assured him. "We came here to visit long ago with Julia and Mamá when she was pregnant with you. I was too small, so I don't remember much."

"Me neither," he whispered. His eyes remained glued to the window, as if not wanting to miss a thing.

The bus station was enormous. Juanito and I stepped off the bus and made our way inside. The crowd was thick, with waves of people moving in different directions. Some were dressed in fancy clothes, others not as much. The really poor wore filthy rags. I felt lost. The only idea that occurred to me was to approach someone and ask for directions to Aunt Hilda's house. But who?

We walked to the ticket counter, gripping our suitcases and the lunch bag. We held hands tightly for fear of being separated by the throng of people. A young man sat behind a counter; we approached him. I placed the suitcase on the ground and the lunch bag on the counter, while holding on to Juanito. With my free hand, I searched my pocket for the paper with Aunt Hilda's address.

"Excuse me, do you know how we can get to this address?" I asked, sliding the piece of paper toward him.

He smirked, ignoring the paper and pointed outside through the big front doors. "Go out there and get a taxi."

"Oh," I sighed thoughtfully. I felt silly remembering that Doña Marta had given me money for a taxi. "That's what taxi drivers do for people, especially the people that are lost." The young man smiled mockingly. "Just give him the address." He slid the paper toward me. "He will punch it into his GPS and take you there."

I took the paper from the counter.

"Let me guess," he said. "First time down from the mountains? Never been to the city before?"

"Thank you," I said, returning his smirk with one of my own. I grabbed my suitcase and turned around to find a taxi.

"What's a GPS?" Juanito asked.

"Shush, Juanito. I don't know."

I looked back at the young man, only to see him mock me, as he slid the lunch bag to the edge of the counter. I tightened my lips, disguised my embarrassment and towed Juanito back to retrieve it.

The street was lined with different colored taxis. The drivers leaned against them, waiting their turns to catch a fare. Homeless people sat along the wall on both sides of the station's entrance. Some begged with a sad look and dirty, outstretched hands.

A driver smoking a cigarette at the head of the taxis saw us. He flicked his cigarette away and made his way toward us. A look of anger was on his face. Fear made the hair on the back of my neck stand up. Juanito squeezed my hand. It was imminent danger. I felt a bit of relief when I saw him looking past us. We turned around as he went by. He pushed a filthy beggar to the ground.

"Back off!" he yelled.

The beggar looked up at him with fear-stricken eyes. He shielded his face from possible blows. When he realized that he would not be beaten, he scurried back to the wall with the others.

"Do you kids need a taxi?" he asked. His tone was surprisingly gentle.

I was speechless.

"Well," he insisted. "Do you, or don't you?"

"Yes," I whispered.

He took our suitcases, led the way to the trunk of his taxi and placed them inside. Then he opened the rear door and motioned for us to get in. We climbed into the back seat with a sense of relief to be moving on. The driver closed the door behind us and got into his seat.

I opened the lunch bag and gave two *pastelitos* to Juanito. We hadn't eaten since breakfast.

"Would you like some *pastelitos*?" I asked the driver. I was grateful and wanted to show our appreciation by sharing our food. It's how we were raised.

"No, thank you," he replied, making notes on a clipboard. "I ate a while ago. Where to?"

I handed him Aunt Hilda's address. He studied it and typed it into the small screen of an electrical device. Juanito and I stared with curiosity. I glanced out the window toward the beggar. He stared at me hungrily as I chewed my food. He seemed hopeful that I might share our food with him. I withdrew two more *pastelitos* and stretched my hand out the window. His eyes went wide. He got up and ran toward me. I closed my eyes hoping that I would not lose my hand.

"Hey," the driver yelled.

He jumped out of his seat and within seconds was by my window. He pushed the beggar violently to the ground before he could get the food.

"I told you to back off!" He said, pointing his finger in the beggar's face.

The beggar remained motionless, shielding his face like a dog afraid of its master.

The driver looked back at me in anger and said, "Don't feed them. They'll rob you of everything you have."

I couldn't believe the cruel ways of the city. "He's hungry," I said, feeling a bit of anger myself. I stretched my hand toward the driver. "You give it to him."

The driver hesitantly took the *pastelitos* and went to the beggar. A look of fear came over the beggar's face. He doubled over and shielded his head, ready to receive the blows he seemed accustomed to. The driver tapped him lightly with his foot. The beggar coiled himself more tightly. When he realized there would be no blows, he moved his arm to peek up at the person standing over him. A look of surprise came across his face when he saw the driver offering him the food. He humbly stretched both hands up.

Juanito and I watched from the safety of the back seat. The beggar took the *pastelitos* to a strange-looking woman and child who sat along the wall. Their clothes were colorful, but filthy. The woman wore a yellow dress, a blue blouse and an abundance of jewelry. She had a dark complexion and didn't look to be the child's mother. The child wore a red jumper with a white blouse. Their heads were covered with colorful bandanas. They looked like they hadn't showered in a long time. Apart from being filthy, the child looked hungry. The woman gave her one of the *pastelitos* and put the other away. Then, the beggar walked back to our window, once the driver was back in his seat. Juanito and I scooted away from the door.

"Thank you for helping me feed my daughter." A sad smile crossed his face, revealing filthy, crooked teeth. His face had scars that made him look dangerous, but when he smiled, he looked gentle. A tear of gratitude ran down his cheek.

The driver was about to get out of his seat again but settled back when he saw the beggar moving away. "Welcome to Guatemala City," he said with a sigh.

Juanito and I were still looking outside, fascinated by the people we saw.

"Unless you have someone else you'd like to invite for dinner," the driver said with exasperation, "we'll go now. I already know the place. According to my GPS, we'll be there in thirty minutes. You kids need to be careful there. It's a terrible place, the worst in Guatemala City."

"What can be worse than all those hungry people at the bus station?" I asked.

The driver looked back through his rearview mirror. "You'll see."

He drove through congested traffic, explaining the different areas of the city, as if my brother and I were tourists. We entered a poor neighborhood where carts filled with scrap metal lined both sides of the street. Some were made from parts of old trucks. The smaller ones were made from bicycles. "All these people live off the city dump," the driver said. "They scavenge for metal or anything else they can sell."

Finally, he pulled over next to a shack built from scrap metal and cardboard. A rancid smell filled the air. "We're here," he said, turning around to look at me for a response.

I was afraid to get out. Everywhere, there were people who looked like the beggars from the bus station.

"That's the place right there," he said, pointing to a shack.

I got out of the taxi. The foul air nauseated me. Juanito got out behind me.

I turned to face the driver. "Could you please wait until someone answers the door?"

"Hurry up, kid. This isn't a good place for me."

Juanito followed me to the front door. I knocked and waited. We looked at each other with sorrow, not knowing what to expect. The door opened with a splintery screech. Aunt Hilda's sunburnt face scrunched at us with distrust, as if the mere sight of us caused her a bitter taste. Her resemblance to Mamá was undeniable. She wore a filthy light-green dress with a bone-colored sweater. Her feet were bruised and filthy in a worn pair of sandals.

"What do you want?" she hissed.

"I'm Rosa, and this is my little brother, Juanito."

Aunt Hilda covered her mouth in astonishment.

"We're your sister María's kids from Santa Rosa." Her eyes widened, she slapped her hands on her waist and smiled. "My God. Rosa, you're so big." She looked down at my little brother. "You too, Juanito. You were born a year after my twins." She then looked behind us. "Where's your mother and Julia?"

"Julia is dead," I said.

Memories from that morning flooded my mind. Juanito and I looked down. Fresh tears rolled down our cheeks as Aunt Hilda processed the tragic news.

"Mamá sent us here to wait for her," I said.

"You poor children," she said, embracing us.

The driver brought our suitcases and lunch bag. He placed them behind us and gave Aunt Hilda a friendly smile, then looked at me. "If you're all set, I'd like to get going."

"Yes," I said, wiping my eyes. I reached into my pocket and paid him. "Thank you for your help."

"It's my job. You kids take care." He turned around and left quickly.

Aunt Hilda picked up our suitcases and ushered us inside. There was a small sink to the left. Wooden boxes hung from the wall to serve as cabinets. A small folding table stood in the middle with four mismatched chairs. A large mattress leaned half-slumped against the wall to the right. She placed our suitcases by the door, as Juanito and I studied her home.

"Come, have a seat." She pulled out the two chairs closest to us. "Tell me what happened." She sat down across from us, ready to listen.

"Julia was killed this morning by her boyfriend, Kike," I explained. "Mamá warned her to not get involved with him, but Julia wouldn't listen." I let out a few sobs. "We were the only ones who saw everything. Mamá sent us here for our protection."

I cried until I was able to speak again. Aunt Hilda listened with a worried look on her face.

"Mamá will come for us. She has to bury Julia first. I think she's going to bury her next to Papá."

"My God," Aunt Hilda said.

I looked at her, teary-eyed. "Can we stay here with you until Mamá comes for us?"

"Of course." Aunt Hilda stood up and gestured for us to hug her. "I'm sorry," she whispered. "I'm glad your mother sent you here to me." She rubbed our backs gently. "Everything's going to be all right. You can help me search for metal at the dump, or whatever else we may find worth selling. This is how we survive ... how we get money for food."

I nodded, wiping away my tears. "We'll help." I looked down at my little brother. "Right, Juanito?"

He looked up with tears in his eyes, nodded and looked down again.

Just then, two small boys walked in with curious looks on their faces.

"Boys, meet your cousins from Honduras. This is Rosa and Juanito, my sister María's kids, the ones I'm always saying that we need to go visit."

"Hello," said the boys, raising their hands slightly.

"Rosa and Juanito, meet my twins. The one on the left is Antonio Jr. and the other is Marcos."

"Hello," we said.

Aunt Hilda went to the sink. She picked up a bag next to it and withdrew a bundle of potato tacos. The small table wobbled when she placed the food on it. Juanito and I exchanged a look. We missed our home.

Aunt Hilda and her family lived in worse poverty than what we endured in Santa Rosa. According to Mamá, she had married a man named Toño, who spent time at cantinas drinking all day instead of working. When he lost his job, they were evicted from their apartment and were soon living in one of the poorest neighborhoods in the city. Their only option was to scavenge the dump for metal scraps. Aunt Hilda lost everything: her dreams, her hopes, her happiness.

The twins dug into the tacos hungrily. Juanito and I watched them eat.

Aunt Hilda frowned when she saw neither Juanito nor me eating. "Come, Rosa," she said. "Let's spread some blankets on the floor. You and Juanito can sleep with the twins." She took a thick blanket from a folded stack she kept next to the mattress. "A good night's rest will do the both of you lots of good."

I gave her a sad smile for trying her best to make us comfortable with what little she had.

"We'll write your mother tomorrow and let her know that you arrived safely."

I couldn't wait to lie down and go to sleep with my little brother. My scalp throbbed with pain from my escape in the jungle. I wanted this awful day to be over. I only hoped that Mamá would come soon.

We were making the bed when Toño stumbled in. He was a big man with a large belly. He wore piles of filthy clothes that matched his grubby beard. He stank of rancid alcohol and looked scarier than many of the beggars we'd seen at the bus station.

Juanito came to my side when Aunt Hilda went to meet him. Toño hadn't noticed my brother and me against the wall. He was so drunk that he had trouble keeping his balance.

"I don't have any money to give you," she whispered, as if knowing what he would ask.

"How much money did you make today?" Toño slurred.

"We have guests, and I need what little I have to feed the twins before they go to school tomorrow."

He stared at her blindly. It was clear that he cared about nothing else but drinking. "Guests?" he asked, trying to maintain his balance. He leaned on the small table for support and sent it crashing to the floor.

Juanito and I hugged each other tighter.

"What guests?" he slurred.

"Two of my sister María's kids have come to stay for a couple of days until she comes for them," Aunt Hilda said, hoping to get through to him.

"What?" he growled. He looked away from his wife and found us huddling against the wall behind him. "Two more mouths to feed?" He looked back at his wife. "Are you crazy? You can barely feed the two hungry brats you have now. They have to leave."

"And go where?" she pleaded. "They're kids. Where could they possibly go in such a big city?"

Toño studied us. I thought that he was considering letting us stay, but I was wrong. I got a bad feeling when his drunken eyes scanned me from top to bottom. Then he looked back at his wife. "Then she'll have to go work at the bar," he slurred, "make enough money to feed all of us." He gave me another drunken look-over.

Aunt Hilda's mouth dropped. "Work at the bar? I won't let you take her there. Take me instead."

"You, huh? No one wants a dirty old woman. Your days are over. I'm going to ask Ricardo to come take a look at her." He took another glance at me before turning around to leave.

Aunt Hilda grabbed him by the arm and pulled him back. "Please! I beg you! Don't do this. She's only a child."

Toño jerked his arm free from her weak grasp and slapped her with the back of his hand. She spun down against the small table, then looked up at him. Hatred filled her eyes. She wiped the trickle of blood with the back of her hand.

"Look at 'er," he growled. "She's not a child. She's all grown. It's time for her to become a woman." He turned around and staggered out the door.

Aunt Hilda rose quickly. She picked up the table and put it back in its place. "Rosa, come here. We don't have much time."

She went to a bag next to the stack of blankets and pulled out a black backpack. She set our suitcases on the table in a hurry and opened them. She stuffed all of my things into the backpack, then wrote something on a piece of paper.

"Take this!"

I took the piece of paper and looked at it with confusion.

"It's the phone number of a woman in Tapachula, Mexico. Her name is Yolanda. She helped your aunt Teresa get to Houston." She tore Aunt Teresa's address from an old letter and threw it in the backpack along with the lunch bag of *pastelitos* and some of the potato tacos.

"Do you have any money?" She stared at me intently.

"Yes," I whispered.

"Then, you must go now."

She took my hand only to slide the backpack onto my shoulders. Before I knew it, the backpack was on, and I was being ushered out to the street.

"Run left for two blocks. You'll see a white taxi with a driver who's missing an arm. His name is Ramón. Tell him I sent you and ask him to take you to the bus station. Buy a ticket to Ciudad Tecún Umán. Find someone there to take you across the Suchiate River. Make your way to Tapachula. There'll be lots of immigrants traveling there. Stick close to them."

We started walking, still listening to her instructions in disbelief.

"When you get to Tapachula, call Yolanda. Tell her you're my niece. She'll find a way to get you on La Bestia."

"But I don't want to go!" I pleaded. "I want to wait here, like Mamá said we should."

Aunt Hilda grabbed my arms lightly. "Listen to me. At any moment, Toño will be back with Ricardo and a couple of others. They'll take you, and they'll have their way with you. When they're finished, they'll prostitute you at the bar. Do you understand? You have to go now!"

"Why me? I never did anything to them."

"Because you're young and beautiful." She turned me around and pushed me. "Now go!"

Juanito stepped out from behind her.

Aunt Hilda grabbed him. "Go, Rosa! Don't worry about Juanito. They're not interested in him."

Juanito cried desperately. I went to hug him.

"I want to go with you," he cried, struggling to get free.

Aunt Hilda pushed me away. "Look, they're coming. Run as fast as you can and get in the taxi." She struggled to hold Juanito.

I followed her gaze over the metal carts and saw Toño coming with three other men. My heart pounded. I gave Juanito a look of distress before I turned and ran in the direction of the taxi. Fear and the instinct to survive made me move quickly. I ran in a crouch, hidden by the carts piled with scrap metal. At the end of the block, I stopped to look back. The four men were at Aunt Hilda's front door. She jumped violently on Toño, buying time, distracting them. Juanito retreated inside. One of the men pointed at me. My body straightened, and I ran for my life. I reached the taxi and jumped into the back seat, slamming the door shut behind me. I didn't bother to check to see if the driver was missing an arm. He looked at me, startled through his rearview mirror.

"Go! Take me to the bus station! Some men are chasing me. Hurry!"

The driver confirmed my fear through his side mirror.

"My aunt Hilda told me to find Ramón, the driver with the missing arm."

The driver gave me a confident look through the rearview mirror and started the engine. He pulled off the curb quickly as I looked out the back window. Toño and the three men were running after the taxi, then came to a tired stop in the middle of the street. Two of the men knocked Toño to the ground and beat him. The other stared at the taxi as it sped away. I removed my backpack and faced forward, relieved to be getting away, yet worried for Juanito.

"What's your name?" the driver asked, glancing at me through the rearview mirror. He was a slim, dark-skinned man with straight black hair. He wore a pair of aviator sunglasses and a blue and white striped shirt.

"Rosa," I answered.

"Nice to meet you. I'm Ramón, the driver with the missing arm. Look."

I looked at his right side from between the two front seats. His right sleeve was neatly ironed and tucked into his waist. I sat back, relieved to be with the right driver.

"Why were those men chasing you?"

"My aunt said that they wanted to put me to work in a bar."

"I believe it. One of the men was Ricardo. He owns La Cueva bar. You're Hilda's niece?"

"Yes."

"Wonderful woman, but bad luck with that husband of hers. Where are you headed now?"

"Aunt Hilda told me to buy a ticket to ... I forgot the name ... Te-something .... Then, cross the Suchiate River into Tapachula, Mexico. There, I'm to call a woman named Yolanda, so she can help me board La Bestia to my aunt Teresa's home in Houston." I spoke the plan as I remembered it. I needed to memorize it.

"That's Ciudad Tecún Umán. Tell that to the ticket agent," Ramón said as he stopped at a red light.

He stretched across the front seat and reached into the glove compartment with his left hand, then continued driving once the light turned green. "I'm going to give you something along with some real good advice."

He handed me a pair of leather gloves. "When you board La Bestia, wear these gloves at all times. The train's covered with slippery grime. If I'd worn a pair of gloves like these, I would've never lost my arm."

I took the gloves and tried one on, then made a tight fist. It felt a bit loose.

"Find yourself a good stone to carry with you. You'll need it to defend yourself. Something not too heavy, so you can handle it easily. If someone attacks you, give them a few good whacks. They'll learn to leave you alone."

I put the gloves in my backpack and listened quietly.

"It's a cruel world. I'm sorry that you have to look for a better life outside your country, but you're worse off sticking around here. That's just the way life is for us Central Americans right now. When you get to the US, people there will call you an immigrant. Don't believe them. You're an American. Our people have been roaming the American continent for hundreds of years."

I looked out my window, thinking about Juanito.

"Many people like me are unlucky and fall off La Bestia … lose a limb. Others have worse luck. They fall underneath and get mauled by her massive wheels. Once you cross the Suchiate River, it's a long walk to Tapachula. Stick close to the crowds until you reach La Bestia. That's about the most important advice I can give a young woman."

I sat back thinking about this Bestia. *Could it be worse than Kike and his gang? Could it have a cruel heart like Toño's? What is this Bestia that I've just begun to learn about?*

Ramón pulled up to the curb. Beggars still sat outside the building. I reached into my pocket to pay him.

"How much do I owe you?"

"Nothing. Save your money, kid, You're gonna need it."

"Thank you. Thank you also for the gloves and for the advice. I'll remember everything you've told me."

"Good luck," he said as he stepped out of the taxi and headed toward the other drivers.

I took the opportunity to retrieve the rest of the money from my shoe before I got out. I only hoped that Doña Marta had given me enough. I went inside to the ticket counter and bought a one-way ticket to Ciudad Tecún Umán. I had no idea what awaited me there. Still confused, I went over and sat down on a bench outside in the departure section. The smell of burnt diesel fuel filled the air. Buses lined the parking spaces. They purred like giant cats waiting to fill their bellies.

Evening set in. Its cool breeze mingled with the smell from the diesel engines. My stomach growled. I dug into my backpack for the bag of *pastelitos* and noticed the bundle of tacos. I took a small bite from a *pastelito*, looking down and chewing slowly. My scalp and neck hurt with every bite.

Toughen up, I told myself. I figured that I had endured the worst that any person could. I convinced myself that from now on, nothing would make me cry.

A large shadow approached me. I kept my gaze down, trying to swallow against fear, afraid to look up and find Toño looking down at me. My heart pounded. I looked up slowly.

It was the same woman from before with the child gripping tightly to her yellow dress. They looked at me with hunger. I dug into my backpack for the potato tacos and offered them with a sad smile. The woman took them and gave one to the child. She put away the rest in her dress pocket.

Her daughter chewed slowly. Her light-brown eyes locked into mine. The woman turned to leave without saying a word, but the child remained silently still, gripping the woman's dress. The woman tried to get her daughter to follow, but the child refused. She looked down at her as if reading her mind. The child gave the dress a firm tug.

"You want to give her one?" the woman asked.

Her daughter looked up and tugged the dress again.

The woman lowered her shoulder bag and opened it. I peeked inside and saw colorful ceramic animals. I looked up at her.

"Take one," she said. "Yaya wishes to give it to you."

I looked back in the bag and saw it. A shiny red rooster partly hidden by other ceramic animals. A memory of Wally's crow echoed in the back of my mind.

The woman shook the bag lightly. "Go on."

I reached in and grabbed the rooster. It was beautiful, identical to Wally. I stared at it, recalling Mamá's words: "Well, it just might be a good omen that Wally wants all of you to be awake and alert every day." It also had a nice weight to it that brought to mind Ramón's advice about a stone.

"Good choice," the woman said, giving me a goodbye smile and walking away. Her daughter followed, looking back. She never smiled.

I studied the rooster in my hand, remembering Julia telling Mamá that I wanted her to make Wally into chicken soup. I remembered Juanito saying that he would never catch him for that. The ceramic rooster brought back so many memories.

"Attention, passengers, the bus with destination to Ciudad Tecún Umán will be arriving in fifteen minutes," a female voice said over the loudspeaker, bringing me back to reality.

I put the rooster in my backpack and flung it over my shoulder. Then I made my way to the ticket counter. An elderly woman sat counting money when I arrived.

"I need to use your restroom."

"Right over there," she said, pointing to a door next to a drinking fountain.

I walked to the fountain and drank my fill. Then I stepped into the restroom to wash my face. I opened the water faucet and looked at myself in the mirror. I looked older, somehow different. I splashed water on my face, then looked in the mirror again, expecting to see my old self, but I looked different. I caught a glimpse of life molding me into someone else. I looked away, frightened, and went back outside to wait for the bus. I wanted to leave the bus station before Toño and the other men came looking for me.

The bus arrived as scheduled. The driver stood by the door taking tickets from boarding passengers. I boarded the bus and took the first available window seat behind the driver. I scooted past a young girl, not much older than Juanito.

The young girl stared at me with curiosity. "What's your name?" she asked, once I was seated with my backpack on my lap.

"Rosa," I answered.

"I'm Wendy. I'm traveling with my mom and dad and my little brother. We're going to …"

"Wendy, leave that young lady alone," a woman said from behind.

I turned to give her the sad smile I had now grown accustomed to.

"You'll have to excuse our daughter. She loves to talk. I'm Angélica, and this is my husband, Pablo."

He smiled and waved hello.

"And this is Pablo Jr. You've already met our daughter, Wendy."

I stretched out my hand to shake theirs. "Nice to meet you."

"I heard you say your name is Rosa."

I nodded and tried to smile, but all I could offer was a frown. "Yes."

"Where are you headed?"

"I'm going to Tecún Umán, where I'm to cross the river into Tapachula, Mexico. There, I'll board La Bestia to Houston to live with my Aunt Teresa."

My eyes filled with tears hearing myself mention my lamentable destination. I turned around to hide my sorrow, reminding myself not to cry.

Angélica looked at her husband with concern.

I was tired. My head throbbed. I closed my eyes to rest them for a second but fell asleep instantly.

Unbeknownst to me, Gato was slumped in his seat at the back of the bus, out of sight.

Mamá

After Julia's funeral, it did not take María de los Santos long to follow her children to her sister Hilda's home. General Jesús Garza, who had paid his respects at Julia's funeral, drove her there. As they approached the city dump, María was astonished by the extreme poverty of the people she saw.

The general parked in front of Hilda's shack and nodded toward it. "According to the GPS, that's the place."

María rushed out of the vehicle toward the shack and banged on the front door.

"María!" Hilda called.

When the two sisters saw each other, they threw themselves into each other's arms, overjoyed to see one another. Hilda cried nervously. Fresh scrapes and bruises were on her face and arms. Juanito came out from behind her and hugged his mother tightly.

"Rosa!" María called into the house.

Hilda turned away in shame.

"Rosa left," Juanito said, looking up.

María looked down at him, trying to understand. Then she looked at Hilda for an answer.

The general and his lieutenants waited with concern.

"Hilda, where's my daughter?" Mamá demanded.

Hilda knelt down. "Please forgive me," she cried.

"Where is she?!" Mamá yelled.

"I had to send her away. They were going to take her."

"Who was going to take her?" General Garza demanded.

"My husband, Toño. He owes Ricardo money for drinking at La Cueva bar. He wanted to sell her to him. They would've raped her and prostituted her at that awful place. I had to send her back to the bus station. I told her to buy a ticket to Tecún Umán, then cross into Mexico and go to Tapachula. I gave her Yolanda's number. She was the one who helped Teresa get to the United States." Aunt Hilda covered her face and cried.

María looked horrified at her sister.

General Garza turned to his lieutenants. "You two, go check out that bar. Call General Hernández to send in a full raid. The rest of us will go to the bus station. With any luck, she's still there." He looked down at Hilda. "I'll need the phone number of this Yolanda woman."

Hilda nodded, then looked at her sister. "María, I'm sorry. It was the only way to protect her from them."

"Everyone, let's go," the general ordered. "To the bus station."

Hilda gave the two soldiers directions to the bar, then gathered the twins to take them with her. When they all arrived at the bus station, everyone went in different directions. No one seemed to know anything. After searching the entire station, María and Juanito sat down on a bench at the departure section. She was overwhelmed with grief, fearing the worst.

"First my Julia, and now my Rosa," Mamá cried.

A colorfully dressed woman walked by with a child tugging at her dress. The child saw María and stopped. The woman stopped as well, when she noticed the child did not move but only stared into María's eyes.

"Let's move along, Yaya," the woman said. "It's none of our business."

María looked up at the woman, teary eyed, then back at the child. The woman tried to pull away, but the child remained motionless. María gasped. She could tell that the child knew something. She slid off the bench and knelt down, meeting the child at eye level. Juanito followed.

"You know who I'm looking for?" María asked, hopeful. "Tell me, little one, have you seen my Rosa?"

The child remained silent, staring into María's teary eyes, sensing her pain.

"We must go," the woman insisted. She tried to move away again, but Yaya remained motionless, then looked up and gave her mother's dress a firm tug. She understood what the child wanted.

"It isn't right to alter destiny, Yaya. It will only cause more problems."

María covered her face and cried.

Yaya hugged her, then withdrew slightly. She wiped the tears from María's eyes with her dirty, little hands, showing no emotion.

María sighed and smiled sadly at the child's tender kindness. Yaya looked up at her mother.

Finally, the woman gave in with a sigh and knelt in front of María and Juanito. "Your daughter came through here yesterday. Twice she gave us food for Yaya. She carries a heavy burden," the woman said as she removed her shoulder bag and opened it.

María and Juanito peeked inside, hoping for a clue.

"Yaya doesn't speak," the woman whispered. "She senses things. She wanted to repay your daughter's kindness. I told her to reach into the bag of omens and pick an animal."

The woman withdrew a shiny red rooster. "Your daughter picked one of these."

María gasped and covered her mouth.

"That's Wally!" Juanito exclaimed.

María took his small hand and squeezed it.

"This animal is the image of her nature," the woman said, in a hoarse whisper. "She is not afraid to fight, even to the death, for she is a fighter. But she also knows when to run. That will save her on her journey. Your daughter will have many troubles and encounter many evils, but she's like a rooster, a fighter."

The woman stood up. "Let's go, Yaya," she said and turned to lead her daughter away.

"Wait!" María called.

Yaya looked back.

"Will I ever see my Rosa again?"

Yaya looked up at the woman, then back at María and walked away without saying anything.

María and Juanito remained on the floor, sobbing in each other's arms. A hand touched her shoulder from behind. She looked back to see the general. Hilda and the twins joined them on the floor.

"She's gone," the general said. "Been gone since late yesterday. I called my contacts in the Guatemalan military. They dispatched a squad to look for her. I'll have my people call this Yolanda woman in Tapachula, Mexico. I promise you that I'll find your daughter."

They drove back to Hilda's home. The only sound heard was María sobbing.

When they arrived, General Garza helped everyone go inside, then instructed, "Please, wait for me here. It seems we've run into horrors at that La Cueva bar. I have to go there and see what we've got."

María, Juanito and Hilda waited a long while in desperation, not knowing what to do next. A few hours later, the general returned.

"Ladies, it may not be a consolation, but we shut the Cueva bar down, arrested the men and are now taking the young girls they had to their homes," he announced.

"Oh my God," María exclaimed.

"At least something good has come out of this horrible mess," the general said.

"Thanks so much, General," María said. "Now, can you help me find my Rosa? She's out there somewhere, lost and afraid."

"I apologize it took me so long," the general said. "We had a lot of interrogating to do. There were twenty-two other girls, some as young as thirteen."

"Oh, no," María said, shocked.

"We need to get your son to San Pedro to testify in front of the federal prosecutor. The Guatemalan government will contact me as soon as they find your daughter. I'm sorry, but there's nothing else we can do here."

"What about us?" Aunt Hilda asked. "When Toño comes home, he won't show any mercy. He'll kill us."

"Toño won't be coming back. He and his drinking buddies are headed to the worst Guatemalan prison."

Hilda's eyes widened. She could not contain her relief.

As much as María wanted to find Rosa, she had Juanito to look after, and she was not about to separate herself from him for any reason. With a broken heart, she agreed to the general's plan.

María held on tight to her son and sobbed all the way back to Honduras. She was troubled by memories of the little girl and her mother who stated that Rosa had to fight to survive. The loss of her two daughters upset her to the point of illness.

"My sweet Rosita," she whispered, "happy birthday." She gasped at her own words. "Be brave. Be smart." She placed her cheek on Juanito's head and cried.

The soldiers drove back in what seemed to be silent anger.

The Suchiate River

"Welcome to Ciudad Tecún Umán," the driver announced. "Since it's three a.m., I'm going to allow you to wait in the bus until it's time to get it serviced. Then everyone must go." The driver knew that most of the passengers were migrants headed for the United States. They had nowhere to wait safely until daylight. Ciudad Tecún Umán was a small town with many migrants passing through. Most were poor and hungry. At night, the small town was not safe. Letting the passengers wait aboard the bus was a kind gesture that everyone appreciated.

Wendy turned to face her parents. "Mom, I have to go to the restroom."

"Me too," Angélica said. "I need to change Pablito and stretch my legs."

"You girls go on," Pablo said. "Please stay together and be careful. I'll wait here with our things."

"Rosa?" Angélica called. "Would you like to join us?"

"Yes," I answered. "I was afraid to go by myself. It's so dark outside."

"Come on," Wendy urged. She took my hand and led me to the door.

We stepped off the bus, taking in a breath of burnt diesel. Angélica followed with Pablo Jr.

There was a line ahead of us, and it took nearly ten minutes for us to use the restroom. Angélica gave Pablo Jr. a sponge bath while Wendy and I brushed our teeth. When I was done, Angélica handed Pablo Jr. to me. He was the cutest baby I had ever held, all smiles and giggles. I couldn't help but share in his unknown joy. I got an awkward feeling in my chest when I caught myself laughing after so much crying the day before. I didn't mind holding him. He brought the healing I desperately needed.

Angélica smiled as she called her son back to her. The child stretched his arms out to his mother. I was fortunate to have found good travel companions. It was dreadful knowing we would soon part ways. We came out of the restroom and headed for a drinking fountain before getting back on the bus.

"You girls try to get some more sleep," Angélica said. "We have a lot of walking to do. You need to be well rested."

She made a good point. I placed my backpack against the window to use as a pillow. Wendy laid her head on my arm. Angélica peeked over the seats and was about to say something.

"It's okay," I said with a smile. I needed her warmth. It provided a sense of protection.

Angélica smiled and sat back.

I was asleep when Pablo returned, but my senses were on full alert. I woke up when I felt someone moving behind me. When I recognized the familiar whispers, I immediately fell back asleep.

I remember I was dreaming. I turned around to see a dark shadow move away from me. I envisioned the child who had given me the rooster. She was offering it to me. I took it just as the shadow touched the back of my shoulder.

I jumped out of my seat, frightened and awake, ready to defend myself.

"I'm sorry," Angélica said, retracting her hand. "I didn't mean to startle you, but we have to get off the bus."

My heart pounded in my chest as I came to my senses. I looked out the window. It was daylight. I felt a bit foolish.

"Are you okay?" Angélica asked with a look of concern.

"Yes," I said with a tight smile. "I'm sorry. I was having a scary dream when you touched me." I grabbed my backpack and put it on.

"Were you having a nightmare?" Wendy asked.

"I don't know. It just felt really spooky, that's all."

"Everyone, make sure that you don't forget anything," Pablo said. He was standing in the aisle with his backpack on, waiting for us to get off the bus. "Check the seats and the floor to make sure you didn't drop anything."

As I got off, I wondered how long I would be able to tag along with them.

"Let's go find ourselves some breakfast," Pablo said, looking at me. "I want to cross into Mexico as soon as possible. We don't want to hang around here too long."

We left the bus station with the crowd heading for the Suchiate River. I was surprised to see that we weren't the only busload headed there. There were two more with men and women of all ages and lots of children. Some of the children traveling alone were as young as Juanito.

It took us twenty minutes to reach the river. Early dawn illuminated the people on the riverbank. Some of them had camped overnight and had fires going. They heated coffee and were frying fish. Others were picking up camp.

We reached a food stand, where a man wearing an apron of the US flag was busy making tacos and taking orders. The aroma was appetizing, but I wasn't hungry.

"How about this place?" Pablo asked. He unbuckled his backpack. "It looks as good as any." He leaned the backpack against the counter and sat down on a stool. "What you got for breakfast?" he asked the vendor.

"Today I have Mexican potatoes with beans, Mexican eggs with beans and Mexican bacon with beans."

"That sure is a lot of Mexican," Pablo said.

"It's the colors of the Mexican flag: green jalapeños, white onions and red tomatoes."

"Sounds good. I'll have three Mexican potatoes with beans and whatever else my wife orders."

Angélica looked at me to see what kind of tacos I wanted.

"That's okay. I'm not hungry," I told her. "Besides, I still have plenty of *pastelitos* I need to finish first."

"You sure?" Pablo asked. "We're buying."

I smiled at their kindness. "I'm sure but thank you."

Angélica and Pablo looked at each other. Pablo nodded toward me as I began walking to the riverbank.

"Rosa, wait!" Angélica called, walking toward me.

I turned around to wait for her.

"Pablo and I were wondering if you'd like to team up with us? We could really use your help with the children, and we'd protect each other until we get to the United States. Besides, Wendy has really taken a liking to you."

A sense of relief came over me. "Thank you. I promise not to be a burden. And you have the most beautiful children."

"Then, we have ourselves a deal," Angélica said, stretching her hand out to me.

I shook it gratefully. "I'll be by the water. Enjoy your breakfast."

"I'll order you a couple of tacos to go in case you get hungry later," Angélica said and then turned around to rejoin her family. She signaled Pablo with thumbs up.

I walked toward the riverbank, looking for a secluded place to think. I couldn't stop dwelling on my dream with the child who gave me the rooster.

The Suchiate River was wide. It flowed calmly with a hidden force. Boats and rafts were crossing people into Mexican territory. I was amazed with how many people were at the river. There were runners all over the place. Their job was to trade currencies with the migrants. They carried the Mexican, Guatemalan, Honduran and Salvadoran bills wrapped around their fingers. Most of the migrants exchanged their national currency for Mexican pesos.

I made my way upstream. The sun was out. I closed my eyes and faced it, warming my face with its delicious heat. There were fewer people the further I went. My mind went back to my dream. *Why was the little girl in my dream?* I needed to think, to find the answers to my questions. *What about the rooster? Why was she trying to give it to me?* Maybe I was being superstitious.

I came upon a huge oak that provided a cool shade. The area looked secluded, peaceful. Part of the oak's shade extended into the river. I listened for people, but all I heard were the watery whispers of the current. I slid my backpack off and searched for the rooster. I felt like it might actually speak to me and provide the answers I needed.

"Here you are," I whispered when I pulled it out, initiating a conversation with the ceramic figurine.

I set my backpack down against the oak and stood contemplating my little red rooster, examining it for answers. I held it up toward the sun, blocking its rays from my eyes. It looked at me the way Wally did from my windowsill.

"What is it with you?" I whispered. "What are you trying to tell me?"

Everything went dark.

Gato

Gato followed Rosa and her friends from a distance. There was no way he could approach her. There were too many people around. Besides, he already had more than enough money to make it to the United States. He did not need any unnecessary attention.

"Hey, you," Gato called out to one of the runners.

The runner stopped to look back at him.

"I have Honduran lempiras and Guatemalan quetzales to trade for Mexican pesos."

The runner stared at Gato. He whistled for support and walked cautiously toward him. He walked to Gato with two older kids who had come from different directions. The runners knew how malicious the Mara gangs were because they had had grave encounters with them in the past. They could identify them easily by their tattoos.

"How much do you want to trade?" the runner asked.

Gato reached into the canvas bag and pulled out the Honduran lempiras and the Guatemalan quetzales. He counted the currencies in front of the runners before handing them over.

"I want large bills," Gato said.

The runner agreed, counted out Mexican pesos and handed them to Gato. Gato twisted slightly to open the canvas bag and put his money away. His shirt lifted from his side, exposing a gun. The runners took a step back.

Gato made his way toward the riverbank. He spotted Rosa walking upstream. Like a jaguar hunting its prey, he began to stalk her, making sure no one followed. His adrenaline picked up with his pace as he saw fewer and fewer people. He slowed down when he saw Rosa stop beneath the shade of a giant oak. He looked around one last time. There was no one around.

Gato picked up speed when Rosa placed her backpack against the tree. He took out his gun as he moved, getting closer and closer. Rosa's back was to him when he swung around from behind and hit her nose with the bottom of the pistol. Rosa fell to the ground. Gato stood over her, looking around to make sure no one saw him. He breathed hard, his heart pounding as he removed the canvas bag and dropped it next to Rosa's backpack.

Gato sat down on Rosa's waist, dropped his gun and clasped his hands on her throat. Rosa could not breathe. Her nose was broken and swollen, blocking her nasal passage, but she opened her eyes and gasped for air. Her head was turned right and her arm stretched out. Next to her hand was the rooster. She remembered with lightning speed: "Find yourself a good stone. Something not too heavy ...."

Rosa looked into his wild eyes. Gato did not care that she was awake, he was so confident in his power over her.

Gato did not see it coming. Rosa swung the rooster at his head and knocked him off her. Then, she slammed the rooster on his forehead, lifted it and brought it down hard on the top of his skull. Blood spurted out and covered his face. He tried to block her blows as she continued to bash him with madness.

Someone yelled. Gato got up, grabbed his gun and ran toward the river. His head was bleeding from several places.

It was Pablo who had yelled. He missed grabbing Gato when the Mara dove into the dark waters of the Suchiate River.

Rosa scurried backward toward the base of the tree, trembling, clutching the rooster tightly.

"It's okay, Rosa," Pablo said. "He's gone."

Rosa was unresponsive, traumatized, fearing Gato would come back. *How did he find me? Was he following me? Why was he here?*

Pablo talked to Rosa trying to bring her back to her senses. "Angélica sent me to find you."

Rosa did not answer, she just looked past him, shivering. She held the bloodied rooster tightly in her hand.

Angélica arrived with the children, followed by others, and she handed the baby to Pablo. She knelt down next to Rosa and hugged her, trying to calm her down. When Rosa felt the safety of her embrace, she cried. Wendy stood frightened next to her father, wondering what had happened to her new friend.

Some of the men searched the river with Pablo, but no one saw Gato in the dark waters. Angélica finally pulled away, but Rosa continued to cry.

"It's okay," Angélica whispered. "Here, let me look at you."

Rosa turned and saw the others behind Angélica. Everyone looked horrified at the damage done to her nose. It lay flat to the left, crushed and bleeding. Her breathing was congested and raspy.

Angélica remembered a towel in Rosa's backpack and got it out. One of the men brought a bucket of water from the river. Angélica wet a corner of the towel and cleaned the blood from Rosa's face. It was swelling. Her eyes and nose were turning black.

An old woman from the crowd stepped forward and looked Rosa over. She knelt down and said to Angélica, "She's in no condition to travel. I have to fix her nose while the fracture is fresh, or she won't make the journey. She won't be able to breathe. Look at me, girl. Everyone here knows me as *La curandera*. My name is Celia, and I can cure people of illness and injury. Want me to fix your nose?"

Rosa squeezed her eyes shut and nodded.

"Lay on your back," Celia said and looked up at Angélica for assistance. "Hold her down."

Angélica got behind Rosa and laid her on the grass next to the big oak. Then she folded the towel and placed it beneath Rosa's head.

Celia tried to pry the rooster from Rosa's hand. "Let go of this thing," she ordered.

But Rosa only tightened her grip.

"Fine," Celia mumbled, then looked at Angélica. "I need you to hold her hands. Otherwise, she'll clobber me in the head with that thing when I straighten her nose."

Angélica agreed and held down both of Rosa's wrists.

Celia sat astride Rosa's waist and held her forehead down with a calloused palm. "This is going to hurt, but you can trust me. I've fixed more than a few broken noses in my time."

She felt around Rosa's nose, causing the young girl to wince and squeeze her eyes shut, trying to resist the pain. The woman then stuck two fingers in her mouth and brought them out dripping with saliva. She turned her palm up and slowly inserted both fingers into Rosa's nose. Rosa's body constricted. The woman's slippery fingers came to a stop on Rosa's broken bones. Celia wiggled her fingers forward, wedging them deeper beneath the broken fragments. Rosa's head tilted back when the woman's fingers slid all the way in. Celia curled her fingers and stretched Rosa's nose up from the inside. Rosa's back arched with the pain, causing her to scream out loud. Rosa wanted to get away but was afraid to move. Celia's fingers rubbed the inner walls of Rosa's nose roughly, making sure the small bone and cartilage fragments were set back in place. Then it was over. The fingers were gone.

Celia got up, keeping her eyes on the ceramic rooster clutched in Rosa's white-knuckled hands. "Sit her up and hand me the towel," Celia requested.

Angélica helped Rosa sit up. Rosa felt dizzy as the woman cleaned her fingers and then placed the towel under her nose.

"Blow gently," she said.

Rosa looked up at her with bloodshot, teary eyes and tried to blow. Nothing came out. The heavy congestion was blocked by her fear of pain.

"You're gonna have to try harder than that if you want to breathe properly," Celia said.

Rosa shut her eyes, taking in courage, and tried again. The pain was intense. Two red clots slithered out from her nostrils, allowing a gust of fresh oxygen to rush into her lungs.

"That's what I wanted to see. Good girl."

Rosa cried softly. *I miss my mom, Julia, Juanito ... my home.*

Angélica pulled Rosa to her feet and hugged her tightly. Rosa cried on her shoulder while Angélica caressed the back of her head.

"We better get you to my tent and into a warm bath," Celia said.

The old woman led the way, followed by Angélica. Pablo and the children went back to the taco stand for their things.

In Celia's tent there was a trough of water next to a table and a small cot against one wall. Boxes were stacked throughout the tent. There were religious relics and statues, and jars with herbs everywhere. Men came in with pails of hot and cold water until the trough was full enough for a bath.

"Take off your clothes and get in the water," Celia ordered.

Rosa set the rooster on the floor and removed her uniform. She became teary-eyed, picked up the figurine and got in the trough. The warm water dulled her pain. Celia and Angélica helped Rosa shampoo her hair and bathe her body.

Rosa submerged her lathered hair into the peaceful stillness of the water.

"I found you some clean underclothes. I'm sure they will fit," Celia offered.

Angélica tenderly hooked Rosa by her underarms and brought her up gently. "Come on, kiddo, you're not quitting on me this easy."

As Angélica was helping Rosa, Celia peppered the water with spices. A sweet fragrance filled the tent.

"Soak in the water for a little while until your body absorbs the herbs," Celia said. "They'll help you heal and attract spirits to protect you."

Rosa sat in the water, cleaning the rooster and trying to put her mind in order. *Wally crowing on my windowsill ... the child in my dream ... the shadow... Gato. How did he find me?*

After an hour, Celia helped Rosa out of the trough and handed her a towel. "Dry yourself. Underwear's on the table. Change behind those boxes." She pointed behind Rosa.

Rosa took the clothes and went behind the boxes. She dried herself, put on the underclothes and wrapped herself in the towel before she came out in search of her uniform and Wally.

"Don't put that on yet," Celia instructed. "Lie down on the cot."

Rosa lay down, and Angélica and Celia placed peeled aloe vera leaves on her face and neck.

"Now get some rest so that you can heal," Celia said.

Rosa held Wally on her tummy and felt the cool sensation from the aloe vera on her wounds. Before she knew it, she was asleep.

Later that afternoon, outside the tent, Pablo asked, "Do you think she'll be able to travel?"

"I don't know," Angélica said, "but we can't just leave her here."

"I'm not saying we should leave her. If she can't travel, we need to move from here to a safe place until she's better. If we cross into Mexico, we can rent a hotel room in Tapachula and have a doctor see her."

"I can travel," Rosa blurted out hoarsely from inside the tent.

Angélica rushed in to find Rosa removing the aloe from her scratches. She had just awakened.

At that moment, Celia came in carrying a basket overflowing with sun-dried clothes. "How's our brave girl?"

"She seems well rested," Angélica said, taking the clothes from Celia and then helping Rosa into her uniform.

"Is it safe to come in?" Pablo called from outside.

"Yes," said the *curandera*.

Pablo walked in and said he wanted to take a look at Rosa. His face filled with sorrow. Wendy came in behind him, carrying Pablo Jr. on her side, his small legs wrapped around her thin waist. She looked frightened.

"Are you sure you can travel?" Pablo asked with uncertainty.

Everyone looked to Rosa for an answer. She seemed hesitant.

Pablo stared at Rosa, waiting for an answer. "If we're going to cross, we need to go now. The boaters are about to quit for the day, and we need to find a safe place to sleep."

Rosa looked at Wendy holding the baby, bravely doing her part. Rosa went to her and knelt down, then removed a lock of hair from her eyes. "I have a little brother, too," she said. "His name is Juanito."

"Are you okay?" Wendy asked, teary-eyed.

"I'll be fine."

"I thought you were going to die."

"It'll take a lot more than that to kill a strong girl like me," Rosa said.

Wendy stared at the dark, swollen areas around Rosa's eyes and nose.

"That's just a bruise," Rosa said. "It'll go away."

Wendy smiled and hugged Rosa the best that she could with her free arm.

Rosa stood up to face the others. Angélica and Celia looked at Rosa with motherly admiration.

Respect replaced Pablo's grimace. In that instant, Rosa became part of their family.

"So, when do we leave?" Rosa asked.

"Now," Pablo said, "if you're ready."

"I'm ready."

Rosa thanked the healer and gave her a hug. Celia was sad to see her leave. Rosa grabbed Wally and stepped out of the tent. The sun was still out. Its heat stung her face. She knew the sun would go down soon. Red trickles ran down her nose into the corners of her mouth. She wiped them off quickly, not wanting Pablo to see them and change his mind.

As they headed for the river, the boater Pablo had contracted saw them approaching and began loading the backpacks that Pablo had left in his care. Rosa was the first to board the boat and sat down at the bow. She looked for her reflection in the water, then looked away, frightened by the image of her deformed face.

The boater pulled the engine rope, and the small motor started with a low purr. They were almost across the river, when he looked back and cursed under his breath. A convoy of Guatemalan military had arrived at the shore, causing migrants to run in all directions.

Pablo and Angélica looked at each other with relief.

"This will be my last trip of the day," the boater said. "The last time they raided the river, they took my boat. I won't let them have this one."

Pablo's family reached the Mexican side and disembarked. The boater helped Pablo unload the backpacks and was soon on his way upstream.

Rosa dug into her backpack for a towel and placed Wally inside. She wiped her nose again and hung the towel around her neck, then put her backpack on.

"Is everyone ready to go?" Pablo asked.

"Rosa, do you want me to help you with your bag?" Wendy asked.

"What bag?" Rosa had not noticed the white canvas bag that was among the backpacks. "All I have is my backpack."

"Well, it couldn't have belonged to anyone at the riverbank," Pablo said thoughtfully. "Only one person comes to mind who could've left this bag behind in a hurry."

"The one who attacked Rosa," Angélica whispered.

Everyone stared at the canvas bag on the ground, fearful of what it might contain.

Tapachula

Pablo looked around to make sure no one was watching from some hidden place. When he felt sure that we were alone, he unbuckled his backpack and let it slide off. He knelt and opened the canvas bag's zipper. Everyone looked down with intense curiosity. Pablo pulled out a bottle of rum. A look of disappointment came across everyone's face, as if they were expecting a genie to be set free. Pablo tossed the bottle into the bushes. Next, he pulled out a man's watch, a cowboy novel and a money bag.

"What's in the small bag?" Wendy asked.

Pablo opened the zipper and looked inside. His eyes grew as wide as his daughter's. The money did not concern him. He was used to being around lots of cash. What troubled him was the person looking to get it back. He looked around once more, making sure that no one was watching. He bundled everything together and shoved it into his own backpack. Having those possessions worried him for the safety of his family. He didn't want to attract unnecessary attention. He buckled his backpack and looked around with uncertainty.

"Let's go. I have a feeling that whoever owns this bag will be looking to get it back."

He flashed me a look. For an instant, I felt he might abandon me. "How are you feeling?" he asked. My face throbbed. A trickle of blood seeped from my right nostril. "I'm all right," I lied.

Angélica came up to me and gently cleaned the trickle from my lips.

"Then, you lead the way," Pablo said. He tried to hide the pity in his face.

"Wendy, you follow Rosa, then Angélica with the baby. I'll steer you from behind and cover the tail. I want all of you to be on high alert from now on for anyone that may be following us. Okay?"

Everyone agreed.

Angélica gave me a baby wipe to keep my nose clean. I walked ahead. I figured that Pablo gave me the responsibility of leading the way to motivate me. The idea that he might be using me as bait crossed my mind, but I doubted that I would see Gato again anytime soon. I remembered hitting him on the head at least three times.

Angélica caught up to me, looking concerned. I tried to look strong by keeping my nose clean and moving along at a steady pace.

"How you holdin' up, kiddo?"

I glanced at her as she walked beside me. The mere thought of speaking sent a stinging sensation throughout my face. "My face hurts, and I can't breathe through my nose," I answered in a congested whisper. "I don't think I can go much further." I felt like I might pass out at any moment. The thought of lying beneath some bushes to die didn't seem so bad, but I kept on.

"You have to keep moving," Pablo said from behind. "Try not to think about the pain. Focus on moving your legs. It shouldn't be too much longer. I'll find us a ride into town as soon as we get on the main road. We'll rent hotel rooms so everyone can rest while I go find a doctor who can come see you."

"Okay," I said hoarsely.

Angélica handed me a bottle of water. I took it and swallowed two large gulps.

"Stop for a second. Let me help you blow your nose," Angélica offered.

"It's going to hurt," I said. Pressure was building in my sinus.

"Just blow softly so that you're able to breathe better," she said, cupping her hand under my nose with a baby wipe.

I did as she told me. My face stung. Two blood clots slithered out. I wanted to cry but was happy to be able to breathe again. However, my nose congested again almost right away. Soon, I was back to breathing through my mouth.

We made our way through paths in the jungle, then onto a dirt road but saw no cars. Pablo was alert for any potential danger that could befall us. I began to slow down. Angélica gave me more water and suggested we rest for a couple of minutes.

"Rosa, I need you to keep a good eye out for this guy," Pablo said. It was his way of filling me with courage. "He may be following us. I need all eyes looking out until we're in the safety of a hotel."

We reached the main highway. Drainage ditches ran along both sides. A large truck stop was visible at a short distance. We pressed on toward it. Walking in a slant on the ditches made it harder for me to advance. I arrived exhausted. Diesel trucks crowded the fuel pumps. I couldn't believe that I had made it this far. I also knew that I couldn't go any further. A two-foot cement border surrounded the truck stop, separating it from the jungle.

"You girls rest here. I'll go find us a ride," Pablo said.

We removed our backpacks and sat down. Even sitting was too much for me. I was tempted to lie down on the other side of the cement border and close my eyes.

Pablo was back in less than five minutes. "Everyone, grab your backpacks. I found a ride to Tapachula. A vegetable merchant agreed to drop us off at a good hotel for two hundred pesos. Let's go."

We followed him to the back of a flatbed truck. It had a load of vegetables he was hauling from Guatemala to the farmer's market in Tapachula.

The merchant removed a guardrail from the rear. Pablo climbed on and moved some boxes around to make room for us to sit. He jumped off and helped us onto the flatbed. We sat in the center watching Pablo and the merchant secure the guardrail. When Pablo felt that it was secure, he climbed into the cab with the merchant.

I leaned back against the boxes and rested my head on Angélica's shoulder as the truck began to move. It was the most uncomfortable ride I had ever been on. The hard surface vibrated and jumped as the truck hit bumps in the road. My face tingled as if covered by a thousand ants. There was nothing I could do but endure the rough ride and hope that it would be over soon.

The truck sped down the highway for what seemed like an eternity. Finally, we felt it slow down and exit the highway. And then it jerked us around the city streets, making continuous stops. Suddenly, the engine went dead, killing the vibrations with it. We stood up to look over the boxes. The truck was parked in front of an elegant building. I had only seen buildings like this in magazines. The outside of the hotel was adorned with short palm trees and a landscape that gave it a tropical look. It was a single story, light-tan building with large windows. Nicely dressed people moved about inside.

Pablo came to remove the guardrail. "Is everyone okay?"
"Are we at a hotel, Daddy?" Wendy asked.
"Yes, sweetie. Come here."
Wendy jumped into her father's arms. Pablo gave her a hug, then put her down. He took the baby from Angélica. I was finally back on solid ground. It felt foreign to my body. We stood on the sidewalk looking tired, beat up and hungry. We really looked like migrants.

We followed Pablo into the reception area and waited while he went to the counter and rented the rooms. Angélica sat me on a cushioned chair. I relaxed and allowed myself a moment to soak up the comfort.

Pablo returned with two keys. I stood up and followed him to our rooms. Many people we passed stared at me with curiosity and concern.

Pablo opened the first door and moved aside for us to go in. Two queen beds were on the left wall. Across from them was a dresser with a television. To the right of the dresser was the adjoining door to the second room. On the far right was the bathroom. Thick, large curtains covered the back wall.

"This'll be Rosa and Wendy's room," Pablo said and went to open the adjoining door. "Angélica, the baby and I will sleep in here."

I had never been in a hotel. I sat down on one bed as Wendy jumped up and down on the other. Angélica handed the baby to Wendy and went to turn on the air conditioner. I removed my backpack and placed it on the other side of the bed. I wanted to get under the covers and go to sleep.

Sensing my intentions, Angélica came to me. "Do you want to blow your nose one more time before you get into bed?"

I nodded and walked to the bathroom. What I saw in the mirror shocked me. A black bruise with purple outlines masked my swollen face and bloodshot eyes. My eyes were so swollen, it was a wonder I could see. I looked down, gripped the counter and cried.

Angélica came in when she heard me. "What's wrong?" I turned away to hide my ugliness from her but found myself looking in the mirror again. "My face!" I cried. "Look at it! No wonder people stare at me. Why did Gato do this to me? Why did they kill Julia? Why does he want to kill me? Why?"

Angélica looked confused. She tried to put together the pieces of information about my past without asking questions—the same ones she didn't want to be asked herself.

"I don't know, honey," she said, trying to console me. "Let's blow your nose and get you to bed."

I nodded.

"You girls make yourselves comfortable," Pablo said on his way out. "I'm going out to find a doctor. I saw many businesses still open."

It was early evening, and in a town like this, accustomed to a steady flow of immigrants, doctors often made house calls well into the night, especially for those in need.

I heard the door open and close. Angélica sat down on the bed and caressed my hair. "When you get better, you can tell me all about this Gato."

I was suddenly awakened by knocks at the door. My heart filled with fear. I backed up against the headboard and hugged my knees, bracing myself.

Angélica rushed to the door and looked through the peephole. "It's Pablo."

She opened the door. He was accompanied by an elderly gentleman carrying a black medical bag.

"There she is," Pablo said.

The man sat down at the edge of the bed. He was careful to maintain his distance and gain my trust. I lifted my face slowly, expecting to see a look of horror.

He smiled tenderly. "Believe me, young lady, I've seen a lot worse. My name is Miguel Gonzales. Pablo has explained your situation to me. What's your name?"

"Rosa," I said hoarsely.

"Rosa, such a pretty name. I'll bet you're really pretty beneath that bruise you're wearing." He paused to study my reaction. "Don't worry. In a week or so, you'll be back to your pretty little self again. Is it okay if I check your vitals?"

I nodded.

"Very well. Stretch out your legs. Try to relax."

I did as I was told and let out a deep breath through my mouth.

"Give me your hand."

He felt my pulse while checking his watch. His touch felt warm and friendly. When he was done, he listened to my heart and lungs with his stethoscope. "I need you to open your mouth and hold this thermometer beneath your tongue."

I opened my mouth. The cold thermometer slid under my tongue.

"Hold it there while I check your eyes and nose."

I nodded.

"Let me know if it hurts. I'll be as gentle as possible." He pushed my eyelids up with his thumb and looked in my eyes. "Now, follow my pen with your eyes without moving your head."

He moved his pen from far right to far left. I followed it, ignoring the thermometer sticking out of my mouth. He moved the pen up high and down low. My eyes chased after it as far as they could.

"Good. I'm going to feel around your nose and look into your nostrils to see if there are any broken bones blocking your sinus."
I winced.
"Oops. Sorry about that." He removed the thermometer and checked the reading. "Is your nose stuffed?"
I nodded.
The congestion had built up as I slept. Angélica came to me with a damp face towel to help clean my nose. She cupped it under my nose as I blew. The fierce pain made my eyes water.
"She shouldn't be blowing that nose," the doctor said. "It could hurt her eyes."
"The healer who fixed her nose said to do it in order for her to breathe while traveling," Angélica said.
"Well, no more blowing. And definitely no more traveling until this young lady is well," the doctor said firmly.
Pablo and Angélica nodded as if I was now their responsibility.
The doctor tilted my head back to look into my nostrils with another instrument, then he examined my ears. "Whoever fixed that nose did a magnificent job," the doctor said. He placed his medical tools in the bag. "I bet there won't be a blemish once the swelling's gone."
Angélica gave me a compassionate smile.
"Your blood pressure and temperature are a little high," he continued, "but that's normal for a person in your condition. Your eye coordination is good. They're just bloodshot. That'll all go away with the bruise and the swelling. Your ears aren't bleeding ... that's also a good sign." He withdrew a notepad from his shirt pocket. "I'm prescribing her some anti-inflammatories, a nasal spray and some pain pills. That should help heal that pretty little nose."

Wendy giggled.

The doctor tore the prescription from the pad and handed it to Pablo. "If you don't feel better after a couple of days," the doctor said, "have Pablo come find me." He stood up and studied me for a moment. "You're a brave girl and you're going to be fine. Take all your medication and rest." He gave me a final smile before looking at Pablo and Angélica. "I can't emphasize this enough. There has to be absolutely no more traveling for her until she can breathe properly." The look on his face matched the sternness of his tone. "Are we clear?"

"No more traveling, doctor's orders," Pablo said, smiling at me.

The doctor looked at me. "Remember to drink plenty of water and eat before taking your medication." He turned and headed for the door.

Pablo opened the door and followed the doctor out. He looked back at his wife. "I'm going to get the medicine and some groceries. I'll be back in a few minutes."

Angélica brought me the two tacos she had bought that morning. I devoured them, fueled by the doctor's positive diagnosis. I didn't realize how hungry I was and, even though my face hurt with every bite, I devoured the food. After eating, I closed my eyes and fell asleep.

Tapachula

I awoke to the sound of cartoons on the television. My pillow was stained from my nasal discharge. I sat up feeling heavily congested. My mouth was dry. I backed up against the headboard to study the room as I came to my senses.

Wendy and her baby brother were on the next bed watching television. Her eyes widened when she saw me.

"Mamá, Rosa's awake!" she called out.

Pablo Jr. giggled with excitement. Wendy lifted him to the side of her waist and came to my bed. They stared at me, waiting for me to say something. I forced a smile.

Angélica came in from the next room. She held a stack of folded clothes. "Glad to see you're awake. How do you feel?"

"My face hurts." I was afraid to mention my congestion for fear of the fierce pain that would follow. "I need water."

"I'll get it for you," Wendy said. She spun around, causing Pablo Jr. more giggles, and headed for the other room.

Angélica giggled at her daughter's glee.

Wendy returned with a bottle of water and handed it to me. I tried twisting it open, but I was too weak. I set it on my lap.

Angélica took it from me and opened it. "Here you go." She handed it to me with a forced smile.

I took the bottle and brought it carelessly to my mouth. A sharp pain on my top lip watered my eyes. "Ow!" I cried out.

"Whoa. Slow down, kiddo."

I drank the water and set the bottle on the nightstand. Angélica and Wendy stared at me with pitiful curiosity.

"I need to use the bathroom." I peeled the covers off and swung my legs out.

Angélica took my hand to help me stand and followed me to the bathroom.

When I stepped inside, I looked at myself in the mirror, hoping that by some small miracle my face would be back to normal. It wasn't. The only difference was that my eyes weren't swollen. A pale-yellow formed around my bruised face. I faced down and let the heavy congestion run toward my nose. I was about to blow when I remembered the doctor's orders. Instead, I forced the mucus to my throat and spit it out.

I walked out and headed back to the safety of my bed. A clean change of clothes waited for me there.

"I bought these for you at a small clothing store that's near the hotel," Angélica said. "I figured you wouldn't wake up while we were gone."

"Thank you for letting me sleep. I mean, thank you for everything."

Angélica took me in her arms and gave me a hug that reminded me of Mamá. "It's nothing."

She held me, giving me the warmth of her healing love. I relaxed in her embrace. I felt I could absorb all of the positive energy this kind woman gave in abundance.

She withdrew enough to look into my eyes. "Everything's going to be all right from now on," she said, caressing the back of my head. "You know why?"

I shook my head.

"Because we're going to stick together like a family until we get to the United States."

I studied her face, feeling her compassion.

"Now, let's get you into a warm bath, so you can eat and take your medicine. I'll prepare the water for you."

She let go and headed for the bathroom.

Wendy came and stood in front of me. "They have a humongous pool here. Come see," she said and turned to lead the way to the far wall and pulled the curtain open enough to look outside.

The crystal-blue water was surrounded by pool furniture and a large variety of tropical plants.

"I've been waiting for you to wake up so we can go swimming. I won't go by myself." She turned to face me. "You wanna go as soon as you feel better?"

I gave her a slight smile. "Okay."

The truth was that I didn't want to go anywhere until the bruise on my face was gone, but it was the least I could do for these kind people.

Angélica came out of the bathroom drying her hands with a small towel. "Water's ready."

I picked up my clothes and headed for the bathroom. The large mirror called to me, but I ignored it and set my clothes on the counter. The tub was filled with warm suds. I stepped into it and winced as I lowered myself into the warm water.

Angélica returned and picked up my dirty laundry. "I'll get your food and medicine ready." She headed out, leaving the door partly open. "I'm going to throw your clothes in the washer first. Washing machines are right around the hall," she called.

I was alone with my thoughts. *Who are these people that demonstrate so much love?* I felt extremely fortunate to have sat with them on the bus. I quivered at the thought of going through this alone.

The water felt wonderful. I bathed myself slowly, letting the warmth engulf me. I rested my head, closed my eyes and prayed that Juanito was okay and that Mamá had picked him up by now. *Did she bury Julia next to Papá? What became of Aunt Hilda? And Gato? How did he find me? God, how?*

After a while, Angélica walked in, breaking my train of thought. "Don't go back to sleep in there, come on out. You need to eat."

I stepped out of the tub and dried gently. The clothes fit perfectly. The underclothes were white cotton. The blouse was tan with a red rose that ran vertical on the left side. The matching pants had the same rose on the right leg. They were comfortably loose. I tied my hair into a ponytail and headed straight back to the comfort and safety of my bed. I felt ugly. I didn't want to be seen.

"Oh, no, you don't," Angélica said. She stopped me before I could pull the covers over my head. "You've had your share of sleep for a while, kiddo. Get up and let's see how the clothes fit."

I stood in front of her feeling a bit shy.

"Do you like the roses?"

I nodded.

"When I saw this cute outfit, I couldn't resist thinking how happy it would make you feel to wear something different. I had to get it for you."

"Thank you."

"Come, sit at the table and eat."

I smiled and did as I was told. Angélica placed a Styrofoam plate filled with beef fajitas, beans, rice, *pico de gallo*, lemon wedges, corn tortillas in front of me along with a cup of Coke with crushed ice. I didn't expect such a delicious feast. My mouth watered with the aroma.

"You want me to brush your hair?" Wendy asked.

Before I could answer, I felt her small hands undoing my ponytail and working the tangles out of my hair with gentle tugs.

"Here's a red hair band to match her outfit," Angélica said and placed it on the table.

"Okay, Mom," Wendy said. She was happy to have some girl-time with me.

She put the band on my hair, pulling it into a tight ponytail. Then she stepped back to examine her work.

"Great job," Angélica said. "I think we may have a future Hollywood hairstylist."

Wendy gave her mother a proud smile.

"Here are your pills and the nasal spray," Angélica said and placed them on the table. "Take the pills after you finish eating. I'll help you with the spray."

I finished eating and swallowed my pills.

Angélica tilted my head back gently and applied the nasal spray to my nostrils. It began working within seconds. I walked to the restroom to spit out the loosened congestion. There was hardly a trickle after that. The congestion stopped, and I crawled back into bed to watch TV with Wendy. I was asleep within minutes.

I woke up the next morning to the aroma of bacon, reminding me of home. I got out of bed and walked to the bathroom. Angélica was at the table setting out Styrofoam plates. Pablo sat at the table feeding his son. I forced a smile as I walked by them. The swelling on my face was gone, except for my nose. My eyes were still bloodshot, but I was recovering.

I returned from the bathroom ready to help Angélica with whatever I could, no matter how awful I looked.

"Can I help with anything?" I asked, feeling a strong urge to carry on.

Pablo looked up at me with a friendly smile. "Good morning."

"Good morning, everyone," I said shyly. "Please forgive my manners."

Wendy rushed by me and sat down at the table. "I'm hungry," she said, looking down at the plate in front of her.

"Speaking of manners, young lady, where are yours?" Angélica said.

"Sorry," Wendy said. "Good morning, everybody."

"I have to go," Pablo announced and stood up from the table. "My new boss will be outside the hotel in a few minutes," he said, handing Angélica the baby. He gave each family member a peck on the cheek before leaving.

Angélica gave me a compassionate smile. "Have a seat. How are you feeling this morning?"

"Better," I said, returning her smile and sitting down for breakfast. It was scrambled eggs Mexican style with beef jerky, chopped jalapeños and tomatoes, refried beans, bacon, diced potatoes, corn tortillas and a cup of juice. I dug into my food.

"Pablo found temporary work with the vegetable merchant," Angélica said. "I told him that he didn't have to work. We have more than enough money to make it all the way to the United States."

"I'm sorry that I slowed you down," I said, afraid to look up. "You've spent a lot of money on this hotel room, the doctor, the medicine."

"No, Rosa," she said, reaching across the table for my hand. "We have cash and credit cards. And besides that, we have all the money from the canvas bag. If you knew our situation, you'd understand why this works out best for all of us."

I wondered what their situation was. I'd been so caught up with myself that I never stopped to think about them. I dared not ask. "One day, when we're all in the US, we'll tell you."

She gave my hand a gentle squeeze and said, "I have an idea. Since Pablo's gone for half the day, why don't we clean up here and go down to the store to buy swimsuits?"

"Yay!" Wendy exclaimed. "We're going swimming!"

"When did Pablo get a job?" The thought of me finding work crossed my mind.

"Just yesterday. He's going to help load and unload vegetables at the farmer's market. It's a short distance from here. He'll work with the merchant who gave us a ride."

"I don't think I wanna go anywhere. I look so ugly."

Wendy giggled. "You're not ugly. You're just bruised."

"You're not here to impress anyone," Angélica said. "It'll do you some good to have a little distraction." She looked at me for an answer.

I said nothing.

"You're looking much better. Don't worry about anything. Focus on getting well so that we can continue this journey, okay?"

"Okay." I frowned. I was afraid of running into Gato again.

Angélica brought my pills and set them beside my food. "Don't forget to take them right after you eat, like the doctor said."

After I ate, I swallowed the pills with some juice and applied the nasal spray. My congestion eased. I stood up and headed for the bathroom feeling the heaviness run toward my throat. I spit the bloody clots into the sink, relieved that they were getting smaller.

We finished cleaning up and got ready to go. Angélica settled Pablo Jr. into her harness. Wendy waited eagerly by the door. Outside, the sun felt bright in my eyes. Its healing rays stung my face, causing an itch around my nose.

"Pablo said not to wander too far from the hotel," Angélica said. "Everything we need is on this block."

We made our way through the crowded sidewalk. Some of the people turned to get a second look at me.

"Look at that poor girl's face," an elderly woman said to her husband.

"What happened to her?" a teenage boy asked his mother.

I walked closely behind Wendy, looking down, ashamed.

"Don't pay them any attention," Angélica said. "If anyone asks you what happened, I'll butt in and make up a story."

"It'll have to be some story," I said.

We walked into the store. Round racks of clothing filled the floor of the shop. Counters covered with folded clothes lined the far wall. A young woman sitting at the register looked up from a magazine and winced at my face for a moment, then went back to reading.

Angélica held up a pair of spandex shorts. "How about these?"

I took the shorts to study them closer.

"Try them on while I find you a matching top."

The shorts looked to be my size, but where did she expect me to try them on?

"Where?" I asked. I looked for the most concealed corner of the store.

Angélica couldn't help but giggle at my confusion. "Excuse me, miss," she called to the young woman at the counter, "is there a dressing room?"

"In here," she said, pointing to a door next to the counter.

I went in and changed into the shorts. They gave me a tight, protective feeling.

Angélica came in and handed me a black top. "How do the shorts fit?"

"Good, I like them," I said, looking down. Then, I put on the blouse. "How much are they? I don't think I can afford the blouse, but I really need these shorts."

"I told you; we have money. Don't worry. Take them off so we can pay. I need to find a sewing kit and something for the kids."

Wendy picked a pink swimsuit for herself and red shorts for her little brother. Angélica paid for our things, and we headed back to the hotel after stopping at a small grocery store to buy stuff for sandwiches.

The room was freezing when we returned. I wasn't accustomed to air conditioning. Angélica turned it off, saying it might be too cold for the baby.

Wendy and I changed into our swimsuits while Angélica changed Pablo Jr. We went out through the sliding glass door behind the thick curtain. A winding trail led us through tropical plants. The scent of greenery mingled with the smell of chlorine, as we neared the pool.

The kidney shaped pool was surrounded by sunbathers while others were in the water. Everyone looked happy, oblivious to the bruises on my face and my bloodshot eyes. Some looked at me momentarily, as if wondering if I was okay. They were reassured when they saw my company. That was better for me. I wasn't a good liar, and I didn't feel like explaining myself to strangers.

Wendy ran and jumped into the pool, trying to make a big splash. Angélica sat at the shallow end with the baby. I sat at the edge with my legs in the water.

"Rosa, get in," Wendy yelled from the opposite side of the pool. "Come on." She was making her way back in a doggie paddle, barely sustaining her head above water.

I pushed off into the crystal water and let myself sink to the bottom until my ears popped. The water was clear. I could see everything. I had never swum in a pool, only the local rivers where Papá worked, where the water was dark green and you never knew what you'd find at the bottom.

I looked up and saw Wendy swimming above me. I pushed myself up from the pool floor as hard as I could and exploded out in front of her, causing her considerable giggles.

"I'll race you all the way to my mom," Wendy said, pointing to where Angélica played with Pablo Jr.

"Okay," I warned, "but I'm really fast."

"Let's see who's faster," she said as she swam toward her mother. "Last one eats a rotten egg."

We swam with all our strength, vying to take the lead. I slowed down to let her win.

"You cheated," I accused her jokingly.

"I'm just a faster swimmer than you," she giggled.

We played in the pool until the afternoon. Everyone else had left for lunch, and we were left with the pool to ourselves. Wendy was the first to complain about hunger. Angélica got out of the pool and entrusted her baby to me while she went to prepare the sandwiches.

Pablo Jr. was excited to change hands. I sat with him in the shallow end, letting him splash and giggle. Wendy swam with endless energy. Pablo Jr. splashed around and babbled to himself. I was startled by a man's growl. Wendy screamed, followed by a big splash. My first instinct was to hug the baby to my chest and get out of the pool.

"Wendy!" I screamed.

"Help!" I wanted the world to hear me.

A man was with Wendy underwater.

"Help!" I walked backward screaming. My heart drummed in my chest. I almost knocked the tray of food from Angélica's hands with my hysteria.

Wendy came out of the water, laughing in her father's arms.

Angélica put the food down on a poolside table and took her son from my arms. She tried to calm me down, but my heart pounded with terror, even as I cried with relief. Some of the hotel guests came out to see what was going on. People stared at me from every direction. I turned and ran inside and stood crying by the elevator.

Angélica came in with the baby, followed by Wendy and Pablo, who carried the food tray. We went to our rooms, where they sat with me and waited patiently, wishing that there was something they could do.

"What's wrong with me? How can something simple trigger so much fear within me? Am I going to be like this for the rest of my life?" I said, looking down and crying.

"Rosa," Pablo said.

I looked up.

"I'm sorry I frightened you. That's the way Wendy and I play when we're in a pool."

"It's okay," I whispered. "It's not your fault."

Pablo looked at his wife, then back at me. "I think it's time you told us your story."

I took a deep breath to stall my crying and closed my eyes. My mind took me back to that morning on our way to school. I tried to remain calm as I told them what happened to my sister. When I got to Aunt Hilda, I remembered the phone number that she gave me for a woman named Yolanda in Tapachula. I rushed from the table to my backpack, hoping that I hadn't lost the number. I found it at the bottom with Aunt Teresa's address.

"Let me see it," Pablo said.

I handed him the piece of paper. He went to the telephone on the nightstand and dialed the number. We waited for a reaction from him. Pablo frowned. There was no answer. He redialed and let it ring until it was obvious that no one would pick up.

"No one's answering." He hung up the phone. "We'll try again later."

"You poor thing," Angélica said. "No wonder everything frightens you." She put her hand on my shoulder. "Why don't you take a warm shower and change into some dry clothes? When you finish, we'll eat."

After lunch, Pablo showed me a tattoo that ran along the outside of his right foot. There were numbers and letters. I didn't understand.

"It's a phone number with my code," he said. "Angélica has one too."

Angélica brought her foot up to where I could see the numbers clearly. It was the same phone number with a different code.

"I think it would be wise for you to get one. This number has been active in the US for over thirty years. The way it works is, I put this phone number with a code matching your description on your right foot. We send a letter to the US explaining why you're fleeing your country. In it goes your code, blood sample and all of your contact information from Honduras, Guatemala and the United States. This is in case anything happens to you. They can identify your remains and return them to your loved ones. If you don't want to get the number, at least send the letter. Think about it. The letter has to go before we leave. We'll be leaving the day after tomorrow." He stood up from the table and headed to their room.

"Okay, I'll do it."

Pablo turned to look at his wife from the adjoining door. Then he looked at me.

"The tattoo. I want it."

"It's the right thing to do," Angélica said.

"I'll get the needle and ink ready," Pablo said. "We'll get started right away."

I gave Angélica my information from Santa Rosa, Aunt Hilda's address in Guatemala and Aunt Teresa's address in Houston. When the letter was ready, she went to her diaper bag for a band-aid, an alcohol pad and a safety pin. Then she pricked my index finger. "That wasn't so bad," she said. It was a tiny sting. Angélica took my hand and smeared blood on a box that she drew on the letter. She cleaned my finger and put a band-aid on it. I signed and printed my name below the box. Pablo and Angélica signed as witnesses.

Pablo was ready with the needle and the ink. He turned his chair to face me and slapped his knee with a smile. I placed my right foot on his knee and braced myself nervously, ready to face the unknown pain of the needle. It took Pablo ten minutes to finish the phone number. I never got used to the multiple pricks.

"Angélica, give me her code exactly how you wrote it in the letter," Pablo said.

"The code is F-RDLS-4-17-1997."

"Got it," Pablo said.

The more I thought about it, the more it made sense to me. I only hoped that it would never come to that.

"While you guys finish," Angélica said, "I'm going to dry Rosa's shorts, so I can sew some of the money from the canvas bag into the waistline. No one will be able to tell it's there when I'm done. We have eight-hundred dollars and five-thousand pesos. We can use them in case of an emergency or if something were to happen to the rest of our money."

Pablo finished the tattoo. He made sure that all the numbers and letters were distinguishable. Angélica put an antibiotic on my foot before I got in bed to watch TV with Wendy. I sank into the comfort of the mattress and fell asleep.

Everyone seemed energetic the following day. The swelling from my face was gone. The bruise was diminishing.

My bloodshot eyes showed signs of clearing. I hardly coughed up any blood clots and my breathing was pretty much back to normal. Angélica was diligent about making me take my pills and using the nasal spray.

While Pablo was working with the vegetable merchant, we cleaned the room. Before noon, Angélica left the hotel to mail the letter to the United States. I spent the rest of the day watching Wendy swim. We killed time waiting for Pablo to get off work and bring us news of his day. He recommended that we get some rest. We would need it for the journey we were to resume the next day.

That night, we washed our clothes and laid everything on the bed to inventory before packing. I exchanged contact information with Angélica and placed her information at the bottom of my backpack along with Aunt Teresa's. Pablo gave me a wristwatch from the canvas bag. I hated the thought of who it might have belonged to. He figured that someone should put it to use.

I didn't want to leave the safety of the hotel, but I knew that I couldn't stay there forever. I decided to go forward, vigilant. I had already experienced savagery in my journey, what else was in store for me? All that I knew is that we would soon board La Bestia.

The Train of Death

I woke up ready to face the unknown. Pablo advised us to eat and to use the restroom before we left. We did not want to feel uncomfortable once we boarded La Bestia.

I examined my face in the restroom mirror. I didn't look as gruesome as before although it still made people stare. I finished getting dressed. My uniform felt clean, as did my socks and my mountain shoes. I fixed my hair into a tight ponytail and took one last look in the mirror. *I'll make it all the way to Aunt Teresa's front door.* I gave myself a compassionate smile and stepped out of the bathroom. I was ready.

Pablo and Angélica moved about the two rooms getting the final things packed. Wendy made her way to the bathroom half asleep. Angélica followed her to give her a bath. I sat on the bed next to the telephone and tried dialing Yolanda's number. There was still no answer. I hated the thought of moving on without talking to her first. There was nothing I could do. I hung up the phone, frustrated with a woman I did not know. Angélica handed me the baby to get my mind off the unknown woman.

Soon, everyone was ready. We gave the room a final look-over. I had everything I needed. Wally was within easy reach in my backpack. I had the pair of gloves that Ramón had given me. I had the most money that I have ever seen sewn into the waistline of my shorts. And I had a watch.

Pablo turned in the room keys on our way out. We made our way to the marketplace while we waited for the vegetable merchant to arrive, our ride to the train yard.

Angélica bought extra tacos to take for lunch and some water bottles for everyone to carry. She made sure that the diaper bag was fully equipped before leaving.

The merchant arrived shortly after we were done buying our supplies. Pablo removed the guardrail and helped us onto the truck bed. We sat down on some cardboard in the center and watched Pablo secure the guardrail in place. Then, he disappeared into the cab.

The vibration of the truck triggered the feeling of invisible ants on my face. I closed my eyes, resisting the urge to scratch. *Soon, I'll be in Houston with Aunt Teresa. Once there, I'll call Mamá and Juanito to let them know I'm safe. I'm going to work hard to send Mamá and Juanito all the help I can.*

I needed to keep my focus on the goal of the journey. I was suddenly anxious to get to Houston. I couldn't wait to see Aunt Teresa, to start my life anew in a country that I'd only heard about from the conversations of others. They had been conversations that never interested me. It never would have occurred to me that I'd leave my family to go there. My eyes watered. I reminded myself to be tough, to think of something else before sorrow overwhelmed me.

There were lots of migrants walking as we got closer to La Bestia's tracks. We saw men and women of all ages and children, lots and lots of children.

The merchant drove into the train yard and stopped behind the crowd of migrants. Pablo got off and removed the guardrail. When we were off the truck, he returned the guardrail to its place and waved goodbye to the merchant. The truck drove away and was soon out of sight.

We walked to the head of the crowd of migrants. Everyone waited patiently for a man talking on his cell phone. Two others stood close behind him. Handguns protruded from their waists.

The man finished the call, then spoke instructions to his men. He walked to the head of the crowd, causing a silence. It was obvious that he was the one in charge.

"Everyone, listen up," the man said. "My name is Héctor. I'll be collecting the fees from those of you wishing to ride La Bestia. Don't be afraid of the men behind me, he pointed at the train behind him with his thumb, they're here for your protection and mine. "The price is four hundred dollars per person."

The immigrants whined.

"Let me finish. It's four hundred dollars if you wish to ride in an empty boxcar. For a hundred and fifty dollars, you can ride on a flatbed. The cheapest fare is riding on the top of the hoppers for fifty dollars."

The migrants spoke among themselves. Most complained about the high prices.

Héctor raised his hands for silence, and everyone looked at him intently.

"No one rides La Bestia for free. Anyone caught aboard without paying will be thrown off. Those of you who pay, like you're supposed to, will receive a ticket. The purple ticket is for the boxcar, the red ticket is for the flatbed and the yellow ticket is for the hoppers. There will be absolutely no wandering around La Bestia. Stay in your own car. When you reach Veracruz, you will show your tickets to my colleagues. They will allow you to finish your trip for another small fee. I advise you to take good care of your ticket. Having said that, who wants to be first?"

"Everyone, gather round," Pablo instructed us. "I think we should ride the flatbed. I brought a tent and a tarp. The tent will protect us from the sun. I don't like the idea of being in a confined space where we could be locked inside."

We agreed with Pablo and covered him while he got the money ready. People were pleading with Héctor to let them ride for free, but he showed neither mercy nor compassion to anyone. He ordered them to go away until they could afford the fare.

When it was our turn, Héctor asked, "How many are with you?"

"Three females, my infant son and myself."

"And how would you like to travel?"

"We can only afford the flatbed."

"That will be seven hundred and fifty American."

Pablo counted the money into his hand.

Héctor put it with the rest of his bankroll and handed everyone a red ticket. When he came to me, he stared at my face and wouldn't let go of the ticket.

I held on to the ticket, expecting him to let go, but he would not. I looked down, afraid to look him in the face, hoping my ticket would not tear. Héctor looked at Pablo. "What happened to her?"

"She was attacked by a Mara at the Suchiate River."

Héctor looked back at me. He lifted my face with the side of his finger, trying to look beyond my bloodshot eyes.

I looked back at him, annoyed, holding onto my ticket.

"Is this true?"

"Yes," I whispered, agitated.

He stared at me a moment longer, trying to discern the truth. Finally, he loosened his fingers.

I pulled my ticket free and moved past him toward Angélica and the kids. I felt his gaze burn my back while Pablo led us to the flatbed. I remembered my gloves, slid my backpack off my shoulders and dug them out. I flashed my ticket to one of the men.

The man nodded toward the ladder. The rungs were dark with grime. I put my gloves on and climbed onto the flatbed. I traded Angélica the gloves for her baby. Once she was on, she gave Pablo the gloves and placed the baby in his harness. Pablo lifted Wendy onto the flatbed, then he tossed their backpacks on and climbed on himself. He returned the gloves once he was onboard.

"Nice gloves," he said. "I have some, too. I wish I would've thought to buy some for Angélica and Wendy."

"A taxi driver named Ramón gave them to me in Guatemala City when I ran from my aunt Hilda's husband. He was missing an arm. He said he lost it riding La Bestia. If he'd worn a pair of gloves, he said, he would've never lost it."

Tall walls guarded each end of the flatbed. A water thermos was tied to the side of each railcar ladder. It was the only thing provided for free by the cartel. There were railroad ties scattered about on the flatbed. Pablo and some of the men moved them around to make room for the tent. Pablo removed the tarp and tent he had tied to the bottom of his backpack and set the tent up against the front end of the wall. Some of the men helped him brace the ends with railroad ties. They stacked some of the ties to the right side of the tent to serve as benches for the long ride ahead. The floor of the tent was lined with the tarp. Angélica spread a blanket over it to make a soft space for the baby.

Wendy and I sat outside studying our surroundings. I was nervous about my encounter with Héctor. The last thing I needed was to be noticed by him and his men. That was asking for too much, considering my face. For an instant, I was glad for the ugly bruises. The thought of hiding behind them consoled me.

I couldn't wait for La Bestia to get moving, hopefully getting me away from Héctor's glare. I thought it would be good to hide inside the tent until we reached Veracruz.

Pablo stood next to Wendy. "You did good by not showing Héctor any fear," he said to me. "I want you to always stick close to us. That goes for you too, young lady. No wandering off, understood?" He gave his daughter a stern look.

"Okay," we said.

Angélica came to sit with us after Pablo Jr. fell asleep on the blanket. The hopper cars in front and back began to fill with migrants.

"Tomorrow at about this time, we'll pass through a town called Juchitán," Pablo said. "Some of the good people there park their vehicles close to the railroad tracks and toss food and water up to the migrants. Others hold out bags for the migrants to stick their arm through the loop as the train goes by. We have plenty of food and water, but I think it would be good to practice hooking a bag safely. We can give whatever we get to the other migrants, in this way, we can befriend them so that we can help each other. What do you girls think?"

The three of us agreed with Pablo.

"If you girls need to use the restroom, there's a bedpan inside the tent with a small roll of plastic bags inside. Just put a bag on the bedpan. When you're done, put a knot on it and discretely toss it overboard," Angélica told us.

Wendy and I nodded.

"How's your nose feeling?" Pablo asked.

"It only hurts if I mess with it, but if I leave it alone it's fine."

"As soon as the train gets moving, I want to teach you girls a few self-defense techniques. They will give you the upper hand with any opponent and can save your lives. We'll also do some light exercises, like push-ups, sit-ups and squats to keep the muscles fit, a little warm-up before the training."

"Yay!" Wendy exclaimed, excited at the thought of learning self-defense.

Pablo looked to me for an answer.

"I'd like to learn to defend myself."

"Good. We'll start as soon as we're out of the city."

It wasn't long before we felt La Bestia's powerful pull. She inched forward, stretching her long vertebrae with loud, metallic crashes. An air horn blasted from one of the locomotives. I felt a sense of relief knowing I would be safe for a while. I felt that there shouldn't be any dangers while the train was moving. Soon, I would be in Houston with Aunt Teresa.

La Bestia made its way out of town. Townsfolk stopped to watch the train filled with migrants. Some waved. A few shook their heads, as if knowing the dangers ahead.

Wendy and I held hands a few feet from the edge. We took our last views of Tapachula. She waved happily at those who waved. Pablo and Angélica joined us.

A warm wind soothed my face as La Bestia picked up speed. Soon we were out of town, passing through farms filled with cattle, goats and miles of green pastures. The train entered a cave made by large trees and branches that covered the tracks for miles. An old vaquero sat on his horse waiting patiently for La Bestia to pass. He leaned forward on his saddle horn and watched the migrants go by. A jackrabbit hung by its hind legs behind his saddle.

"All right," Pablo said. "Time to have some fun. Let's get started on your training. Stand over here in the open area next to the tent."

Wendy and I did as we were told and faced Pablo. He stood before us with his hands behind his back, as if he were a real drill sergeant and we his new recruits.

"Today is our first day of workout and training," he said. "I want you to give me twenty push-ups, twenty sit-ups and twenty squats." He moved in a drill-sergeant demeanor. "Go all the way up and all the way down. We have twenty minutes to do them. Follow my lead in sets of ten. Are you ready?" He looked at us sternly while keeping an eye on the tent where his son slept.

"Yes," Wendy answered, with enthusiasm.

"Then let's partner up. I'll partner with Angélica. Wendy and Rosa will be partners throughout the exercise. Everyone down for the first set of push-ups. I'll allow you to do them on your knees if you need to."

La Bestia made its way north at full speed. We began our first day's workout on her pulsating back, feeling her vibrations resonate throughout our bodies. By our third set, we were out of breath and strength. I couldn't move another muscle. Pablo allowed us a water break. That was enough to gather our strength for the final round.

"Now, ladies, these are the easiest and most effective self-defense techniques that I can teach you in a day. If you learn to use them exactly as I'm going to teach you, they could save your lives. If you're ever in a situation where you're forced to use them, make sure that the first strike is delivered accurately. Your opponent won't give you a second opportunity. You have to make the first strike count."

Some of the migrants gathered around to listen to Pablo's instructions.

"The first part of your lesson is to memorize what I'm going to tell you. Repeat after me. Number one: if your opponent can't see, he can't fight."

Wendy and I whispered the lesson.

"Number two: if your opponent can't breathe, he can't fight." He waited for Wendy and me to repeat it. "And number three: if your opponent can't stand, he can't fight. I want you to look at your partner and say this over and over until your muscles are very much aware of what you're saying."

We all repeated the three phrases.

"Now, again, repeat after me."

We repeated the phrases again. It took us ten minutes to memorize them.

"Now, back to number one. If your opponent can't see, he can't fight. I'm going to teach you how to blind your opponent using what we call the eye gouge. You girls, as defenseless as you may think you are, actually have a great advantage over your opponent."

"What advantage can a girl have over a grown man?" I blurted out but apologized immediately.

Pablo smiled. "The element of surprise." He gave us a moment to think about it.

"Let me explain. If an attacker comes at you, even if he has a knife in his hand, you mustn't be afraid. Only act like you are by raising your hands to your face with your palms facing out." He raised his hands in demonstration. "Make sure that the hand you plan to use to gouge his eyes has the fingers split in a V, like this."

We mimicked his hand gesture. Some of the migrants followed Pablo's instructions, especially the younger ones.

"Angélica, I want you to come at me, as if you have a knife in your hand. Watch carefully, girls. This is where the element of surprise lies."

Angélica lunged at Pablo.

He raised his hands, acting scared. Wendy laughed at the show her father was putting on. Soon, we were all laughing, including the migrants. Pablo stopped and looked at his daughter with the demeanor of an angry drill sergeant. "And what, may I ask, is so funny, young lady?"

Wendy wasn't buying it. "You're acting like a scared little girl, Daddy," she said, between giggles.

"Will you please let us know when we can continue with our lesson?"

"Okay, sorry."

Pablo smiled at his daughter. "The reason for acting scared is to let your opponent think just that. In doing so, you bring down his defenses enough to jab your fingers deep into his eyes, like this." He demonstrated the technique again without further interruption from his daughter. I began to understand the element of surprise.

"Remember, once you strike there's no turning back. You have to make it count. The pain in your opponent's eyes will be so intense, it will send a shock to his brain, causing him to drop whatever's in his hand. When your fingers are behind his eyeballs, he'll try to grab your wrist to pull your fingers out. Curl your fingers and gouge his eyes out." He waited a moment to let the technique set in our minds. "Don't show your opponent any mercy. He wasn't going to show it to you. If your opponent hasn't let go of his weapon, grab his wrist and hold him so that he doesn't pull away. But if he drops his weapon, grab him by the back of the head and gouge his eyes as hard as you can. Don't worry about hurting him. You'll be doing the world a favor if he was trying to hurt a girl. Remember, if your opponent can't see, he can't fight. I want you to practice this technique with your partner from a safe distance. Be careful not to hurt each other. Try to improve the speed of your jab. When I'm confident that you've memorized the technique, we'll move on to the next."

Pablo walked around us, studying our training. "Aim at your opponent's eyes with your mind by guiding your fingers over his nose and into his eye sockets." He stopped to look at me. "Imagine a real bad person. See yourself going deep into his eyes and ripping them out."

I closed my eyes and saw Gato's face in front of me. The thought of hurting him gave me a valor I'd never known. I savagely dug my fingers into his eyes. The satisfaction of my mindful revenge gave me great relief.

After we got the feel of the technique, Pablo decided we were ready to move on to the next lesson. "If your opponent can't breathe, he can't fight. This next technique is called the hand knife. Your weapon will be the inner edge of your hand." He demonstrated the edge of his hand in a striking motion. "If your opponent comes at you with a knife, like the beautiful Angélica is about to demonstrate, dodge the weapon by turning slightly sideways and grabbing your opponent's wrist. With lightning speed, strike the hand knife to the throat." He motioned for her to come at him with the imaginary knife. "Simple, ladies. Now, same as the last lesson. Practice the technique until it feels natural to you. I want you to feel how it works. Tell yourself, as you practice: 'If my opponent can't breathe, he can't fight.'"

"Wow," I whispered, amazed.

Pablo repeated the technique with his wife a few times until Wendy and I got the hang of it. A smile came over my face. The techniques gave a boost to my confidence. We practiced until our bodies moved gracefully. I was hungry to learn more self-defense. My mind and body absorbed the lessons rapidly. I assured myself that the next person who tried to hurt me would regret it.

"How are you girls feeling so far?" Pablo asked.

"I can beat you up, Daddy," Wendy said. She raised her right knee to a crane pose. Everyone laughed at her silliness.

"It seems somebody's far more advanced than I thought." Pablo folded his arms across his chest, waiting for Wendy to finish clowning around. "Can we move on, or would you like to teach us your moves?"

"You can continue," Wendy said, giggling.

Pablo gave her a smile before returning to his drill sergeant mode. "The last technique I'll demonstrate with Angélica is called the groin snatch. If an opponent comes at you from behind, hugs you around the waist and pins your arms to your sides …" He demonstrated with his wife, giving us their right-side view. Angélica reached her right hand behind her and gently grabbed hold of his crotch. A devilish grin flashed across her face. Pablo looked at us cross-eyed.

The migrant men winced and crossed their legs in imaginary pain.

"Easy, honey. We're married, remember," he whispered. "Don't be afraid to grab your opponent by the testicles, as my wife is so gently demonstrating. Grip tight and pull away from the body."

Angélica let go in the direction of the pull, and Pablo released her. She came over and stood next to Wendy and me.

"If your opponent can't stand, he can't fight." Pablo put forth his hand in a tight fist. "Squeeze hard and pull away from the body. His pain will be so intense, it'll knock him out. We like to refer to this as 'fade to black.' Practice this technique with each other until you feel you have it."

We practiced the groin snatch until we got it right, then we practiced the prior techniques again. We practiced until we were too tired and hungry to continue.

"I think it's time for lunch," Angélica said. She led the way into the tent. We ate *carne guisada* tacos with a slap of refried beans. They were cold but delicious.

Pablo went into his backpack and pulled out the canvas bag. I looked away from it. Remembering who it belonged to filled my chest with butterflies. He noticed my discomfort and put the bag away. He tossed me the cowboy novel and went back to eating.

"What do you want me to do with this?"

"I thought it might be a good idea if you sat outside the tent and read to Wendy and some of the other kids, help keep them distracted."

"He's right," Angélica said. "A good story will make this ride go a little smoother."

"It'll keep your mind occupied and not let you dwell on your past," Pablo said.

I read the back of the novel, acknowledging their point. It was a love story about a ranch hand and the rancher's daughter that ends in a gun battle.

After lunch, I sat with Wendy on the railroad ties. La Bestia vibrated, demonstrating the strength it wielded beneath us, slithering mechanically north at full speed. Migrants of all ages gathered around to listen.

"Are you a teacher?" a little boy interrupted.

I looked at him momentarily, thinking about his question. "No. I should be in school like you. But someday, I'll be a teacher."

"You have a pretty voice for reading stories," he said. "I miss my teachers from school." He looked down, thoughtful, saddened by his absence from school. Then, he looked up and smiled. "Will you be my teacher while we're on this train?"

My smile grew, stinging my nose. "I'll try my best."

I continued with the story. Everyone listened in silence. Butterflies in the pit of my stomach interrupted my reading. I looked toward the top of the hopper. Héctor stood at the edge, looking down at me, his arms folded across his chest. I tried to continue reading, but I couldn't concentrate. My sentences came out broken.

Gato

After having escaped the angry mob that had come to Rosa's aid by the riverside, Gato stayed hidden in the dense jungle for days, subsisting on the flesh of snakes and iguanas that he trapped and occasionally sneaking out at night to see what he could find to eat in the farmhouses nearby. He even lost his way for a couple of days, unable to recover his bearings, not able to follow the sun through the dense canopy of the forest.

Early morning light began to overcome the darkness on the day when Gato decided it was safe to emerge from his green refuge and continue his journey north. It would be daylight soon, and he still needed to travel undetected until he reached the railroad tracks. The cartels that controlled the migrant routes had spies everywhere. He needed to be as inconspicuous as possible. He finally found his way to Tapachula and walked through the streets with his hands in his pockets. His right hand gripped the .38 revolver. He was cold, tired and hungry.

It was still dawn and very chilly when he walked down a deserted street. This was the best time to steal something to warm himself—anything. People were still sleeping. He passed several residences, but their tall, iron gates were locked. He passed alleys, looking for something to steal or someone to rob. He would settle for the filthy jacket of a homeless man if he could find one. He seemed to be out of luck. Then, he saw something that made his heart jump. A boy in his late teens riding a motor scooter came to a stop at a traffic light. A stack of pizza boxes were tied to the rack behind his seat.

Gato calculated the situation, and his feet took action. He needed to get to him before the light turned green. The boy looked slightly bigger than Gato, but Gato had a gun in his hand. He hopped onto the scooter behind the boy and sunk the barrel of his .38 into the boy's lower back. He held on to the boy's waist with his left arm. The light turned green. The startled boy was in shock. He looked around for help, but there was no one.

"Turn around and drive back the same way you came," Gato whispered into his ear twisting the barrel of the gun into the boy's ribs.

The boy had no choice. He made a slow U-turn.

"Make a left at the next alley. Don't try to do anything stupid. I won't think about pulling the trigger."

The boy did as he was told.

They came upon a large dumpster. "Stop right here," Gato said.

The boy stopped, fearful of what might come next.

"Get off."

The boy got off the scooter and faced Gato. "You have the scooter. Take it and go."

"Nuh-uh. Give me your cap and sweater." Gato put down the kickstand and got off.

The boy handed over the clothing. Gato put them on, careful not to take his eyes off the boy. "Give me whatever money you have."

The boy handed over 500 pesos and some change, turning his pockets inside out.

"Now give me all your clothes."

The terrified boy removed his clothes and handed them over. Gato took the clothes and stuffed them into one of the scooter's saddlebags. The boy stood naked in the morning chill, covering his genitals.

"Turn around."

The boy began to cry. "Please don't kill me. I gave you all I have."

Gato pointed the gun at his head. "I said turn around."

The boy turned around slowly, sobbing gently, expecting to die. "You don't have to kill me," the boy said, with a shaky whisper. He closed his eyes wondering if he would hear the fatal gunshot.

The blow from the gun butt hit the boy in the back of the head. Darkness overcame him, and he collapsed next to the dumpster.

"You're lucky I'm saving my bullets," Gato sneered as he got on the scooter and raced out of the alley looking much like its previous driver. Gato rounded the corner and drove in the direction of the railroad tracks. The unconscious boy laid by the dumpster.

Gato reached the tracks and followed them out of town. He continued for miles until he entered a heavily wooded area. Large trees hung their massive branches high above the tracks. He stopped in a secluded area where he could rest from the bumpy ride. His stomach growled at the delicious smell of pizza. He untied the pizza boxes and sat against a tree to see what kind he was fortunate enough to have scored.

The first box contained a pepperoni and cheese pizza. The second had sausage and cheese. The third was a Mexican breakfast pizza with beans, eggs, sausage and salsa. Gato stacked the three pizzas in one box and took a triple stack for himself. He bit into the three slices at once. They were delicious. He had not eaten like this for the last two days. When he was done eating, he used the tie straps from the scooter to secure the box and make a shoulder strap. That would hold the box safely while he boarded La Bestia.

He went back to the scooter and changed into the rest of the boy's clothes, then sat on the tracks to tie the laces on his new shoes. He looked up and saw a vaquero and his horse some fifty yards downwind on the opposite side of the tracks. The cowboy was busy gutting a jackrabbit. He lifted the carcass by its hind legs and tied it to the back of his saddle. The horse let out uneasy snorts. The man walked toward the tree, picked up his rifle and looked around warily. He soothingly petted the horse on the neck while studying his surroundings, looking for whatever was making his horse nervous. He slid the rifle into its holster and led the horse a few feet down the tracks and then mounted. He rode away from Gato, heeding the animal's warning.

Gato climbed a tree with the thickest branches that hung over the tracks. He was safe until La Bestia came speeding through. He had jumped on and off of trains before. Other than a few cuts and bruises, he had never hurt himself. He had seen others fall and lose an arm or a leg. Some were mauled under the massive wheels and left behind for the vultures. This far out of town, La Bestia would be traveling at full speed.

Gato could barely make out the horse and rider now. He settled on a strong branch and waited. A distant air horn sounded. La Bestia was coming. He thought about climbing down and hopping on, but he figured that he would not be noticed if he jumped on the train from above. All he needed to do was jump on the platform and hold on. The air horn sounded again, closer this time. His heart pounded with anticipation. His adrenaline accelerated in tune with his memories of the train's speed.

La Bestia came into view. He was anxious to climb on and find a place of solitude where he could sleep. The train had five locomotives, followed by different cars, all filled with migrants. As the train sped below him, he tried matching his jump to the train's speed, but La Bestia was going too fast. He was seven feet above the tallest hopper, and he started to have second thoughts, when his eyes grew wide. A girl wearing the same uniform as Rosa's was on a flatbed car. Her back was to him when she sped by. She held the hand of a younger girl. *Was that Rosa?*

It was too late to back down. La Bestia had sped by so fast, he barely caught sight of her. He needed to find out if that was her. Fewer migrants were visible. Two men lying on their backs caught a glimpse of Gato in the branches. He waited to put some distance between them. The last thing that he needed was migrants asking him questions. He prepared himself to jump, calculating the speed of the hurtling cars. With Rosa fresh in his mind, he leaped like a cougar through the leaves.

Gato landed on the center platform of a hopper, but the train was going too fast. The platform was slippery with grime. The metal beast slithered out of his grasp as he scratched wildly, trying to hold onto anything. His hands caught the ledge of the car. He hung on, the pizza box hanging from his shoulder. He looked down for a safe place to land. This fall was going to hurt. If he broke a leg, he would never be El Gato again, but he was not about to fall into La Bestia's iron jaws—to be eaten alive. If he was lucky, he would land safely and get back on; but he doubted that. He was too high. He would have to push off to avoid the iron wheels. Beneath him the rock bed was speckled with debris from previous repairs.

His fingers were slipping, and he was doomed for sure. Then suddenly, the two migrants who had spotted him were pulling him up.

"Hold on, we got you," the bigger one said.

Within seconds, he was crawling onto the platform. He lay on his back, panting and watching the speeding branches above. His heart beating furiously. "Thanks," he told the two men.

Both wore rugged clothing and ball caps. "You're welcome," said the smaller of the two. "We saw you up in the branches and were curious to know if you made it."

"Yeah," the bigger one said. "You're lucky we were curious. Otherwise, you'd be in a lot of pain right now."

"Or dead," the smaller one said.

Gato thought about their words, when the larger one said, "You better not let Héctor, the train boss, find out you got on without paying."

Gato studied the men. They were a threat. They knew his secret and could blackmail him. They would not hesitate to sell him out.

"What you got in the pizza box?" the smaller one asked. "Is it pizza?" He reached for the box.

Gato slapped his hand away. "It's my pizza." He reached into his pocket and gripped his .38. *These two deserve to die, but I can't make a scene by shooting them off the train.* "It's all the food I have."

"We saved your life," the bigger one said. "That pizza will buy you some time with us. Give it to us, or I'll toss your skinny ass over."

"Or," the smaller one said, "we could tell Héctor, and he'll just give us the pizza as a reward. You know, a finder's fee." He let out a goofy laugh and reached for the box again.

Gato slapped his hand away a second time.

The bigger one took a step toward Gato, who drew his .38 and pointed it at their heads.

The men froze.

"Go ahead. Reach for it one more time."

The men stepped back with their hands raised at chest level.

"You think you can rob me? Don't you know what I am?"

The men shook their heads.

"Empty your pockets."

The men did as they were told. They each had a yellow ticket, a few loose coins and a wad of beef jerky wrapped in brown paper.

"Don't shoot us," the bigger one said. "My brother and I were just hungry. We don't want no trouble."

"Sometimes you don't have that choice," Gato sneered, took their belongings and put them in his pockets. "Turn around."

The brothers turned around nervously, not knowing what to expect.

"If you shoot us, Héctor and his men will hear the gunshots," the bigger brother said.

Gato kicked him off the train. "That's why you're jumping off."

The smaller brother did not wait for Gato to kick him over but jumped of his own accord.

Gato saw the brothers hit the rock bed and roll to a stop against splintered railroad ties. He watched them shrink, then vanish, as La Bestia sped on. He then looked around the top of the hoppers to see if anyone saw them fly off. No one was in sight. The last few migrants were at least ten cars ahead of him. Gato sat to rest for a moment, then looked up in time to see two men running toward him from the front. They jumped from car to car against the speeding train.

Gato opened his pizza box and grabbed a piece. He left the box open, hoping to draw their attention to the food.

"What are you doing back here all by yourself?" Héctor asked.

"I came back here to eat my pizza. It's all the food I have."

Héctor eyed Gato suspiciously. "Let me see your ticket."

Gato withdrew a yellow ticket from his pocket and handed it to him. Héctor inspected the ticket and handed it back to Gato, then looked down at the pizza.

"That's a lot of pizza," the other man said. Both of them reached into the box and grabbed a couple of pieces.

Gato hid his anger.

"Finish eating and join the others," Héctor said. "We don't like anyone riding by themselves."

Gato secured the pizza box and hung it on his neck and shoulder. He followed the men forward, confidently leaping behind them from one railcar to the next. They cleared La Bestia's iron jaws with each jump, until they reached the other migrants. Héctor and his companion stopped at the edge of the last car. They could not jump any further.

Gato sat down at a distance and waited for them to leave. Then he could search for the girl that looked like Rosa.

Héctor stood at the edge of the car, looking down with his arms folded across his chest. He could not help but stare at the beautiful girl with the black eyes. She was surrounded by migrants listening to her read a book.

"Omar would like her," Héctor said to his companion. "She could bring in a lot of money from his clients. Let's find a way to take her."

Rosa

I closed the book and looked around. I hadn't realized I had the attention of all the migrants on our railcar. Héctor appeared and disappeared every now and then. I got tired of watching out for him. We were on the same train. I was probably going to be seeing a lot of him.

"That'll be all for today," I said with a forced smile.

A lament erupted from the small crowd.

"Will you read again tomorrow?" the young boy asked.

"Yes."

He smiled, satisfied, and moved away to sit with the others.

Evening came, and everyone made themselves comfortable with what little they had. This was going to be our first night riding La Bestia. Everybody wanted to get the first day over with. The migrants lay on the floor, some covered with small blankets, others simply curled up next to each other with whatever they had on.

Pablo called everyone into the tent for the night. My place was at the end, against the wall. Wendy was to sleep next to me, followed by Pablo Jr. and Angélica. Pablo would sleep across the entrance.

"This is just like going camping," Wendy said to me. "Have you ever been camping?"

I was lying on my back, feeling the vibration of the iron beast's velocity from rail to rail. Fond memories of camping by the river's edge flooded my mind. "Yeah," I said, reminiscing. "Sometimes my dad would have a lot of work fishing the river. Our family would go with him and camp at the riverbank along with other families. It was a lot of fun. We ate fried fish with bacon and cornbread cooked over the campfire. We swam all day. It became a tradition."

Everyone listened quietly.

"I'll never forget how my sister Julia and I would lie outside our tent talking to other girls under the stars. Sometimes, all we did was look for shooting stars until we fell asleep."

"I wanna go look for shooting stars," Wendy said.

"Count some sheep, honey, and go to sleep," Pablo said.

Angélica and I laughed.

"Da-ad, stop being a meanie."

I woke the next morning with my arms around Wendy. My body ached all over. The vibrations brought me back to reality. I looked for Angélica, but only Pablo Jr. lay asleep beside Wendy.

I reached for my backpack to find my toothbrush and toothpaste. I withdrew my ceramic friend and gave him a thankful smile. "I'm sorry for telling Mamá to cook you when all you wanted to do was help me. Please keep waking them up every morning." I kissed its beak and put him back in my backpack. I found my toothbrush, put a layer of toothpaste on it and then shoved my backpack into its corner. I crawled over Wendy and the baby, carefully making my way out.

Pablo and Angélica stood by the edge of the railcar talking to some of the other migrants. I walked by with a closed smile, keeping my morning breath to myself. The water from the thermos was cold. I splashed water on my face and rubbed my eyes. It felt nice. I brushed my teeth and spit the foam out between the cars. My hair felt like messy tangles in the wind.

Angélica walked up to me. "Good morning, kiddo. How'd you sleep?"

"I'm sore," I complained. "I don't know if it's from the workout or the constant vibration." I hugged myself, shuddering against the morning wind.

Angélica lifted my face with her fingertips. "Your bruises are fading. Soon, you'll be back to normal. This'll all seem like a bad dream." A motherly smile shone across her face.

"Did I just hear somebody complain about the workout?" Pablo asked from behind. He came and stood next to Angélica.

I pulled away from her embrace, feeling guilty for my self-pity.

"Don't mind him," Angélica remarked.

"Don't worry," he said. "We won't work out again until tomorrow. Except for self-defense techniques, you have to practice them until they become a part of who you are." He put on a serious face. "Those are an everyday must. If you want, I can teach you a few good kicks."

Wendy poked her head out of the tent. "I'm hungry."

"I'm hungry, too," growled Pablo, "and I'm going to eat you! Grrrr!"

Wendy screamed and withdrew back into the tent. Pablo rushed in after her.

"Pablo, you're going to wake the baby," Angélica said.

"That's okay. The boy sleeps too much."

Angélica and I followed him into the tent. We ate a piece of sweet bread with cold coffee. The bread was beginning to get hard, but I ate it appreciatively. Outside our tent were people who didn't have anything to eat.

"How about if I put together some peanut butter, honey and banana sandwiches for lunch?" Angélica asked.

"Yay!" cheered Wendy. "Those are my favorite." She turned to me. "Have you ever tasted them?"

"No, but they sound good."

"We'll see what we can grab from the good people of Juchitán," Pablo said, thinking of the day ahead. He looked at me. "Do you wanna try grabbing a bag of supplies?"

"I don't know how."

"There's two ways to do it. One is to lay on your stomach at the edge of the railcar and grab a bag."

"Pablo, she's a girl," Angélica protested.

"The other," Pablo said, looking from his wife to me, "is to hook bags from the ladder."

"How do I do that?"

"You climb down the ladder and hook your right arm through the top rung to lock on. Hook your left arm straight through the bag loop and then bring up your catch," Pablo explained. "If you don't think you can do it, it's okay. I don't want you to get hurt."

"I want to. Just show me how."

We came out of the tent and walked to the edge of the railcar. Deciding between the filthy floor or the greasy ladder. I opted for the ladder. Pablo climbed down the ladder and looked up at me to follow his instructions. "When you get down here," he yelled against the wind, "lock your arm around the top rung like this and hook your left arm through the bag loop." He demonstrated the action, as the strong wind blew against his body.

"Okay," I nodded.

He climbed back onto the car and asked, "You wanna give it a try?"

I turned around and headed to the tent to get my gloves. I came back out, putting on my gloves. I was anxious to get on the ladder and try Pablo's grab-bag technique. Everyone saw my determination. I walked past them toward the ladder.

"Rosa, be careful!" Angélica yelled into the wind as I climbed down.

La Bestia raced through the open plains. The ground moved at an incredible speed a short distance below my feet.

"Lock on to the top rung firmly," Pablo yelled over the pressing wind.

I did as I was told, feeling my feet firmly planted on the last rung. I dared to let myself hang out as far as I could. The cool wind massaged my sore muscles and my bruised face. My uniform glued to my body. The wind bathed my hair.

"Why are you putting her through this?" Angélica asked. "We don't need anything else."

"There's a good reason for this," Pablo said, watching me closely. "She's learning to conquer her fears. She needs to experience bravery and learn to be daring if she's to start a new life in another country. Plus, these experiences will take her mind off the tragedies that she's been through."

"But you're training her as if she were a man?"

"Because she has to be as tough as a man in order to make it on her own. You, Wendy and the baby have me. Rosa has nothing but her youth and beauty. And tragedy is a companion of beautiful women. When we part ways, she'll be on her own with evil men along her path ... even after she reaches her aunt in Houston. That's why it's crucial for her to learn to survive."

"Hold on tight!" Angélica yelled.

I looked back at Angélica, then faced forward. I closed my eyes, getting a blind feel of La Bestia.

"You'll need to concentrate on looking straight through the target," Pablo yelled. "When they start getting close, ignore the face of the person holding the bag. Focus on putting your arm through the loop."

"Okay," I yelled back.

I stretched my arm in a hook, cutting through the wind. I felt confident. A rush of adrenaline ran throughout my body. I climbed up to the platform and down a few times to gain confidence against the iron beast. The soreness in my muscles made me tense and alert.

"All right, show off. We can see you're obviously a natural," Pablo said.

We practiced our self-defense techniques for the rest of the morning. Pablo added a few kicks, some jabs and a fast get-up. We ended our training when the air horn blasted.

La Bestia alerted motorists as it approached a railroad crossing. Our surroundings indicated that we were on the outskirts of Juchitán.

"Go to the ladder, Rosa," Pablo said. "Hurry. I'll go to the ladder on the other side. Angélica, stay by the tent with the children."

I put on my gloves and climbed down the ladder. I felt strong and confident, as if I had done this a thousand times. I locked onto the ladder, ready for what came next.

Other migrants were positioning themselves on their bellies at the edge of the railcar to try to grab whatever they could. Some came down from the hoppers to position themselves on the lower platforms.

Ahead in the distance, people stood along the tracks with bags at their feet. Some parked their vehicles close to the speeding train.

La Bestia moved at full speed. I leaned out as far as I could, testing my hold on the ladder. I felt strengthened by my determination to help Angélica and her family. With the wind pressing against me, I relaxed. The people came closer by the second. A heavy-set woman, wearing a red folkloric dress, stood in the bed of a truck. A bag was in her hand. The truck was filled with supplies. Two young men stood next to the truck tossing lunch bags to the top of the hoppers.

La Bestia did not slow down with compassion for the hungry migrants on her back. The two men were steadily tossing bags. The woman and I made eye contact as she came closer. She held a bag ready for me to hook. I signaled with my four fingers that I was ready. She reached down for two more bags and matched the loops. She held them out ready for me to hook my arm straight through. I tightened my sore muscles, keeping my sight on the hole in the loops. The woman grew as she got closer. In a split second, she was in front of me and gone the next. My body twisted with the weight of the bags, popping my back in three places, but my arm held firmly to the top rung. I swung back to face the ladder and closed my eyes for a second to let my heartbeat calm down. I turned to get a glimpse of the woman. She was barely visible. There were no more vehicles. A migrant fell from the railcar as he stretched for a bag. People moved away from him when he hit the rock bed and rolled to a stop. A painful expression drew across his face. He stood back up with his catch and ran to grab onto a speeding railcar.

I turned to face the ladder and climbed onto the platform with my catch.

Angélica and Wendy stared at me with astonishment as I handed them the bags. I went to see Pablo. He climbed onto the railcar with bags and handed them out to some of the migrants.

"Please share," he told them.

This was enough intensity for one day. I went into the tent to put my gloves away. I lay down in my spot and closed my eyes, letting the train's vibrations massage my back. I was sore, tired and in desperate need of a shower. I closed my eyes to ponder my situation. So many bad things had happened this past week. I missed Mamá and Juanito ... and Julia, who was gone forever. I missed Doña Marta's *pastelitos* and Mamá's chicken soup. Feeling homesick, I fell into a restless sleep.

A couple of hours later, I opened my eyes to Wendy's touch on my shoulder.

"Rosa, Rosa, wake up. You have to come see this," she said.

"What's the matter?" I asked, propping myself up on my elbows.

"Come see," she repeated. "It's beautiful."

I crawled out of the tent to find us surrounded by enormous mountains and a cool breeze. La Bestia sped on, never seeming to tire. Everything went completely dark as the train plunged fearlessly into a tunnel.

Pablo turned on a small flashlight and led us into the tent. He stood outside until the darkness passed. It was almost ten minutes before daylight reappeared, and we came out of the tent to find the enormous mountains behind us. The train's horn blasted as we crossed a long metal bridge, high over a lake.

The next area we hurtled into had grassy plains on both sides. It was a beautiful country. We stood at the edge of the car admiring hundreds of head of cattle grazing.

Gato

Gato woke up early the next morning to study everyone around him while they slept. The majority were children. None had anything worth stealing. He felt thirsty and went to the lower platform where the thermos was fastened. He splashed water on his face and drank his fill. Then he urinated over the edge. Thoughts of Rosa came to his mind. He buttoned his pants and crossed to the next railcar. He went to the right side and peeked around the wall at the sleeping bodies.

Gato recognized the two who were awake and standing by a tent. They were the man and the woman who had been traveling with Rosa.

His heart accelerated rapidly, and adrenaline changed his demeanor into that of a feline predator. He withdrew and leaned against the wall, taking slow breaths to calm his anxiety. Life was giving him a second chance to kill her.

Where's Rosa? He took another careful peek and was back against the wall within seconds. *She has to be inside the tent.*

He waited to see if she would show her face, but there was no sign of her. He crossed back to the hopper and climbed to the top. This time he kicked some immigrants out of the way and sat close to the front. From there, he could watch for her without being noticed. All he had to do was raise his head enough to peek at the tent. He untied his pizza box and grabbed two pieces. He took big bites, lifting his head slightly every now and then to see if Rosa appeared. After he finished eating, he shifted forward to where he could relax and keep his eyes on the tent. The next time he looked, Rosa was coming out. *There you are. I won't fail this time. Why else would fate keep putting you in my path?* Gato was happy with his good fortune. He studied her every move. Her nose was slightly swollen, and she still had black patches around her eyes. He touched his own wounds, remembering the scene at the riverbank. She disappeared around the wall for a few minutes. Gato guessed she was at the water thermos. She came back around and stood talking to the woman.

Gato lay still, planning his attack. *My bag has to be in that tent.*

He watched them throughout the morning as she practiced grabbing a bag from the ladder. Gato laughed when he saw her practice kicks and jabs with the young girl. He would have to make sure that Héctor and his men were not around. He was not worried about the migrants, but Héctor's men were different. Some of them were ex-military.

I need to get rid of the man traveling with Rosa. Then, I'll make her give me my money, shoot her and jump off the train.

The immigrants positioned themselves to grab bags from the people by the tracks. *There's too many people around, I'll have to wait until we're out of the city*, he told himself.

Héctor came into Gato's view on the hopper across from the flatbed. The leader stood at the edge looking down at Rosa. Gato understood his intentions.

I better move fast, or I'll never have another chance to *get my money back and kill her.*

Rosa came up from the ladder with an armful of bags.

Héctor and his men stepped back to avoid being detected by her, confirming Gato's suspicion.

Rosa handed the bags to the woman and the young girl, then she went to check on the man on the other side. When Rosa saw that he was okay, she went into the tent and did not come out for a while.

Gato watched Héctor and his men as they kept an eye on their prey. They passed a bottle of liquor around and smoked marijuana. He recognized the sweet aroma that blew in his face. He knew that it would be dangerous to get to Rosa with Héctor and his men close by. He lay down on his back to think. Every now and then, he stole a glance at the tent for signs of the girl, then at Héctor and his men. They were having a good time, laughing and drinking. Some of the men kept an eye on the tracks for anyone trying to jump on La Bestia.

Gato grew tired of waiting for the men to leave. The rest of the migrants sat enjoying whatever food the people of Juchitán had put in the bags.

A chubby teenage boy approached Gato. "I'll trade you two tacos for a slice of pizza."

Gato looked at him and slapped the tacos from his hand.

The frightened boy picked up his food and went to sit down as far away from Gato as possible.

Huge mountains could be seen in the distance. Soon, La Bestia would be surrounded by them and enter a long dark tunnel at full speed.

I wonder who'll be dumb enough to get knocked off the train.

Every time that Gato came through this tunnel, some unwitting individual always got knocked off by the low clearance. They tumbled between the trains and were mauled to a gruesome death by passing trains. The screams lasted seconds, sometimes nothing more than a yelp, muffled by La

Bestia's deafening racket. *Maybe I can push the man off at the entrance.* He looked toward the mountains. They were still far away.

One of Héctor's men made the others cry with laughter as he made goofy faces and moved his body in a sexual manner.

Gato lay on his back and stared at the cloudy sky. He pulled his hoodie over his cap and ran his fingers over his head wounds. He thought about getting rid of the man traveling with Rosa. The more he thought about it, the better sense it made to push him off at the tunnel's entrance. Héctor and his men would surely go someplace safe until the train resurfaced.

I just have to catch him by the edge when Héctor and his men aren't around. I wish I could throw his ass between the railcars.

Gato dozed into a partial sleep. When he woke up, he looked toward the tent for Rosa. She was still inside. Héctor and his men were still there. Only the mountains grew closer as La Bestia raced toward them. He lay back and dozed off again.

He woke up and looked in all three directions for any change or opportunity. Other than the nearing mountains, nothing else had changed. He closed his eyes. On the third time he woke up, he was surrounded by the huge mountains. He sat up and pulled out another slice of cold pizza. He took a bite and looked toward the area of the tent. Rosa and the young girl were outside.

Gato drew back.

Rosa and her companions went up to the edge of the flatbed to admire the scenery. The tunnel was approaching. Gato looked behind him for any possible victim. The only person in danger was the chubby kid who had tried to trade his tacos for pizza. He was sitting at the end of the hopper with his back to Gato.

La Bestia blasted her horn to warn of the approaching tunnel. Héctor motioned to the immigrants to lay down. Then he and his men disappeared.

Gato moved quickly. It was now or never. He flung the strap over his shoulder and hurried down the ladder. It would be perfect timing if he could push the man off before the tunnel. He climbed down to the flatbed, then leaned his back against the wall before taking a peek. Everything went pitch black followed by a short scream. Gato was too late.

Scattered beams from a flashlight danced on the tunnel walls. He could see the man was ushering Rosa and his family into the tent. Once they were safe inside, he stood guard at the entrance. Gato cursed himself for not coming down sooner and seizing the opportunity. After several minutes of darkness, light reappeared. La Bestia shot out of the mountain like a missile. He peeked around the wall again. One of Héctor's men was coming toward him.

Gato climbed back up to the hopper's platform and urinated off the side.

The gunman came around and faced him. "What're you doing down here?"

Gato turned to look at him casually. "Can't you see, I'm taking a piss."

The gunman jumped over the coupling with expert agility and waited for Gato to finish. He was in his early thirties with a muscular build. The grip of his gun stuck out from his waist. He faced Gato with an authoritative posture.

Gato zipped his pants and turned humbly toward him.

"Let me see your ticket," the gunman said over the racket of the train.

Gato reached into his pocket and accidentally withdrew the two tickets that he had taken from the migrants.

The gunman looked up at Gato with confusion. He was close enough for Gato to smell the alcohol on his breath. Gato suddenly threw his weight against the gunman, pushing him off balance. The gunman stumbled backward and down between the railcars. He clung by his fingertips to the platform, his eyes filled with terror. His legs kicked wildly beneath the belly of the beast. Its jaws worked to suck him down with each passing tie.

"Help me!" he pleaded.

Gato drew his gun and squatted to look down at the gunman. He knew the man's grip would soon falter. He pointed at the gunman's head. "Pow, pow," he whispered, enjoying the look of terror on the man's face.

"Don't kill me! Please, I can help you!"

"Don't you know what I am?"

"No." His fingers were slipping.

"I'm a Mara."

He raised his gun and brought it down fast on the gunman's head. The man's fingers gave way, and La Bestia swallowed him in an instant.

La Bestia blasted its horn, as it crossed a bridge over a large body of water. In the blink of an eye, below the tracks was a blue abyss.

This would've been another good place to push him off, Gato thought as he looked around to make sure no one saw him. Then he crossed to the flatbed and caught his breath with his back against the wall. He stole a peek to see where Rosa was.

La Bestia cleared the bridge and raced through a cattle ranch. Gato saw Rosa and the young girl holding hands, admiring the countryside. Next to the girl was a woman, and next to her was the man he assumed was the young girl's father.

Gato looked around, and no one seemed to be watching the four figures. He focused on the adult male, gripped his gun firmly and charged straight into the father with his shoulder, forcing Pablo off the train.

Now that Pablo was out of the way, he could finally overpower Rosa and take his revenge.

Héctor

"Daddy!" Wendy screamed.

I turned to see who pushed Pablo off the train.

Gato was pointing a gun at my head, confirming my fears.

Angélica pulled Wendy toward the tent.

Gato tilted the gun, licking his lips, ready to shoot.

"Why did you do that?" I yelled, ignoring the gun. "He didn't do anything to you! Neither did I, or Julia, or Hermán! Leave us alone!"

"Where's my fuckin' money?"

"What money?! I don't have anything of yours."

He took a step closer, and I raised my hands in fear, my palms facing out.

"Don't act stupid. It was in the bag I left at the river, where I should've killed you." He noticed the watch on my wrist. "The same bag you got that watch from."

I looked at the watch and lost my breath.

"Give me my money, or I'll kill you."

"Go ahead! Kill me!" I shielded my face and turned away, expecting a bullet to rip through me. "I'm tired of running from you! I'm tired of all this!"

Wendy cried behind me. Angélica nervously tried to calm her.

Gato's complexion changed. He pointed the gun at Wendy. "I'm not asking you again! Give me my money, or I'll shoot the girl!"

"No!" Angélica screamed, shielding her children. "Please, God, don't let him hurt my babies!"

I lunged at his eyes, screaming. Gato pointed the gun at me and pulled the trigger. "Click, click, click." The gun misfired as my fingers slipped into his eye sockets. They came to a stop. I curled my fingers to gouge his eyes, but his eyeballs slid around my fingernails.

Gato dropped the gun and pulled away, covering his eyes in pain. I took a step back and kicked him in the groin as hard as I could. He grabbed his crotch, grunting with pain. He bent forward. He lifted his head, trying to see through the damage in his eyes.

If your opponent can't see, he can't fight.

The eye gouge worked. Tears of anger rolled down my cheeks. I moved to his right side, stiffening the hand knife and swung it fast at his throat. Gato fell on his back, struggling to breathe. He choked, scratching wildly at the sky, trying to grab oxygen with his hands.

If your opponent can't breathe, he can't fight.

I wasn't afraid of him now. This was the time to put an end to him. I knelt my right knee on his stomach and swung my hand deep into his crotch, taking a firm hold of whatever genitalia I could. I squeezed tight and pulled away from his body.

If your opponent can't stand, he can't fight.

Gato screamed. His body arched, and he took hold of my arms. He could've fought me, but he only held on, trying to resist the pain, breathing through clenched teeth. A surge of strength came over me, and I squeezed harder, trying my best to rip his genitals away. Gato soiled himself, releasing a foul odor. His body went limp.

We call this "fade to black" Rosa thought recalling Pablo's lesson.

"No!" I screamed. Now you know what it feels to feel pain, especially the one you caused me."

I let go of his crotch and dug my fingers back into his eyes. Gato was unconscious. I continued to gouge his eyes, screaming at him to wake up. My fists pounded his face, trying to revive him through pain. The foul stench was not enough to stop me. I needed to make sure that he was blinded forever, so he would never hurt anyone again.

A gunshot rang out. I fell on Gato. Realizing that I was okay, I continued to beat his face, using my fists as hammers. "Die!" I cried.

Another gunshot came from the top of the hopper. Héctor came down, followed by three others. He lifted me by the waist and pulled me off Gato.

"What the hell is going on here?" Héctor asked.

He picked up Gato's gun and cracked the cylinder to see if it was loaded. There were bullets in some of the chambers. He spun the cylinder and closed it, then stuck the gun in the waist of his pants.

I couldn't stop crying, even though I wanted to find the right words to explain.

"That's the Mara who assaulted her at the Suchiate River," Angélica said between tears. "He pushed my husband off the railcar. Please, sir, you must stop this train and let him get back on. We can't continue without him."

She was nearly hysterical but managed to regain control for the sake of her children.

"First of all, lady, I'm not the conductor," Héctor said. "And second, what is that god-awful smell?" He looked down at Gato. "Goyo!"

"Yes, boss," the biggest of the three men accompanying Héctor said, stepping forward.

"Tie him up and take him to the empty boxcar. We'll question him at the train yard."

Goyo frowned, then rolled Gato onto his stomach and tied his hands behind his back and then did the same to his feet. "He stinks really bad, boss," Goyo said. "Maybe we should just kick him off the side."

"Can't. We need to get some information from him," Héctor said.

Goyo frowned. He lifted Gato easily and threw him over his shoulder and marched away.

And that was the last I ever saw or heard of Gato. I felt that my problems were ending there, but the cartel members had other things in store for me.

"You, come with me," Héctor ordered me.

I trembled, "What?"

Angélica hugged me and her children close. "Why?"

"She has to explain to the boss what happened and everything that she knows about this Mara," Héctor said.

"But she's already told you everything. Please, don't take her away from me. With my husband gone, she's all I have to help me with the children."

I couldn't understand. *Why does his boss need me to explain the attack to him?* I began to panic.

"Look," Héctor said, "come with me willingly, or I'll have one of my men tie you up and carry you like the Mara. As soon as you tell my boss what happened, you can come back to your friend."

"Okay, okay," I said, raising my hands in a gesture of peace. "I'll go."

Héctor swung his arm toward the hopper and bowed.

"Ladies first."

I went ahead of Héctor and his men, glancing back at Angélica and the children. Her face was filled with horror. She looked away with sorrow when she saw Héctor climb the ladder behind me because she saw how he looked up my dress, then smiled down at his men. Once on top of the hopper, Héctor motioned for me to follow Goyo. We reached the edge where a railroad tie was laid across the gap. I stood still, wondering if it was safe to walk across.

"Go on," he said.

I stepped onto the tie. The ground below moved at incredible speed. I took a deep breath and walked across quickly. Goyo moved fast ahead.

I thought of Pablo when I walked across the next railroad tie, then I remembered the migrant who fell and got back on quickly.

He has to be all right. Hopefully he'll be back with Angélica soon.

A long ladder lay along the center of the next boxcar. I thought nothing of it when I reached the hatch.

"Stop right here," Héctor said.

His men surrounded me. A horrible feeling came over me. I peeked over the side, contemplating my jump.

"Don't even think about it," Héctor said.

One of his men opened the hatch and dropped the ladder into the darkened boxcar.

"Go down," Héctor said.

Fearfully, I looked into the dark hole. Women's faces, semi-hidden in darkness, peered up at me. I turned to face Héctor and his men. They were too close. My heart drummed with panic.

"Please, I'm only trying to get to my aunt in the United States." My eyes filled with tears. "I need to work, so I can help my family."

"I'm sure you will … eventually. Right now, you must go down the ladder, or my men will throw you in. Your choice."

"Who's down there?" I looked down the hatch again, contemplating my escape through my peripheral view.

One of his men closed in behind me when he guessed my intentions. I stretched my hand toward his face to stop.

"Just more beautiful girls like you," Héctor said.

"Okay, okay," I said, giving in.

I put my foot on the top rung and began my descent into the dark boxcar. The sorrow on the girls' faces became clearer the lower I went. With misery, young women looked up at the newest arrival.

Pablo

Pablo's first instinct was to roll on impact. That was the way he had been trained in the Guatemalan special forces. He hit the rock bed and rolled to a hard stop against the broken end of a railroad tie. The greasy wood failed to cut through his clothing but banged him up, nonetheless. It struck his left side, missing his lower rib by an inch. The flannel shirt protected him from a cut but not from what was surely a large black and blue welt. The impact was hard enough to knock the wind from him, and there was no time to catch his breath. He held it, ignoring the pain, and looked toward the end of the train. The caboose was coming at incredible speed.

Questions of who might have pushed him sprung to mind, but he quickly shunned them. Now was not the time. His only concern was getting back to his family. Without him to protect them, they could be lost forever. With a rush of adrenaline and a breath of air, he sprang up from the rock bed. As the ladders raced at incredible speed, he ran with a limp, careful not to fall and lose time. He held his arm against the lower left side of his chest, trying to ignore the pain. The fear of losing his family was much greater.

Pablo did not need to look back to know the caboose was fast approaching. He sprang for the passing ladder of a boxcar.

His hand jerked and slipped from the greasy rung. He fumbled forward but managed to regain his footing and his momentum. He swallowed large gulps of air, running along the sloped rock bed and swung at the next ladder. He missed it completely. He took a quick look behind. It was his last chance. Pablo held his breath and dove sideways, stretching his arms as far as he could. La Bestia jerked him forward, pulling his arms viciously from their sockets, violently trying to shake him off its tail. His legs flailed. The speeding ties bit at his feet, conspiring with the iron beast. He took a deep breath and curled his arms until he was able to place his left knee on the bottom rung. He was so relieved to have made it this far and looked up at the top of the ladder that led to the small platform at the back of the caboose. Once on top, he looked at the empty tracks in the wake of the train.

Now safe, Pablo looked up, trying to stretch out the pain on his side. He was breathing hard, his body cramping in multiple places from the injuries he had sustained. The most severe pain came from his lower left side and his right calf. He was grateful for his steel-toe boots. Otherwise, all his toes would have broken.

He closed his eyes to breathe easier. He did not care about the pain. Getting back to his family was his priority. He needed to move before the pain grew too much to bear. La Bestia was long and pulled many cars. His family was at the neck. There was a long way to go before he reached them.

Pablo lifted his shirt to look at his left side. A bruised lump had developed below his ribcage. He felt it with the tips of his fingers. A sting ran up to his armpit. He wanted to lie down and rest, but he needed to check his leg. He pulled his pant leg up. A dark bruise covered most of his outer calf. He took a deep breath and took a step toward the door of the caboose.

He hoped that there was someone inside to help him. The caboose was empty.

Pablo limped inside. A water thermos was at the entrance. Pablo put his mouth beneath the nozzle and drank. He searched for a first-aid kit—there was none. He limped out of the caboose, applying pressure to his left side with both hands. His injuries choked him. He made his way around the small, railed platform rimming the caboose and moved forward, dragging his shoulder on the wall for support.

God, please let my family be okay.

He made his way from railcar to railcar, his pain becoming unbearable. He advanced a quarter of the way until the pain was too much to bear. It sucked the air from him. He needed to rest, to renew his strength. Black dust blew in a whirlwind inside the empty coal car. He looked to get to the next railcar, but there were many more cars to go. He would have to make the best of this. He sat in a corner away from the swirling dust. The lump on his side was the most painful. He stretched his legs, trying to find a painless position. Lying on his back was his only option. He pulled his collar over his nose and closed his eyes.

Everything's going to be okay. I just need to rest some of this pain away. He thought about his family and tried to ignore the pain.

The air horn blasted at early dawn, startling Pablo awake. His body felt stiff when he tried to move. He pulled his collar down. A black mask of coal dust covered the upper half of his face. New pains awoke throughout his body, but he had renewed strength. He looked at his watch. Five a.m. "Damn it!"

Pablo stood up. The muscles in his back and around his waist ached from the fall. The uncertainty of his family's well-being sent a rush of adrenaline throughout his body. He climbed out of the coal car and made his way forward, fueled by his determination to reach his family. It was early daylight when he opened the entrance of the tent. Angélica's eyes grew wide with fear when she saw his masked face. She moved to protect her children.

"It's okay. It's me."

"Pablo?"

"Daddy!" Wendy cried.

She rushed to her father's arms and hugged his neck tightly. Pablo knelt and patted his daughter's back reassuringly. Angélica made her way around Pablo Jr. and joined their embrace. She cried with relief.

"I need to lie down for a second," Pablo said.

Angélica and Wendy let go of him, and he crawled deeper into the tent and settled next to his son. Wendy curled into the safety of his protection on his other side.

Angélica reached over her daughter and ran her fingers through his coal-dusted hair. "Are you okay?"

"I took a hit to my lower left side, took my breath away."

"Lift your shirt and let me see."

He pulled his shirt up enough for her to see the dark bruise. "I'm sorry I couldn't get back to you sooner. My right calf got banged up. The pain was unbearable." He looked around. "Where's Rosa?" he asked, fearing the worst.

Wendy lifted her head to look at her father. "They took her away, Daddy."

Pablo looked at his wife.

"It was Gato who pushed you. You were right. He came looking for his money."

Pablo frowned.

"After he pushed you, he pointed the gun at Rosa and threatened to shoot her if she didn't return the money. She told him she didn't have it, so he pointed the gun at Wendy."

Pablo felt an emptiness in the pit of his stomach.

Angélica covered her face and cried. "I was terrified."

Pablo let her cry it out until she could continue.

"I hugged Wendy and Pablito with my back to him and prayed to God that the bullets wouldn't go through me and …" She looked down and cried some more.

Pablo sat up and held his wife. He imagined her fearfully protecting their children.

She drew away to look in his face. "That's when Rosa attacked him. She did everything just like you taught her. Gato pointed the gun at her and pulled the trigger."

Pablo looked down, breathless.

"I heard it," Angélica said. "I was expecting the bullets to hit me in the back, but the gun misfired. He shot a few times. Rosa nearly killed him. He was unconscious when the men came to see what the fight was about. They tied him up and took him away. I explained everything to them, but Héctor insisted that Rosa go and tell the story to their boss personally. He said they would bring her back."

Angélica was interrupted by a burst of tears. "She saved our children, and they took her," she said between sobs. "I saw their intent. They're going to hurt her!" She looked down and cried.

Pablo lay on his back, deep in thought.

"You must be hungry," Angélica said, wiping her eyes. She moved around nervously as she made sandwiches.

Pablo and Wendy took the food Angélica prepared along with bottles of water.

They ate slowly.

"I was so afraid," Angélica continued. "I didn't know if we'd ever see you again. I planned to get off at the next stop and call the number and wait for you, hoping you were okay."

Pablo winced. "That would've been the wise thing to do."

Angélica remembered Rosa's pain medication and went to the diaper bag. She handed Pablo two pills. "They're Rosa's. They'll help with the pain and bring down the swelling."

Pablo took the pills and lay down. He closed his eyes to think while the medication took effect. He was asleep within minutes.

Angélica woke him at noon, when La Bestia slowed to enter Mexico City.

Pablo felt sore, but not enough to stop him. He and Angélica tore down the tent and packed everything up quickly. Some of the migrants mentioned that they would be switching trains at the train yard.

>>>

La Bestia came to a full stop. Héctor stood at the top of a hopper getting everyone's attention. He waited for the crowd to quiet down. "I need everyone to get off the train and follow my men. They'll lead you to a place to wait for a few hours until we're ready to move on. Stay put until we tell you which train to get on. Do not go wandering around the train yard. It could be bad for your health." He pointed to a couple of men on the ground. "Follow those men."

Pablo got his family off the train and took the opportunity to talk to Héctor.

"Stay here with the children," he told Angélica, "I'm going to ask for Rosa."

Angélica looked distraught.

Pablo quietly climbed to the top of the hopper where Héctor stood with two of his men. Their backs were to him. He looked around, hoping to catch a glimpse of Rosa moving in the crowd, but no one even looked like her.

"Excuse me," Pablo said, in the humblest tone he could muster.

The three men jerked around, surprised to see him there.

"What?" Héctor said. "Who the heck told you to come up here?"

His men drew their guns and pointed them at Pablo.

Pablo raised his hands and lowered his head in humble respect. "No one. There's a girl traveling with us. Her name is Rosa."

"Is she related to you?" Héctor asked.

"She was entrusted to us by her family in Guatemala. They're waiting for her in Dallas, Texas," Pablo lied. "We need her back in order to continue our journey."

Héctor smiled and folded his arms across his chest. "She's okay. My boss allowed her to call her family in Dallas. They agreed on a price to get her there through some of our contacts." Héctor looked at his men and laughed. He looked back at Pablo with a mad expression. "Now, get your ass off my train before I have my men throw you off."

The two men took steps toward Pablo, forcing him back and down the ladder. He joined his family and put on his backpack in a hurry. They followed the crowd to a junkyard of railcars. No one was left to guard them. Pablo took his backpack off and unrolled the tarp in the shade for Angélica and the children to wait.

"Listen to me," Pablo told his wife.

Tears flowed from her eyes. She knew her husband's compulsion. There was no point trying to dissuade him from going to look for Rosa.

"I'm just going to have a quick look around," he said, reading her mind.

"Pablo," she whined.

"I'll be all right. Just stick to the plan."

Pablo snuck away from the crowd. He did not intend to be away for too long, only enough to have a quick look. With a speck of good luck, he hoped to find Rosa and escape the train yard. He crept through abandoned rail cars, cursing himself for putting his family in such a bad position. Although he was a firm believer that everything happened for a reason, he had clearly underestimated the journey through Mexico and wished he would have arranged for other means to get out of the country. The train yard was enormous. He searched everywhere with no luck.

She could be anywhere by now.

He reached an intersection that led to a warehouse in the distance. He was almost across, when a cargo truck came fast around the corner. The diesel engine roared by, grinding its gears. Pablo dove out of its path. He looked back at the truck. It had a tan canopy. The truck did not slow down until it was out of sight.

He crossed a maze of boxcars before getting close to the warehouse. His body still ached, but the medication was doing wonders for him. When he reached the warehouse, there was no one there. He snuck away in a hurry. Within minutes, he was back with his family.

He told Angélica everything that he had witnessed and how he had searched for Rosa without any luck.

"Poor Rosa," Angélica said sorrowfully. "I hope she has a chance to call the number."

"Yeah, but for now I have to ditch the backpack and get us out of this train yard."

Rosa

I descended down the ladder into the darkness, horrified of what awaited me. The lower I went, the more terrified the faces I saw were. I stepped off the last rung and looked around, trying to adjust my eyes to the dark. The ladder flew up behind me. I looked up in time to see it pulled out. The hatch dropped with a metal crash that echoed in the dim darkness.

A flashlight hung upside down at one end of the car. A woman stood next to it holding a smaller flashlight. A musty odor filled the boxcar. Some women looked at me with curiosity. Others cried softly in each other's arms. I hugged myself, quivering with fear as the woman with the flashlight walked toward me.

"What's your name?" she asked, pointing the light up to my face. Despite the glare, I could see that she wore a yellow top with shorts.

"Rosa," I said in a frightened whisper. I looked from her to all the sad faces that slowly surrounded me.

"I'm Yolanda," the woman said, coming into the light beam. She had a thick scar running down the left side of her face, giving her a lazy eye. Her deep crow's feet revealed her age. "Let me show you around and tell you what Omar expects."

"Who?" I asked.

"Omar's the big boss. That's all you need to know. Follow me."

She led me to the opposite corner, by the hanging light, to a five-gallon bucket with a roll of newspaper on the lid."

"That's the toilet. If you need to use it, remove the lid; do your thing. When you're finished, put the lid back on and leave everything like you found it. We keep it covered to keep the odor from stinking up the boxcar. It's bad enough that we haven't showered in days."

Next, she led me to a row of dirty mattresses lining part of the wall. Filthy blankets were scattered across them.

"That's where we sleep," she said casually.

Then, Yolanda sat down on a milk crate away from the light and crossed her legs. She reached into her bra for a pack of cigarettes and shook it. The butt end of a cigarette sprang out. She extended the pack to me.

I shook my head, nauseated by my new environment. Some of the girls gathered around me as if they wanted to tell me their stories or to listen to mine. They needed to hear words of courage. Their hopeful expectations ate at me, as if I had the answers to their problems.

"Why am I here?" I asked Yolanda.

She lit her cigarette and said, "We're all here because we owe money to the Mexican cartel. Some of us owe money for drugs, others for passage to the US. Some of us are simply kidnapped until we pay whatever they say we owe. We're headed to Juárez to be sold into prostitution until we pay our debt."

"What!" I said, astonished. "I don't owe the Mexican cartel anything."

"Me either," echoed some voices around me.

"Were you traveling alone?" Yolanda asked.

"I was traveling with a family from Guatemala."

"Maybe they sold you to them for a free fare. God knows, I've seen it done a thousand times."

"Pablo and Angélica would never do anything like that to anybody!" I snapped.

"Well, whatever, you're here now. Understand this: attempting to escape will only get you killed or, at the very least, beaten. Besides, the side doors are locked from the outside, and the hatch only opens from the top. Even if you did manage to escape, there are men outside with guns who would just love a reason to use them."

I placed my hands on my head and tried to make sense of her words.

"My advice is to do what they say. When we get to Juárez, we'll see what happens then. Maybe, I don't know, you can run away from whatever bar they stick you in. Or maybe you'll be one of the lucky ones that ends up a mistress to one of the heavy bosses. They always get first pick of the new girls."

Yolanda looked at me as if reading my mind. "The only time they lower the ladder is whenever they bring a new girl or when the men come down to pick some of the girls to go up with them."

"Uh, where do they take them?" I blurted out, fearing the answer.

Yolanda leaned forward from the dark wall. "What do your worst fears tell you?"

I saw the answer in her eyes. My mouth opened in protest, but no words came out. I was listening to my fears.

"Exactly," Yolanda said, an expert at reading sorrow. "Listen to your fears and prepare to face them ... go with them. Think of the worst that can happen to you and expect it. That way if it doesn't go as badly, you won't suffer."

I didn't want to hear anything else from her. Her words only fed the horrible feeling in the pit of my stomach. I walked away to sit by myself against the wall. I hid my face behind my knees and braced myself for whatever came next. The frustration was overwhelming. After a few minutes of mindless thinking, I lifted my head to look around. Some of the girls were gathered around Yolanda, lighting cigarettes. They watched me, knowing my thoughts. Something told me that they knew more than what Yolanda had told me. *What else is there?* I hid my face again.

"What's your name?"

I looked up to find a young girl looking down at me. She was a chubby, big-boned Native American. Her hair was cut short like a boy's. She wore a dirty, brown T-shirt and jean shorts. Her hands were big for a girl, but her voice was like an angel's: soft, musical.

"Rosa," I whispered.

"I'm Cecilia."

"How old are you?"

"I turned thirteen last month."

"You're so young." I studied her childish face. "How did you end up here?"

"I lived with my grandmother. She died a month before my birthday. Her friend took me in. She's the one who cut my hair like a boy's so men wouldn't want to touch me." She frowned, running her fingers through her short hair. "Everyone I know told me that I was going to be a prostitute like my mother. She lives in California. That's where I'm going. I'm going to find her and probably be a prostitute with her."

I couldn't believe what she was telling me. "Who told you that you have to become a prostitute?"

"Everyone where I lived. They said that the young girls who don't have anyone to care for them become prostitutes in order to get money to eat."

I frowned. "That's not true. You don't have to believe that."

"I didn't have anyone to go live with, so I figured that if I was going to become a prostitute, I would do it with my mother in California."

"You can't believe everything people tell you, especially if it's bad. And becoming a prostitute is very bad! Bad, bad, bad!" I closed my eyes, leaned my head back against the wall and took a deep breath. "You have to believe in what's right, do what's right, expect it …. Then, you receive it." I looked into her eyes. "Good things do come true." I wondered where my words were coming from.

Cecilia went quiet. She looked down, deep in thought, as if I'd ruined her plans. "The girls with Yolanda are already prostitutes."

I looked at the girls smoking with Yolanda and felt pity.

Cecilia sat down in front of me with her legs crossed. She rested her elbows on her legs with her palms on her cheeks. She looked like a big child.

Another girl sat down next to Cecilia with her legs crossed.

"I'm Jazmín."

"How old are you?" I asked.

"Nineteen."

"Where are you from?"

"The capital of Honduras. I was sold to these assholes by the man who I thought loved me. His name's William. He has the most beautiful eyes and lots of muscles. But inside, he's rotten to the core."

"I'm sorry."

"Don't be. That's what my ex-boyfriend does for a living. He makes young girls fall in love with him, then heartlessly sells them to devils like the ones here."

Another girl introduced herself, "I'm Patricia."

"How old are you?"

"Sixteen. I'm from Guatemala."

"How did you end up here?"

"I was trying to get to Philadelphia to live with my mom. The coyotes that agreed to help me said that when they got me there, I could work as a waitress for some of their people's restaurants until I paid my debt. And here I am."

More girls gathered behind Cecilia.

"I'm Liliana."

"I'm Olivia."

"I'm Elena."

"I'm Diana."

And this is how we got to know each other. We all came from different countries, we shared similar, tragic stories. Some were from as far away as Colombia, while others were from southern Mexico.

When the top hatch opened, letting in a few rays of sunshine and fresh air, the men lowered grocery bags tied to a rope. Yolanda was the one to receive the bags. The men then pulled up the rope and slammed the hatch shut, leaving us again in dim darkness. Then, Yolanda handed out sweet bread and bottles of water to us.

Later, I heard the women and girls whisper to each other, wondering which of them would be selected to go up with the men. They were so frightened by the possibility.

"I don't think any of you should go with our captors," I told them. "We must resist as long as we can. Maybe we can escape." I hugged my knees and looked up at the hatch. "We just have to find a way out of here."

I looked at Cecilia, and she agreed with me. She walked to the mattresses, picked through the blankets and brought two back.

"Let's lie down and cover ourselves," she said.

I ignored that the blankets were filthy and moved out of her way. She folded one in half and laid it on the floor, then rolled the edge to make a pillow. She moved the blanket up to a wall. We lay down and covered ourselves. The blanket scratched my arms. It was so gross. I sighed, and kept my eyes fixed up on the hatch, horrified, as if it were to suddenly open and make our worst fears come true.

"I'm not going to be a prostitute," Cecilia said. "When I find my mom, I'll go to school and be really smart, so I can work with animals. Then, with all the money that I make, I'll buy a big house for me and my mom."

"Those are great plans."

"I had a big orange cat when I lived with my grandma. I was the only one who could feed him. He was very aggressive. I even healed him one time after he got in a fight with a big dog that survived the attack …"

Her conversation was cut off by a loud screech. Light entered the boxcar. The ladder came down fast. Cecilia and I stayed under the covers. The rest of the girls gathered around the ladder.

Four armed men descended. Héctor came down last. Three of the men carried short machine guns while Héctor carried only his holstered sidearm. "Tomorrow at noon, La Bestia will stop in Mexico City," Héctor said. He studied all the sullen faces. "I'll need five ladies to come up and entertain a few of my police associates. Those who come up will have to shower." He smirked. "We don't like dirty whores. You'll be fed well while you're out. Those of you who are picked, must do exactly as you are told, so my associates don't have to beat you up. That will only piss them off … and their anger will be nothing compared to what I'll do to you. Are we clear?"

The girls shared a panicked look with each other as Héctor proceeded to pick out who would go up. He pointed and said,

"You ... and you ... and you..." until he had four. Then, he moved his flashlight around from one face to another as he made his way over to me. The flashlight came to a stop on my partly covered face, exposing my bloodshot eyes. Cecilia was curled up close to me, fully covered, trying hard not to be noticed. I turned away, but the light stayed on me.

"Get up," Héctor ordered.

I didn't move. He was going to have to kill me.

He came closer, and I jumped to my feet, ready to defend myself.

Héctor jumped back. He didn't expect me to get up so quickly. He kept the light in my eyes, trying to blind me.

I shielded my face, pretending to be afraid. My palms faced him, ready to strike as soon as he was within reach. When he saw who I was, he moved on. One of the men grabbed my arm and pulled me forward.

"Not her," Héctor said. "She belongs to the boss."

Yolanda grinned at me.

Héctor flashed the light in Jazmín's face. "You, be ready to go with the others."

He turned, headed toward the ladder and climbed halfway up. He turned and said, "Remember, ladies, tomorrow at noon." With that, he climbed up and out and slammed the hatch shut.

My blood boiled with anger and my heart filled with compassion. Those evil men didn't deserve to live. How could they do so much evil?

Feeling sad for the selected girls, I put my chin on top of Cecilia's head and cried. "Let's lie down," I said.

Cecilia pulled the blanket over us, and we held each other until we fell asleep. We woke up the following morning to the hatch opening, bringing our nightmares to reality. Our hearts beat hard, anticipating the worst. To our relief, it was only the supply bags, but deep within I knew that it was only a matter of time before Héctor came back. No words were exchanged from above or below. Yolanda untied the bags and passed out the bread and water.

"I had a dream that we were looking for my mom, and we got jobs making movies," Cecilia said, starting the morning's conversation.

I encouraged her wishful thinking, trying to get her mind off the horrible situation we were in. But fear and agony produced a knot in my throat. It choked my breathing. A tear escaped my eye.

"Why are you crying?" she asked, wiping away the tear.

I couldn't fight it any longer, I cried in her arms just like the night before.

"Everything's going to be all right," she whispered, caressing my hair. "You'll see."

La Bestia came to a stop after a while, it must have been noon. Héctor and his men came down and took the five girls without resistance. I supposed there was no point in fighting. The men were going to do what they wanted.

Before long, the sliding door of our boxcar opened to reveal the long bed of a cargo truck backed up against us. To the right, there was a three-foot gap between the cargo bed and the boxcar. I thought about jumping out and making a run for it, but that would mean leaving Cecilia behind. We had to escape together, and we would have to wait for the right moment.

Cecilia and I were last to cross into the cargo bed. As we got closer, I looked through the gap. There were armed men on the ground. My escape would have been futile. I looked into the cargo bed for a place to sit with Cecilia. I was relieved when I saw Jazmín and the four others sitting on a bench against the far wall.

Cecilia walked close behind me, clinging onto my dress.

A gunman came in through the gap and stood, apparently waiting for something.

Cecilia was about to set foot into the truck, when he jerked her away. I spun around to see him toss her through the gap. Cecilia screamed.

My chest filled with horror as I lunged after her. Something hard hit the back of my head, and I fell down. My vision blurred, and I was dragged to the center of the cargo bed, where I was left unconscious in a puddle of my own blood.

I never saw Cecilia again.

Pablo

Héctor reappeared on La Bestia hours later. He looked freshly showered and wore black tactical clothing. His pants were tucked neatly into his military boots. A bullet-proof vest protected his chest. It had the initials "MC" over a large map of Mexico on the back. A side arm was on his belt with extra clips. Dark aviator sunglasses covered his eyes. A short machine gun with a folding stock hung from his right shoulder. Three men dressed similarly accompanied him. The migrants waited for instructions to re-board La Bestia and continue their journey.

"We need to get out of this train yard and find some other form of transportation," Pablo said to Angélica. "They look like they're getting ready for war. We can't be subjected to any more of this danger."

Angélica looked perturbed. "But won't we be exposed if we travel by bus, or plane? If the police find out who you are, they'll kill us themselves and collect the bounty from the cartel."

Pablo needed to reassure her of their safety. "Mexico City is one of the biggest cities in the world. There are millions of places to hide long enough to make contact with a good friend of mine. He's the head of DEA in Tucson. He'll help us. I won't know what his plan will be to get us out of here until I speak with him."

Angélica looked into her husband's eyes, she trusted him with her life.

"We need to separate ourselves from the crowd so we can get out of the train yard and find a safe hotel," Pablo said. "You and the kids will have wait for me there while I come back tonight and have another look around. With any luck, I'll find Rosa. She has to be here."

Angélica was speechless, but she knew what her husband did for a living.

"I told Héctor that she was entrusted to us until we reached Dallas."

"But Rosa's aunt lives in Houston."

"Exactly. You know what he told me?"

Angélica shook her head, not quite understanding.

"He claims that his boss spoke to Rosa's family 'in Dallas' and that they agreed on a price for her safe transportation."

"Oh my God, no!" She placed her hands on her face in disbelief, fearing Rosa's fate.

→→→

"Everyone, it's time to go!" Héctor ordered. "Follow us so we can board. We're scheduled to leave in less than an hour. Whoever isn't on board forfeits their ticket."

Pablo and his family lagged behind the crowd. Once in a safe zone, he diverted his family to an abandoned boxcar. He removed his backpack and loaded the canvas bag with what he needed most. Then he hid the backpack beneath the boxcar. He flung the bag over his shoulder and led his family toward a chain-link fence. Pablo put his gloves on and removed the bottom fence ties. He lifted the fence enough to get his family through. Angélica lifted the fence from the other side for him. As they walked away, Pablo made a mental note of a burned-out campfire. They walked through light brush and cactus until they reached a dirt road. They hoped to catch a ride from a passing vehicle, but the locals refused to have anything to do with migrants. Finally, an elderly man in an old pick-up gave them a ride.

They picked a hotel that seemed to have tight security. Pablo checked his family in at the front desk, then led them to their assigned room. It had a double bed, nicer than the one in Tapachula. Pablo had no time to waste. He jumped in and out of the shower, catching just a glimpse of his wounds as he passed the mirror. He kissed his wife and kids, then headed out the door.

He took a taxi to a small surplus store, where he bought dark clothes and the largest pocketknife he could find. He changed in the store's restroom after paying and threw his dirty clothes in the trash on his way out. Once out on the sidewalk, he looked for another taxi but spotted a cellular store across the street. He went in and bought a prepaid phone. Outside, he dialed the number of his friend in Tucson.

"DEA headquarters," answered a female voice. "How can I direct your call?"

"Jim Austin, please." He looked out to the horizon. The sun would go down soon. He thought to tell her to hurry.

"One moment, please."

It took two rings for Pablo to hear his friend's familiar voice. "This is Austin. How may I help you?"

"Jimmy. It's me. Pablo Reyna."

"Pablo!" He rose to his feet from the seat at his desk. "How are you? How's your family?"

"I'm good. They're good."

"Man, everyone's worried sick about you. We thought you were taken by the cartel. You know they've got a high bounty on your head. I also got a call from General Garza in Honduras telling me that you're headed this way with your family ... aboard La Bestia, no less."

"How did he find out?"

"Are you traveling with a teenage girl named Rosa?"

"Yeah, I mean, I was."

"The general and the mother were tracking her and found out about you helping her at the Suchiate River."

Pablo thought for a moment.

"Pablo, you there?"

"Yeah. Maybe I should've taken a chance and called sooner."

"We could've flown you out of there a long time ago."

"I was trying to protect my family. I couldn't trust anyone. All the phones are tapped. Most of my comrades are looking to sell me out and collect the bounty. The only way that I could get my family out of the country was with the migrants headed for the US."

"We'll get to that in time, but for now give me your location so that I can have someone pick you up."

"I'm in Mexico City, but I'll only go with the DEA. I can't trust the Mexican authorities."

"I understand. I'll fly out there personally, and then we'll fly back together. Can I call you back at this number?"

"Yeah, I just bought this phone."

"I'll get back with flight confirmation."

"Hey, Jimmy, one more thing…"

"You got it, buddy."

"Do me a favor and call General Garza. Tell him that Rosa's been taken by the Mexican cartel. I'm trying to find her and hopefully get her back."

Pablo gave Austin a quick summary of Héctor and the train yard.

"I'll have my best contacts ready to raid as soon as you give word."

"I'll call you back when I have something solid."

Both men hung up and went to work.

Pablo waved down a taxi to take him back to the hotel. Angélica had the children showered when he walked into the room.

"How about dinner at the hotel restaurant?" he asked.

Angélica agreed with a dim smile, and they walked to the restaurant. The overdue family dinner will help pass the time until it was dark enough for Pablo to sneak around the train yard undetected.

"I called my friend in Tucson," Pablo said, once they were seated. "He's coming to personally fly us to the US. If I find Rosa, we can take her with us and get her political asylum through his government contacts."

"But how will you rescue her from all those gunmen?" Angélica asked with a worried look.

"Jimmy has some good law enforcement contacts here. As soon as I find her, I'll call him, and he'll then call the Mexican authorities. They'll be forced to act because the intel is coming from the American DEA."

"I see."

After dinner, Pablo led his family back to their room and prepared to leave again. His body still ached, but the need to help Rosa and the anger he felt were greater. He took two more of Rosa's pain pills and looked at his watch.

"Don't worry," he told Angélica and kissed her.

She looked down sadly.

He kissed the children and promised not to be gone long.

Armed with the pocketknife and a small flashlight, he left the room and waved down the first taxi he saw.

The entrance to the train yard was heavily guarded by armed men. Pablo had the taxi drop him off on the dirt road closest to the fence where they had crawled through earlier.

He reached the burned-out campfire and picked up a piece of charcoal. He smudged it across his face and arms, then crawled under the loose fence. Pablo moved through the space like a ghost, snooping through every boxcar and toolshed. He found nothing.

The warehouse was directly under the bright moon. He made his way toward it as if guided by divine justice. He continued checking everything along the way. He didn't want to miss anything. Something inside told him to hurry. He came upon the warehouse from the right. Slivers of light escaped through the crevices of the boarded-up windows.

"Cough, cough."

Pablo froze.

"Cough, cough."

Pablo followed the coughs to an outhouse and hid next to the door. He held the pocketknife at neck level in a tight grip. His lips tightened as he held his breath. The door flew open, and a man in black tactical gear stepped out. He was looking down, buckling his belt. Pablo grabbed him from behind and put the tip of the small blade to the man's jugular.

The man raised his hands and froze.

"Don't make a sound, or I'll bleed you like a pig," Pablo whispered.

He took the man's side arm and felt the hammer with his thumb. It was cocked back. Pablo lowered the safety.

"What the ...?" the gunman said.

"Shush," Pablo whispered in his ear, inspecting his surroundings. He twisted the blade enough to draw blood.

The gunman's heart accelerated.

"Get on your knees."

The gunman went down slowly, and Pablo pistol-whipped him hard on the side of the head.

The gunman fell unconscious.

Pablo dragged him away from the outhouse and stripped him of all his weapons: a short machine gun with a folding stock, a large knife, tie-rods, a flashlight and a gun belt. He used the ties to bind the gunman's hands behind his back. He then tied his feet. Pablo worked in a hurry, making sure no one was coming. He tore off a piece of the gunman's shirt, gagged him and secured the gag with another piece of shirt tied around his head.

Pablo put on the gun belt, hung the machine gun on one shoulder and flung the unconscious gunman over the other. Pablo carried him off into the darkness to an abandoned boxcar close to the fence. He dropped the gunman into the boxcar. The man grunted as he regained consciousness. Pablo climbed into the boxcar and slid the door shut. He shone the light in the gunman's eyes. A devilish grin appeared on Pablo's face.

Héctor lay at Pablo's feet bound and gagged. He looked up at Pablo, his eyes wide with terror.

Pablo squatted and grabbed Héctor by the jaw to look into his eyes. Pablo slapped him. "I'm going to ask you a few questions. First, I need to know if you're going to cooperate. Or do you need to feel the pain in order to talk? It's your choice."

Héctor nodded and coughed.

"I guess that's a 'yes'?"

Héctor nodded again.

"I'm going to remove the gag. If you yell, I'll pick the other option. You won't like it. Understand?"

Héctor nodded.

Pablo shined the light on Héctor's knife. "You have good taste in knives," then slid the blade between Héctor's cheek and the cloth holding the gag. He wiggled it roughly, cutting the cloth and Héctor's face.

Héctor winced and spit the gag out, then coughed. Blood ran down his face. "Who are you?"

"*I* ask the questions, asshole."

"My men will know I'm missing. They'll come looking for me. When they find you, they'll kill you."

"Well then, we better not waste any more time and get started. Where's Rosa?"

"Rosa?"

Héctor stared at Pablo's face. There was something familiar about his voice. "It's you. The man traveling with the girl who beat up the Mara."

Pablo smiled. "I taught her well."

"I told you. We spoke to her people in Dallas. She's on a flight to the border. Our people will pick her up there and get her to her family."

"You're lying. I mentioned Dallas to give you the opportunity to lie and help me make my next decision. Last chance. Where's Rosa?"

Héctor frowned, realizing he had been played.

"Where is she?" Pablo asked angrily. He grabbed Héctor's chin and forced him to look at him.

"I don't know where they took her."

"You know exactly where they took her. You seem to be someone with a little bit of power."

"She's gone."

"Gone where?"

"She was sold, along with twenty other girls."

"To whom?"

"Our people in Juárez."

"Where are they now?"

"All I know is they loaded them in a cargo truck with a tan canopy."

"Shit!" Pablo quickly gagged Héctor.

Héctor stared at him, defenseless, his eyes bulging with horror for what would happen next.

Pablo stood up. He shined the light in Héctor's eyes again and then knocked him cold with the butt of the gun he had confiscated. He then dialed Jimmy's number.

"Pablo, how are we doing?" Jimmy asked.

Pablo told him everything he found out and gave the exact location of the train yard, including where he would hide Héctor. "If I don't call you back in a half hour, send them in, but not until then. Give me time to gather strong evidence and take some pictures."

"My contacts are ready. I'll be by the phone."

Pablo slid the boxcar door open and jumped out. He made his way back to the rear of the warehouse. A gunman stood away from a metal drum, watching the fire. Pablo crept as close as possible, pistol forward, looking for a chance to take him out quietly. He snuck behind the gunman and pistol-whipped him on the temple. The gunman collapsed. Pablo stripped him of his weapons, tossed them and dragged him into the darkness. He gagged him and tied his hands and feet. Then he headed toward the front of the warehouse.

Pablo reached the front corner, gun drawn and peeked around. There was no one in sight. The door next to the garage was partly open. He looked inside, but saw nothing, only a light at the far end. He squeezed through the door, trying his best not to make a sound, and made his way toward the light. A gunman was busy hosing blood from a stainless-steel table. A blood-covered two-by-four leaned up against the entrance. He frowned at the thought of its purpose. He holstered his weapon and picked up the two-by-four. He walked behind the gunman, raised the piece of wood like a bat and swung. The impact struck the man on the neck; he dropped the hose and fell. Pablo raised the piece of wood again and brought it down on the side of his head like a golf club. The man convulsed for a moment, then lay still. Blood came out of his ear, mixing with the red water. Pablo took pictures with his phone. He shut the water off and walked out.

When he reached the burning barrel, he pushed it over with the two-by-four, then stood it upside down. He kicked it away and scattered the burning contents. There were bones, most with roasted flesh on them. He covered his face with his free arm, trying to avoid the smell. When he caught his breath, he took several pictures.

Pablo walked back to the fence and texted Jimmy. He shared all the pictures he had taken.

A few minutes later, the phone rang. It was Jimmy. Pablo shared the gory details and where he had left the men bound. Jimmy called Interpol on another phone.

Pablo made his way down the dirt road. A small canal ran along the road. He stopped to wash some of the charcoal from his face. When he finished, he looked toward the warehouse. The place glowed with red and blue lights.

The next morning, Pablo and Angélica lay in bed watching the local news. The news anchor reported the raid at the train yard and the taking down of a cartel operation. Pictures of the gunmen captured were shown along with those still at large. He mentioned the remains of two burnt bodies. One male and one female.

Angélica gasped.

Pablo hugged her close.

Jim Austin walked into the hotel lobby later that day to meet Pablo and his family. They were scheduled to fly out of Mexico City on a government plane at their earliest convenience.

"Pablo, please tell me the truth," Angélica said, once they boarded the plane. "Were those Rosa's remains they found?"

"I don't think so. We won't know for sure until we request a DNA sample," Pablo sighed. "These psychopaths target young women traveling alone. Héctor confessed that they sold Rosa along with twenty other girls to some people from Juárez. Right now, all we can do is hope that she's okay and that she'll get a chance to call the number we told her to call."

They sat in silence as the plane reached its cruising altitude. The thought of Rosa being sold into Juárez, where more than three-hundred women were missing, terrified them. They tried to speak in whispers to keep Wendy from listening to their conversation.

Wendy sat quietly staring out the window with Rosa's backpack tightly against her chest. She turned to face her parents with silent tears. "Rosa's alive and I'm going to save her things until she comes for them."

The Desert

I woke up on the floor of the cargo truck. My head pounded. My mouth was dry. My eyes were partly closed, seeing only blurry legs. I struggled to gather my senses. "Cecilia?" I whispered, lifting my head slightly. I looked around the cargo bed, my head throbbing. "Cecilia?"

The other girls looked at me sadly. The men guarding the entrance laughed at me.

I sat up feeling dazed. Half of my face was asleep. I put my hand on my cheek and felt the imprint of the wooden floor. My cheek was smeared with slobber and blood. I touched my head where I had been hit. My hair was crusty and moist. I looked at my fingertips, rubbed the fresh blood between them and then looked at the drying puddle of blood on the floor.

The girls kept looking at me. I focused my sight on the rear, hoping to see an opening, an escape route. There was a slit at the center of the canvas, but a gunmen sat at each side.

"Don't even think about it, Tiger," said the one on the left. "You might not wake up next time." He patted the stock of his machine gun and laughed. Someone touched me from behind. I jerked away. It was a girl. I tried to remember who she was. I finally recalled. Jazmín. She led me to a bench opposite the gunmen.

"My head hurts," I whispered, looking around. "Where's Cecilia?"

"I don't know," she answered, her whisper barely audible. "She's not here, they threw her off the boxcar when she was walking behind you. Don't you remember? You tried to help her, but the man on the left hit you with his machine gun." She handed me a bottle of water. "Drink this."

I guzzled the bottle in three gulps.

"I brought back two tacos from my visit with the men. Take one. I'll eat the other."

I looked at her with profound sorrow. She had been forced to prostitute herself for food and was now sharing some of it with me.

"No, I couldn't." I pushed her hand away. "It doesn't feel right, taking food that cost you so much."

"You've got to quit pissing them off. And we need to eat, no matter the cost." She shoved the food into my chest. "Here."

I took the taco, acknowledging her point.

"I heard them say earlier," she whispered with food in her mouth, "that we should be in Juárez by tomorrow evening."

My eyes widened slowly. "We have to be ready to escape the first chance we get."

Jazmín frowned with pity. The look on her face told me she was afraid.

After a long while, the truck came to a stop. The gunmen jumped out to help the girls out. When it was my turn, I saw the biggest full moon—destiny's cosmic way of watching me. A gunman stretched his hands out to me; I ignored him and jumped off. This added more stress to my pounding head.

"All right, then," he said. "Help yourself."

A light breeze hit my face. The sun finished its shift, leaving the evening's responsibilities to the bright moon. We were in what appeared to be a deserted ranch, it was the remnants of a luxurious estate but was now run-down. The truck was parked behind the old mansion.

"Okay, ladies. My name's Cuervo. I'll be in charge of your safe transport to Juárez. You have half an hour to use the restroom and stretch your legs. I plan to drive all night, and by tomorrow, you will all have what I like to call 'job security,' eh?"

"Cuervo," called one of the gunmen, "I thought we were going to have our fun here with the girls, like always?"

"Not this time. We have to keep moving, boss' orders. We've got big problems in Mexico City. Omar wants the girls delivered as soon as possible. Don't worry, these precious little things will entertain us in Juárez." He looked over the girls. "You ladies, step inside and find a restroom."

Jazmín and I looked at each other. I was lucky not to have been raped by them thus far, but I felt the time was fast approaching. I was determined to escape before that happened or die trying. There was no way that I would submit to the will of these evil men.

We were led through the back door into a big kitchen. The appliances were missing and in their place were piles of trash bags. We walked into the living room filled with more trash and bottles of beer and alcohol.

Jazmín and I looked for an empty bathroom with a shower. We found one in a bedroom suite. Jazmín made sure that the bedroom and restroom doors were locked before we bathed ourselves.

"Hurry, we haven't much time," she said. "Get in the shower and wash your head so the wound doesn't get infected. I'll wash your blouse in the sink."

I didn't think twice and undressed quickly. The hot water burned my scalp. I let out a few sobs. Red water ran down my legs and feet.

I told myself to toughen up, there was no time for crying. There was a used bar of soap on the soap dish. I used it to lather my hair until there was no more red in the water. When I got out, Jazmín was wringing out my blouse. She shook it a few times and looked at it. The blood stains were out.

"You're going to have to put it on wet."

I took the blouse and got dressed. Jazmín covered my wound with a tight ponytail. It was the best she could do to prevent an infection.

We came out of the bathroom after making sure that we had used every second of the half hour. We wanted no time to spare in the company of the gunmen.

Through this experience, Jazmín and I bonded with a sense of survival that could never be broken. She felt more like a sister than a friend. We united our strength with the inner will to fight for our freedom, for our lives. It was us against them, and we were determined to win.

One of the men spotted us when we came out the back door. All the girls were already in the cargo bed.

"There they are, Cuervo," a gunman said.

Cuervo watched us as we walked toward the truck.

"Watch out for that one," said the gunman who had hit me. "She's a tiger."

"Which one?"

"The one that looks like a raccoon."

Cuervo studied me as we walked by. "I like tigers ... and raccoons," he whispered in my ear. "Hell, I like all kinds of animals," he sneered.

The gunmen laughed.

I leaned on Jazmín, acting sick, improvising the defenseless technique that Pablo had taught me.

"Get these girls on the truck and let's move out," Cuervo ordered. "We have a long distance to cover."

When we were all accounted for, we headed for Juárez. Jazmín and I sat in the same place. I liked that spot because I was able to keep an eye on the gap and the gunmen.

We rode in silence for most of the night, dozing off and on against each other. In the morning, we were woken by the gunmen as the truck pulled into another ranch house. This one was much smaller than the last. We were ordered to use the restroom quickly. An old woman stood at the back door handing out sack lunches when we came out. Pity was written on her wrinkled face as if she-too-were a slave to these men.

We boarded and were soon on the road again. I couldn't help but focus on the gap. *You only have one opportunity to strike, so make it count.* Pablo's words resonated in my mind.

Some of the younger girls had moved closer to the gunmen and flirted with them.

"Jazmín, look." I nodded toward the men. "The girls are distracting them. We could use that to our advantage and dive through the gap …. Then, we run."

"I don't know, Rosa. That sounds dangerous."

"Of course, it's dangerous. But it's nothing compared to being forced into prostitution or worse."

"I'd rather wait and try to escape from wherever they put us to work."

Noon came and, soon after, evening. But no city. It was obvious that the driver was taking back roads. The bumpy ride seemed to have no end.

Suddenly, the road became smooth, advising me that we were getting close. We overheard the gunmen tell the women and girls that we were in Juárez and that they would soon be having their fun.

Dusk was upon the city. Lights from the vehicles behind us flashed through the gap. Colorful lights from business signs flashed by.

"As soon as the truck slows down and the men are distracted getting ready to bring us down, we make a run for it," I whispered in Jazmín's ear.

"I don't want to die."

"We won't. We have to try and get away before we get to where we're going. They'll lock us up again," I said looking into her eyes, "if we don't go now, we may never have another chance."

"There has to be another way. They have guns and they'll use them. You don't know them."

"I've seen enough to know them."

We braced ourselves as the truck came to a screeching stop at a traffic light. Prismatic lights shined through the gap. At the top, the full moon peeked into the cargo bed as if it was following me. It called to me.

The gunmen were distracted hugging and fondling the girls, who were resisting the unwanted attention. The entire scene made my stomach turn. I sprang for the gap.

One of the gunmen pushed a girl at me but missed. I landed on my palms, inches away from the vehicle behind us. The impact sent a shock of pain up to my elbows, but I stood up quickly and sprinted toward the oncoming traffic. My entire body ached, but the rush of adrenaline thrust me onward, fueling me with the will to survive, filling me with a renewed sense of freedom. I ran through a large intersection, dodging cars, trucks and an occasional bus. Some came one way, honking their angry horns, and some went another way. I put my hands on the warm hood of a car that came to a screeching stop. The frightened driver locked eyes with me.

"Come back!" the gunman yelled.

I didn't look back. I ran for my life against incoming traffic. I ran like I had run out of the jungle the morning Julia was murdered. I ran until I reached the sidewalk and kept going, trying to put distance between the truck and myself.

When I slowed down to catch my breath and looked behind me, I saw the truck moving away with the traffic. Then I saw the gunman getting closer. He was making his way toward me in a crouch between moving vehicles.

I sprinted until I reached a restaurant. The place was packed with people inside and outside. Some of the customers sang along with mariachis who played their music on the sidewalk. I ran right through the crowd. The people looked at me joyfully, oblivious to my problems, living in their own happy worlds, much different than mine.

"Hey!" a waiter yelled. He was taking an order at a table full of customers. "You can't be running in here." He looked at me for an explanation.

I wanted to talk to him, but I was breathing too hard. I tried to come up with the right words, but I didn't know where to start. I looked away from him to the entrance. The gunman stood outside, watching me through one of the big windows. He spoke on the phone.

I ran toward the back through a pair of cantina doors that led to a big kitchen. I didn't see the waiter balancing a large tray of dishes over his head and crashed into his chest, knocking him flat on his back. Dishes covered with food shattered around us. I landed on my butt, breaking my fall with my palms. Pain shot through my wrists, but I was instantly back on my feet. I ignored the pain and ran past the fallen waiter to the back and looked around for a safe place to hide.

A young boy dragging a trash can came through the back door.

I ran out the back into a dark alley. The truck came from my right. The gunman came from the left. I caught the door before it closed, went back inside and locked it behind me.

The boy with the trash can was helping the fallen waiter clean up the mess. I flew over the boy and through the cantina doors.

"There she is!" a waitress yelled.

"You, stop!" a man in a black suit yelled. He was surrounded by employees.

I ran toward the bar area and hid behind a large fish tank. I looked through the tank of colorful fish toward the front window. My heart pounded.

A hand grabbed my shoulder from behind. I spun around and swung my foot into the man's crotch. A roar of laughter erupted from the bar. The man in the black suit bent over with a pained expression, his hands on his genitals.

"Good job," a woman said.

I ran toward the front door, determined not to let anyone put their hands on me. I ran outside, looking for any sign of the gunman or the truck. Neither of them was around. I walked through the crowd, having regained my breath, ready to sprint.

It began to drizzle. The people made their way indoors. Several taxis were parked along the street. I ran into the back seat of the closest one and lay low, slamming the door behind me.

"Go," I cried. "Please."

The driver saw my fear through the rearview mirror.

"Go!" I screamed.

"Okay, okay," the driver said. "Where to?"

"Anywhere. Just go!" I was in tears. "Please, before they come. I can pay you."

I felt relieved when he pulled away from the curb and into moving traffic. I lifted my head slightly to look out the rear window. The only thing I saw were bright lights through the falling rain.

"Okay, kid, talk to me," the driver said. "Who's following you?" He looked at me through his rearview mirror for an answer.

I didn't know where to begin.

"Are you all right? You look pretty beat up."

I told him a little about my story from Mexico City until now.

"You need to go to the police. They can protect you. Is that okay with you?"

I wondered if that was a good idea. The police seemed to be corrupt everywhere. "Okay," I whispered.

We arrived at the Juárez police station within minutes. The driver parked a few spaces from the front doors. I jumped out the back before he could put the car in park and ran inside.

"Wait for me," the driver called.

In the light rain, another taxi came to a stop a short distance away. Cuervo sat in the passenger's seat.

Juárez

I ran through the rain and into the police station. There was a long bench secured against the wall. Across from the bench was a counter that separated the waiting area from the officers' cubicles. An elderly man in uniform, well past his seventies, stood behind the counter shuffling through papers. Behind him sat a secretary with small, square glasses. She typed rapidly.

"I need help!"

The old man, with an ID tag that said Arturo Méndez, lifted his gaze with calm scrutiny, gathering his thoughts.

"Please, help me!" I looked back toward the door.

"What seems to be the problem, young lady?" Officer Méndez said.

I looked into his eyes, at a loss for words, wondering if he was trustworthy. I didn't know where to start.

The elderly officer waited patiently for me to respond.

How can this old man help me? "I need to talk to a female police officer."

"Hold on. Let me see if Marisol will see you. She's the only female detective here." He turned around and headed calmly toward the cubicles. "I believe she's getting ready to leave."

The old officer stopped at the entrance to one of the center cubicles and spoke to the person inside, looking toward me. I kept my eyes on the door, expecting the gunmen to rush in at any moment. These people were taking too long. I looked around for a place to hide, but where? The thought of leaving crossed my mind.

"Marisol, there's a frightened young lady at the counter who only wishes to speak to a female officer. She looks like she's been roughed up."

"Just my luck, Arturo," Officer Álvarez said. "I'm running late, and someone comes in wanting to specifically speak to a female officer!" Frustrated, she stood up from her desk and walked out of her cubicle toward me. Arturo followed. She didn't look happy.

I wondered if I'd made a mistake by asking to speak to a female officer. What else could I do? I couldn't trust an unknown man—police officer or not.

"I'm Officer Álvarez," she said, lifting up part of the countertop and inviting me through.

I stood, frozen, put off by her facial expression.

"Well," she asked, "are you just going to stand there, or do you have something you'd like to tell me?" She studied my face for an answer. Then she let out a breath of frustration. "What's it going to be? I don't have all night."

I led the way to her cubicle, longing for the protection of office walls. I would at least be out of sight for a while. I hoped that whatever came of this, my pursuers would grow tired and move on.

Officer Álvarez stood at the counter, watching me. She looked at Arturo for an answer. He shrugged his thin shoulders and went back to shuffling through papers. She closed the countertop and followed me to her cubicle.

Her head shook with disapproval. "Have a seat," she said. She walked past me, pointing to an empty chair in front of her desk.

I sat down, feeling somewhat relieved to be in the presence of a female authority figure. Her cubicle looked messy. Boxes and folders were stacked on the floor. She took a notepad and pen from her desk drawer and sat down. Her eyes fixed on me, ready to take notes.

"What's your name?"

"Rosa de los Santos. I just turned fifteen. I'm from Santa Rosa de Copán, Honduras."

"What happened to your face?"

"I was attacked by a Mara."

"Is that why you're here? You wish to file a formal complaint?"

"No. I mean, yes, but that's not the only reason I'm here."

"Yes, Arturo," she said, looking behind me. I followed her eyes.

"There's a taxi driver at the counter. He says we owe him a fare for bringing this young lady here by way of emergency."

Álvarez looked from Arturo to me. "Really?" She let out a sigh of frustration and stood up and grabbed her purse. Without saying a word, she walked around the desk and went to the front counter, where she took the driver's information and paid the fare, then returned to her seat. She looked more frustrated than before. She picked up her pen, not bothering to look at me.

"Where were we?"

Just then, I heard a phone vibrate in the next cubicle and a voice answer, "This is López."

All I could hear was some man's voice shouting something about a girl ... a restau ... *Oh, no!*

"Hold on." López stood up from his desk and peeked into Álvarez's cubicle. He returned to his seat, and I could not hear anything else, except, "I'll call you later."

Officer López got up and came to Officer Álvarez' cubicle. I turned to look up at him. Chills covered the back of my neck and arms. He was accompanied by the strong aroma of cologne and cigarettes. He stood 6'1", had a long pointy nose on his skinny face. He had wavy black hair and a goatee. He wore a white-and-gold silk shirt with white alligator boots. The look on his face was untrustworthy. He squatted to my eye level to get a better look at my face.

I turned away from him and continued to give my statement to Officer Álvarez. She was beginning to show interest, taking notes of everything I said. When I reached the part about the tattoo on my foot, she set her pen down and looked at my feet.

"Let me see it," she said and went to a filing cabinet for a camera.

I removed my shoe. She knelt down and studied my foot. She took pictures of my face and tattoo. Her frustration changed to compassion.

"I'll try the number on her foot," López said after taking a closer look at the tattoo to dial the number. He stepped away. "There's no answer."

I assumed he was lying. I looked down, feeling my hope shatter. It was hard to hold my tears. I put my sock and shoe back on, thinking he had dialed a wrong number on purpose. I was about to protest, when Officer Álvarez spoke.

"We'll try again later. Right now, I want her full statement."

I continued with my story until I ended up at the police station.

"You poor child," Officer Álvarez said. She placed her hands over mine and gave them a gentle squeeze, then rested them on my lap. "You remind me of why I became a police officer twenty years ago."

My eyes watered with relief when I saw her sincerity. I was safe.

"It's getting late. We have to get you to the orphanage, where you can have a place to stay. You need to rest. We'll find a way to call your mother tomorrow morning and send you back to her as soon as possible."

I nodded.

"She must be worried sick. Come."

I took her hand and stood up.

"Listen, Marisol," López said, "you've had a long day. You've been wanting to leave to take care of some personal business. I'll take her to the orphanage. Go home."

He tried to take my arm, but I shook him off and hid behind Officer Álvarez. "I'm not going anywhere with you," I hissed.

His eyes widened and he raised his hands in a peaceful gesture. "Okay, okay. I just wanted to help."

Officer Álvarez placed her arm around me to demonstrate her protection. She eyed López suspiciously. "I'll take her myself." She looked at me and smiled. "The day's pretty much over, anyways."

We walked out of the police station into the drizzling rain. Officer Álvarez' car was parked out front. I got in the passenger seat. The interior was cluttered with household items. The back seat was piled with boxes of clothes.

Officer Álvarez noticed my curiosity. "Casualties of divorce," she said as we pulled out of the parking lot.

The orphanage was a large, white building on the same property of a Catholic church. A light bulb above the metal door illuminated the large porch. She parked in the front and looked at me with a smile.

"Let's hope the twins are awake."

"Twins?" I asked, thinking of orphan girls.

"The nuns who run the orphanage."

She got out of the car in the drizzle and opened my door.

I was having second thoughts about losing her protection. "Why can't I stay with you?"

"It's against policy to take anyone involved in a case to our homes. It's a big no-no. Come." She gave me her hand. "No one's going to hurt you here."

I got out of the car and followed her to the front door. She knocked loudly with the metal knocker. A small window in the door slid open, exposing an agitated, wrinkled face behind large-rimmed glasses.

"Do you know what time it is?" the wrinkled face asked.

"I'm sorry to bother you so late, Sister, but I have a young lady who needs a safe place to stay until I can send her back to her mother in Honduras. She's been through a lot this past week. It's a miracle she's even alive."

The wrinkled face eyed me up and down, verifying Officer Álvarez's statement. The window slammed shut.

For a moment, I thought that she wouldn't accept me, until I heard the lock open. The metal door screeched inward. Two identical nuns stepped out into the light of the porch. They wore the same rimmed glasses. Large crucifixes hung over their habits at their waists.

"How are you, Marisol?" the shorter nun asked.

"We haven't seen you at Mass in such a long time," the other said.

"I know. Please forgive me, Sisters. I've been really busy with work, the kids ...."

"That's no excuse to ignore your spiritual obligations," the shorter nun said.

"Prayer does help," said the other.

"This is Rosa. She's literally been fighting for her life since she was forced to flee her home in Honduras. She witnessed gang members murder her older sister and their friend."

The twins studied me for a moment, then comically smiled at the same time.

"I'm Sister Geraldina," the shorter nun said.

"And I'm Sister Otila," said the other.

"We'll take her from here," Sister Geraldina said, ushering me inside.

"I'll be here to pick you up first thing in the morning," Officer Álvarez called behind me.

I looked back as I was ushered further into the orphanage. I caught a glimpse of Officer Álvarez's worn face for the last time. The metal door closed with a crash that echoed throughout the building. I was led through a corridor adorned with paintings of Jesus and statues of saints with lighted candles at their feet.

"Stop right here, child. Light a candle to Saint Jude," Sister Geraldina said.

I knelt down in front of the saint's statue, and Sister Otila lighted a long match and handed it to me.

"Now say a quick prayer," Sister Geraldina said.

The first thing that came to mind were the men chasing me, but I recited the "Our Father," anyway.

"That's enough, child," Sister Otila said. "Let's get you in the shower."

We crossed a waiting room with a crucifix on every door and stopped at a closet. Sister Geraldina went in and grabbed some pajamas, a towel, a washcloth, clean underclothes and some packets of shampoo. She handed everything to me and led me to the showers.

"Use the shampoo to wash your hair and body," Sister Otila said.

"It kills everything from lice to ticks," Sister Geraldina said.

"Every girl that comes in from the streets has to take their first shower with this medicine," Sister Otila said.

"It's a three-in-one," Sister Geraldina said.

"Shampoo, body wash and conditioner," Sister Otila said.

"While you shower, we'll prepare a sandwich for you, so you can eat something before bed," Sister Geraldina said.

After the nuns left me, I got undressed and stepped into the shower. The warm water felt so good. I cleaned myself thoroughly, feeling a calm wash over me.

I missed the showers at home. Mamá always warmed water for me in the fireplace. I would mix it with cold water and shower with a big cup. I wanted my old ways back. I wanted to go home.

I got out of the shower holding back my tears and put my spandex shorts on over my underwear. The pajamas were mismatched. The top was light-blue and the pants had white-and-yellow vertical stripes. I folded and set my uniform neatly on the bench next to my shoes and went to find the twins. A light was on in an archway in the hall that led into the kitchen. I walked slowly, trying not to let myself be heard.

"Did you see her eyes?" Sister Otila asked.

"God knows what that girl did to deserve such a beating," Sister Geraldina said.

I stepped away and walked back to the showers to wait. I sat down on a bench and looked at my filthy uniform. *I'll find some soap and wash it tomorrow. Even if I have to wait in these ugly pajamas for it to dry.*

Sister Otila walked in holding a plate and a glass of juice. "Eat this, so we can get you to bed."

I took the food and ate hungrily.

"When you're done, look in that closet for a pair of sandals. Don't walk around leaving wet footprints everywhere."

I felt foolish for spying on them, but I couldn't trust anyone, even twin nuns.

The juice and sandwich lifted my spirit. I searched the closet and found a pair of sandals in a pile of old shoes. They were used but in good shape. I tried them on. I ran my fingertips along the thin scabs of the tattoo on my foot, thinking about my friends. The fear of never seeing Angélica and her family crept over me. I shook it off, put the sandals on my feet and picked up my shoes and uniform.

Sister Otila looked me over for cleanliness. "Come with me, child. Your bed is ready."

I followed her down the hall. Sister Geraldina stepped in behind me from the kitchen. I looked back at her, but she walked in a trance-like state.

I was led to the end of the hall. Sister Otila stopped at the door and looked at me. "Listen good, child. Don't go creating a ruckus."

"Get in bed and go to sleep," Sister Geraldina added.

Sister Otila opened the door. The dormitory was dimly illuminated by nightlights plugged into the outlets. I walked inside and so did Sister Geraldina. Bunk beds lined the long walls. Tables were scattered in the center.

Sister Otila led me to an empty top bunk and pointed to it, then she brought her finger to her lips.

I nodded.

The nuns made their way out, checking the sleeping bodies along the way. I stood next to the bunk until I heard the door close behind them.

Silence overwhelmed the dormitory. It was too quiet compared to what I'd gotten used to in the past few days. I placed my shoes beneath the lower bunk with my neatly folded uniform over them. The bed frame and ladder brought back memories of La Bestia's greasy ladders. I took hold of the top rung and climbed. The mattress was soft. The linens smelled fresh, nothing like what the girls and I had endured in La Bestia's belly. I thought about Cecilia and Jazmín, hoping they were okay.

I was extremely tired and got under the covers. My body sank into the comfort of the mattress. My eyes closed before my head hit the pillow, yet after a few breaths I couldn't sleep. Adrenaline still flowed throughout my body, telling me the night was far from over. The slightest sounds emanating from the sleeping bodies opened my eyes with vigilance. I lay awake feeling tired. And when someone poked the mattress from beneath, I jumped off the bunk. I was ready to fight.

"Whoa," said the girl on the bottom bunk. "Take it easy, Tiger." She was propped up on her elbows.

"Don't call me that," I warned.

"Okay. So, tell us your name."

"I'm …" I looked behind me. Young girls of different ages were gathering around. Others were climbing down from their bunks. "… Rosa," I whispered.

"I'm Aleida." She moved her legs out of the way, patted her mattress and smiled. "Sit and tell us what brings you here."

Aleida's skin was pearl-white. Her hair was wavy black and thick. Her big brown eyes with thick eyebrows added luminescence to her pretty face. She was beautiful.

I felt a friendly calm and sat down on the edge of her bed. All the girls were up and waiting for me to tell them my story. Some were as young as six. Others, like Aleida, were Julia's age. All of us wore mismatched pajamas.

I began my story from the morning when Julia, Juanito and I were on our way to school. The girls listened with astonishment. I finished by explaining how I was brought to the orphanage.

"I'm sorry about your sister," Aleida said. "We know how you feel. We've all lost someone. You must be exhausted."

"You can't even imagine." I looked down.

"You didn't by any chance talk to an Officer López when you were at the police station, did you?"

"No. I mean, yeah. He was there listening. He offered to drive me here, but I refused. I was just really scared of him. Officer Álvarez brought me here."

Aleida's eyes went wide, and she frowned.

"Why? What about Officer López?" I asked.

Aleida took my hands. Her touch felt soothing on my injured palms. "Listen to me carefully. I don't want you to panic, but everyone knows that López is one of the most corrupt police officers for the cartel."

I let out a sigh of frustration.

"I'm still in danger here, right?"

"We're all in danger. Girls like us disappear from here all the time. The twins claim that we run away. I think they simply turn a blind eye for their own safety."

I let go of her hands and reached for my clothes and shoes beneath her bed. Without saying another word, I changed back into my uniform.

I was grateful for the shower, the food, the clean underclothes. I couldn't stay where they could easily pick me up. It was time to go back to my new way of life—a life on the run.

Aleida watched me get ready with curiosity.

"If everyone knows that he's so corrupt, why don't they arrest him?" I asked, lacing my shoes with discontent.

"No one does anything because the cartel's too powerful, even for the police."

"What happens to the girls?"

All the girls, from the youngest to the eldest, looked down and shook their heads sadly.

"How do I get out of here?" I asked Aleida. "You can leave out the front door whenever you like. But I wouldn't do that if they're following you. It's better to sneak out through the bathroom window and jump a brick fence into the apartments behind the orphanage." I waved goodbye as I headed for the door.

"Wait," Aleida called.

I turned around with my hand on the doorknob.

"Where will you go?"

"I need to get to a pay phone, then find a way to cross into the US."

"But you don't even know how to get across the river."

"I'll just head north until I reach the river, then swim across."

"Where in the US do you plan to go?"

"Houston or Phoenix."

"I know someone who can get you across safely, but you need money for that."

I let go of the doorknob. "How much?"

"Fifteen-hundred pesos. It's actually a very good deal. Other coyotes charge three thousand. If you get caught trying to cross the river without paying, the cartel will make an ugly example of you. This coyote can help avoid all that."

"How well do you know the coyote?"

"His wife's a good friend of mine. We met here a couple of years ago. She ran off to marry him."

"Does he work for the cartel?"

"I'm sure he pays them something for using the river to make money, but he's not like a cartel member or anything."

"I don't know ... I don't have any money."

"I have an idea. Let me go with you. We can find a job to help us save money to pay the coyote. I know where we can get some work, I've done it a few times before."

I thought about it for a moment. I had more than enough to pay for the both of us, but I couldn't trust her with that knowledge. I needed to move fast, and she knew her way around Juárez.

"Okay, but hurry. We need to go now."

"Whoopee!" She swung her legs out of bed and gathered her things. In a matter of seconds, she was in tight blue jeans, a red blouse and white sneakers.

"Are you coming back?" a sad-faced little girl asked, hugging a naked Barbie to her chest.

"I'll come back like always," Aleida said, looking at all the gloomy faces. "You all know me. I'll just help her get across the river."

"Will you bring us a surprise?" the little girl asked.

"You know I will."

The little girl's eyes watered, and she threw herself at Aleida for a teary hug. Aleida kissed her forehead before letting go.

"I'm going to tell Doña Lupe to bring you some tacos, okay?"

The little girl nodded.

Aleida walked past me, sniffling. "Come on."

I followed Aleida out of the dormitory. She turned to look at me with her finger to her lips. "Shush."

The nuns were in the kitchen with their backs to us when we crept past. Aleida looked back and shrugged, flashing a mischievous smile. We reached the shower room. The plate and the empty juice container were still on the bench. I would've never guessed that, an hour later, I would be making another escape through there.

Aleida opened the window at the end of the room. A cool breeze came in, followed by a cacophony of crickets. They seemed to warn me of the unknown territory I found myself in. She placed her hands on the high ledge and lifted herself onto the windowsill. Then she jumped into the darkness.

"Come on," Aleida whispered.

I placed my injured hands on the high ledge and tried to lift myself onto the windowsill. The pain was too intense. I tried again, trying to ignore it. It was unbearable.

"What's taking you so long?" she whispered from the darkness.

"My hands hurt."

"Hold on." She moved around in the dark, being careful not to make a sound.

I looked at my palms, wondering how much further I could go.

A five-gallon bucket appeared at the window. "Here, use this to step on."

I brought the bucket in, stood up on it and climbed onto the windowsill with a twinge of pain. I jumped out. I was expecting to feel pain in my feet, but I landed on a thick carpet of grass. I adjusted my eyes to the dark, looking around for my new friend.

Aleida came into view and closed the window behind me. "If I leave it open, the mosquitos will have a feast on my sisters."

"You have sisters in there? Why didn't you bring them?" I whispered.

"No, silly. That's what we call each other. We're all sisters here." She smiled tenderly. "And now you're going to be my sister, too."

She took my hand and led me to the back. A thick wooden table stood against a six-foot brick wall. It wasn't like the one

Papá had built, but it was strong enough to support the weight of us both.

"Can you climb the rest of the way?" Aleida whispered over the noisy crickets.

I tried to get on the top ledge. I let go when I felt a surge of intense pain shoot from my palms to my forearms.

Aleida noticed my discomfort. "Hold on."

She jumped off the table and ran back to the window. I looked back and caught a glimpse of her butt over the windowsill. She was back on top of the table with the bucket in no time. With two easy steps, she was on the top ledge.

"I'll go first," she said.

Before I could say anything, she jumped into the darkness. "Come on," she urged from the other side.

I climbed to the top and sat on the ledge.

"What are you waiting for?"

I could barely make out her shadow. My mind said jump, but my body disobeyed. I feared the jolt of pain I was going to inflict on my feet. Having injured hands was bad enough. I would never get away with injured feet.

"It's okay. There's nothing but soft grass down here."

I closed my eyes, feeling butterflies in my chest, and pushed off against my will. I landed on the grass and felt no pain.

Aleida took my hand and led me through the dark corridors of the apartments and out the front gate. "Let's go this way and check if they're following you."

We ran, holding hands, to the street corner, rounded to the next corner and stopped. Aleida poked her head around the building. She sighed with surprise and leaned against the wall, wide-eyed, breathing heavily.

"What?" I whispered.

She rolled her eyes with her mouth agape. "He's following you. López' car is right there! Look!"

I peeked around the corner and recognized the vehicle that Aleida referred to. My heart pounded. I brought my head back and stood next to her in shock.

"Did you see it?"

"Yes. I remember it from the police station. It was parked next to Officer Álvarez's car."

The rush of adrenaline combined with panic almost made me choke.

"Let's go," she said, taking my hand.

Aleida led me through the dark streets of Juárez. We ran through neighborhoods, cutting through alleys and apartment complexes, hiding from incoming headlights, until we came to a street where we felt safe enough to walk. We headed for a light that illuminated a taco stand at the end of the street.

"Hola, Doña Lupe," Aleida said excitedly to the woman running the stand.

Aleida sat down on a stool at the counter and made herself at home. I stood behind her feeling fear and panic.

"Aleida, *m'ija*, how are you?" Doña Lupe asked lovingly. "I was wondering when you were going to show up."

"You know me. I must spend some time with my sisters at the orphanage."

"And who's this frightened little thing with you?"

"This is my new sister, Rosa. She came to the orphanage a while ago. I had to help her get away. The cartel's looking for her."

"Aleida, stop. She doesn't need to know," I said.

"Oh yes, she does."

"Oh yes, I do," Doña Lupe said.

She walked around the counter and took my frightened body into her arms. Doña Lupe was about 5'5", a dark-skinned woman in her early fifties. Her salt-and-pepper hair was tied in a ponytail. She wore a tan blouse with a long denim dress. An apron with strawberries covered most of her upper body.

"You poor child," she said tenderly. "It's okay, you're with Mamá Lupe now."

I looked behind her.

Aleida was putting on a clean apron. "What can I help you with tonight?" Aleida asked from behind the counter.

Doña Lupe held my injured hands and looked into my eyes. "Aleida, everything's ready to serve any customers who come by. I'll be right back." She turned to me, and said, "My God, you look like you're about to fall over. Come inside, so you can get some rest."

With her arm around my shoulder, she led me behind the taco stand and through the front door of her small home. I was instantly absorbed by her loving warmth.

"You can sleep there," she said, pointing to a long couch in front of the living room windows.

I sat down on the couch and waited while she rummaged through a small closet.

She returned with a fluffy pillow and a colorful blanket. "Here. When Aleida comes in, she can spread some blankets on the floor for herself. Make yourself at home. You girls can stay as long as you like. Tomorrow will bring its own sorrows."

I nodded with a half-frightened smile, placed the pillow at one end of the couch and covered myself with the blanket. I was tired of running, tired of fighting for my freedom, tired of fighting for my life. I started to fall sleep.

Doña Lupe hurried outside to help Aleida attend to a customer. The headlights of a car illuminated the living room, where I was finally able to sleep soundly.

Cuervo & López

"So, where's the girl?" Cuervo asked.

"Relax," López said. "She's at the orphanage, probably sleeping like a baby by now. I couldn't just take her from Álvarez by force. I'm a police officer and I have to keep up appearances. Besides, things are getting hot around here on account of all the missing women. Even the *gringos* are starting to put pressure on us. We need to rethink our business if we want it to last."

"Rethink our business ... as in more money for you?" Cuervo raised his eyebrows curiously. "I'm sure Omar and all of the other bosses would love to hear your ideas, *pendejo*."

"Hey, it costs money to keep people quiet and look the other way, or to get a heads-up when the military's coming."

"It's not my call. But I'll tell you what ... if you wish to keep enjoying the lavish lifestyle, like that new car, those silk shirts and alligator boots, I suggest you shut up and take me to the girl."

"Okay, okay, you get so damn emotional!"

They drove in silence to the orphanage. López parked half a block away from the front door.

"There she is," López said.

"Where?"

"In there."

"Well, go in and get her."

"Don't you fear God? Let's wait until she comes out in the morning. She's not the first girl we take from here."

"Wait until morning?" Cuervo asked, frustrated.

"When she comes out," López said patiently, "you hide in the back. I'll tell her I'm here to help her call the number on her foot. We will come to make the call from my car, once she's in, I will lock the doors and drive away. You will then be able to take her. We're not going in after her. The Catholic Church has way more connections than any of your bosses. So, relax. Tomorrow morning, I'll drop the two of you off and collect my money."

"Sounds easy. It better work, for your sake."

"You better get something straight. Number one: I wasn't the one responsible for getting her here. And two: she got away from *you*."

Cuervo stared at López with death in his eyes.

"Look, she's inside with the nuns. Where could she possibly go? She's from Central America. She has no one here. Just follow my plan until morning."

Cuervo sighed, not liking the idea.

They sat in silence, unaware of the two girls spying on them from the street corner.

"Let's go get some gas and something to eat," López said, starting the engine. "I know a good taco stand."

Cuervo agreed, and they drove around a few corners until they pulled into a gas station. The two men went into the store while an attendant pumped the fuel. They returned with drinks and headed for the taco stand.

The bright headlights blinded Aleida, illuminating the small home behind her. A woman moved around inside. The woman saw the headlights and rushed outside.

Aleida shielded her eyes with her right hand.
López killed the engine and exited the vehicle.
"What kind of tacos would you gentlemen like this evening?" Aleida asked with her best welcoming smile.
Doña Lupe rushed to her side.
López and Cuervo sat down on stools, admiring the young girl's beauty. Wicked smiles flashed across their faces.

Pablo

"General Garza?" Pablo asked over the phone.
"This is he. How may I help you?"
"Sir, this is Pablo Reyna speaking."
"Well, son, it's about time you called."
"I received a call from Jim Austin with the DEA in Tucson," the general said. "Mr. Austin said you called him from Mexico City. I was relieved to know that you and your family are okay."
"Thank you, General. We're in Phoenix now. My family's safe."
"Mr. Austin mentioned the kidnapping of a young girl, Rosa de los Santos, by the Mexican cartel. Apparently, she was taken while riding aboard La Bestia, and now she may have, according to you, been sold into prostitution along with twenty other girls. Is that true?"
The general had not mentioned what he knew to Rosa's mother, María. He could not bear to see the poor woman lament a second missing daughter. That type of heartache has been known to kill.
"Yes, General, that is true .... Sir, you there?"
"Yes, just trying to figure out how to break the news to a mourning mother. She specifically asked me to keep her

informed on any news. I've been buying time until I heard from you."

"Yes, unfortunately, it's true. But I have a good feeling that we'll hear from her soon."

"Why do you say that?"

"I was able to teach her some emergency self-defense techniques. She picked them up quickly. Tough girl. I say, you wait a few more days before you tell her mother anything."

"You think so?" the general asked. "It's been really bothering me deep in my gut whether or not to tell her."

"I can positively say she will be fine. She beat up a Mara by the name of Gato, one of her sister's murderers."

"This doesn't sound like the incident at the Suchiate River, or is it?"

"It's not. Although in that particular incident she defended herself quite well.... She almost killed her assailant. She hit him with a ceramic rooster the size of a softball. I wish you could've seen it when she held it in her hand. The thing was covered with blood and hair from the times she let him have it. I almost caught him, but he dove into the Suchiate inches from my grasp. He left behind a white canvas bag with a lot of money and other stuff that I'm sure he'd stolen."

"That delinquent left his bloody paws along his path," the general growled.

"I'm not sure how he found Rosa aboard La Bestia. But it was his bad luck. He must have been watching us, waiting for the right moment to push me over the side. I was barely able to get back on. By the time I made it to my family, the cartel had taken the Mara and Rosa."

Pablo could make out the general's anger in his breathing.

"According to my wife, after he pushed me over, he pointed the gun at Rosa and demanded the money back. She didn't have it. I had stashed it in my backpack. So, he pointed the gun at my daughter and threatened to shoot her. That's when Rosa attacked him with the techniques I taught her and beat his ass."

"So, Gato didn't hurt Rosa on the train?"

"Negative. But that's when this Héctor, the guy in charge of collecting the fees for the cartel from the migrants, took them both. I'm pretty sure they tortured and killed Gato at a railroad warehouse in Mexico City. Rosa was loaded in a truck with other girls and driven to Juárez. I took my family out of the train yard and put them in a safe place. That's when I called Jimmy."

"So, it was you who gave the intel on the human trafficking."

"Yes, sir. I went back to the train yard at night to look around and try to find Rosa."

"What did you see?"

"The first subject I took out was none other than Héctor himself."

"Go on."

"There's not much after that. They haven't caught the leader that goes by the name of Omar, but I think they're onto him."

"I hope so," the general said. "I hope you're right about Rosa."

"I can't explain it, but I know we'll hear from her soon. I tattooed a phone number on her right foot. I also mailed a sample of her DNA to the DEA Headquarters."

"We'll have to wait and see what happens these next few days. That young girl is out there fighting for her freedom, maybe even for her life. Keep me posted on the slightest news."

The men said their goodbyes and hung up.

Pablo stepped out to the patio of their new home, a house provided by his friends at the DEA. Angélica was flipping burgers on a small grill. Wendy and Pablo Jr. played in a plastic pool.

Pablo set the phone down on the table and hugged his wife from behind.

That's when the phone rang.

Rosa & Aleida

It was nine in the morning when I opened my eyes. I felt rested. The wound on my head pulsated in sync with my nose, hands and other parts of my body, reminding me of what my life had become, teaching me the price of freedom. I was free, and it was worth the pain. I sat up on the couch and stretched my arms as high as I could. A morning yawn escaped my lips.

"Look who's finally up," Doña Lupe said.

I turned around to see who it was, trying to piece together my memories of the night before.

"Did you sleep okay?" Doña Lupe asked.

I nodded, remembering her name and the kindness she had shown me.

"Good morning, Doña Lupe."

She sat at the kitchen table in her pajamas, steadily cutting away at a pile of raw beef with a sharp butcher knife. The strong aroma of coffee engulfed her cozy home. I felt peace, a peace I hadn't felt since Kike killed Julia and Herman. I remembered the girl who helped me run away from the orphanage. If it weren't for her, I'd be back in the brutal hands of the cartel. I searched the floor, but she was not there.

"Did you lose something?" Doña Lupe asked from behind the pile of beef.

"Where's Aleida?" I asked.

She looked at me as she cut away with blind ease. "I sent her for groceries, so we can have us a big, delicious breakfast. She also mentioned calling Amanda to see about crossing you two as soon as possible."

That was the best news I'd heard in a long time. I felt the strong urge to get to a phone and call the number on my foot. I closed my eyes. "Thank God," I whispered.

"Are you going to stare at me all morning, or do you want to get up and take a shower?" she asked with a teasing smile. "The shower is outside, through this door behind me, on your left," she said, pointing behind her with the butcher knife. "I have lots of clothes that you can look through when you come out."

I swung my legs out from under the blanket and stood up to fold it. A big blood stain stared at me from the pillow. I panicked, worried that I had ruined it. The blanket slipped from my hands. I hugged the pillow to my chest, trying to hold back tears. I felt ashamed. I walked toward her, expecting a frown before she kicked me out. I reached her side, teary-eyed, clutching the pillow tightly.

Doña Lupe looked up at me with concern. "What's wrong, child?"

I showed her the stain. "I'm so sorry," I said between sobs. "If I can borrow some soap and water, I promise I'll do my best to clean it."

Her eyes widened. I didn't know what to make of the look on her face.

"Where did all this blood come from?" she asked, rising from her seat.

I touched the crusty blood in my hair. "From here."

She put down the knife to study my head. "Did someone hurt you?"

I nodded.

Doña Lupe hugged me to her bosom and let me cry. Her hand caressed my crusty hair.

I looked up at her. "I'm sorry I ruined your nice pillow," I whispered. "I was just so tired of running that …"

Doña Lupe placed her finger on my lips. "Hush, child. Don't you worry about that. What I need you to do is get in the shower so I can take a closer look at your wound. Okay?"

Her motherly voice soothed me. I buried my face into this unknown woman's shoulder and nodded.

Doña Lupe took another look at my blood-encrusted hair, then looked up in prayer. "Dear God, why do you allow such evil men to hurt your defenseless children?" She drew away and looked into my eyes. "You don't have to be afraid anymore. You're safe with me. Later, you can tell me all that's happened to you. Now, get in the shower and wash your head really well."

I stepped out into the cool morning to find the shower stall. A small, oval mirror hung above the sink. I looked at myself. The bruising around my eyes had faded into a pale yellow. My bloodshot eyes looked better.

I set the water temperature and stepped in. The hot water stung my head. I winced and stood still, my eyes and lips shut tight. The water pressure rinsed my head and hair. I opened my eyes to see the shower floor pink with diluted blood. When the stinging subsided, I used large amounts of shampoo to wash my hair.

I stepped out of the shower and wrapped a towel around my body. My uniform was filthy; I would borrow soap to wash it. I put toothpaste on my finger and brushed my teeth the best I could. It tasted cool and refreshing. The mint taste brought back my sense of freedom. Feeling clean, I headed back inside.

Aleida was putting groceries away with her back to me. Doña Lupe was busy clearing the table. I tried closing the screen door silently behind me. Aleida turned around when she heard me and smiled. "*Buenos días*, Rosa."

Doña Lupe looked up at me from what she was doing. Her expression told me that she was waiting for me.

"Hola," I said with a small wave.

"Sit right here," Doña Lupe said, pointing at the chair in front of her.

A large tube of antibiotic ointment sat on the table next to a brush, along with some colorful hair ties.

I followed her instructions, and she immediately went to work searching for the wound on my head. I winced at her gentle tugs. She applied a thick coat of antibiotic ointment and pulled my hair into a tight ponytail, securing the wound. She reminded me of Wendy, Cecilia and Jazmín. I closed my eyes, hoping they were okay.

"There you go," Doña Lupe said. "The cut isn't that bad. I see no reason for you to see a doctor here. Better for you to see one on the other side." She smiled and left to help with breakfast.

Aleida moved about the kitchen as if it were her own. She wore the same jeans and shoes from the night before. Only her blouse had changed to a dark purple. She caught me staring at her blouse and studied my uniform. I felt embarrassed.

Aleida smiled, reading my thoughts. She measured me from head to toe. "What do you think, Doña Lupe? Does she look like a six or an eight?"

"I don't know what sizes I have. I'm sure there's something there that'll fit her. She's welcome to go through everything after breakfast. You two need to eat. I have a feeling that you girls have a long day ahead."

Aleida sat down across from me. Doña Lupe placed our plates in front of us. The food looked delicious. There were sunny side up eggs set over a corn tortilla and a slice of fried ham, diced potatoes and refried beans. She placed a stack of flour tortillas in the center of the table before taking her seat.

Aleida inhaled the delicious aroma and gave me a cross-eyed, goofy face.

"My kids send me pallets of clothes from the US to sell," Doña Lupe said, initiating the conversation. "Sometimes the clothes are new, sometimes they're used. I don't need much and give most of it away. My two sons work in construction, and my two daughters work as cashiers in supermarkets. The girls attend a community college at night."

I listened to her as I ate my breakfast.

"They want me to go live with them in El Paso, but I refuse to go. As long as I know they're safe on the other side, I can help so many homeless children here," she continued. "Too many young women have disappeared. Most of them factory workers. There's just as many missing boys. Everyone assumes that they run off and join the cartels."

She went on about the theories behind the more than three-hundred missing women of Ciudad Juárez. Aleida's countenance turned sad. Her chewing slowed as if choked by a memory. I looked at Doña Lupe, wanting to learn more about what was going on in that city. I felt like a small victim to something much bigger and worse than I had previously thought.

I looked at Aleida, who was no longer eating but lost in thought.

Doña Lupe looked at Aleida as if asking for permission to go on. Aleida nodded with watery eyes.

"Yes," Doña Lupe whispered, "young women are killed randomly, but others in good health have become targets for their organs. They are always finding their remains in the desert surrounding Juárez."

We picked at our breakfast.

"How can human beings be so monstrous?" I asked. "I don't understand how a man can gain satisfaction from torturing and killing defenseless women."

Doña Lupe frowned.

I force-fed myself against a nauseated stomach. It was hard to know what lay ahead with wicked men everywhere. I needed all the energy I could get.

"Amanda said she would be here to pick us up at one," Aleida said, breaking the silence, tears rolling down her cheeks.

I got the impression that Doña Lupe had brought back a memory for Aleida, but I didn't dare ask.

Doña Lupe went to her side, took her hands and pulled her into an embrace. Aleida buried her face in the motherly bosom and cried. It was a cry I knew too well. A cry of loss, of hopelessness. A cry of defeat.

"It's okay, *m'ijita*," Doña Lupe whispered. "Sandra's in a better place now. You need to be strong for her, okay?"

Aleida lifted her teary eyes. "I miss her."

"I know."

Aleida buried her face again and cried softly. I realized how sad I felt knowing that I wasn't the only one who had to endure horrible tragedies. I looked down at my injured hands and cried.

Doña Lupe motioned for me to join their embrace.

I rushed around the table to them.

Doña Lupe brought me in next to Aleida. Once again, in the company of women I hardly knew, I felt love and healing ... the magical power I felt in Angélica's embrace ... the love I missed so much from my mother.

"This is why I'll never leave Juárez," Doña Lupe said. She tightened the hug before letting us go.

We took our seats, wiping our tears.

"Now all we need to figure out is how to come up with three thousand pesos," Aleida said. She wiped the mascara that ran down her face with the tears.

"I have some things to sell," Doña Lupe said, going for her purse.

"I have the money," I announced and looked down to hide my shame for not trusting these good women earlier.

Aleida looked from Doña Lupe to me. "You do?"

I lifted my gaze to theirs. "Yes."

They looked at me with curiosity.

"Actually, I have a bit extra."

Right then and there, I took off my spandex shorts and unstitched the waistline enough to pull out some of the money.

Aleida's jaw dropped open.

I counted out five thousand pesos. "There's some hundred dollar bills also."

Doña Lupe and Aleida stared at the money in awe, then at each other and back at me.

I smiled shyly, waiting for them to say something.

"You sneaky brat," Aleida said with a mischievous grin. "Why didn't you tell me you had this?"

I shrugged. "I didn't know who to trust. But after getting to know the two of you, it was time for me to put the money on the table."

Aleida and Doña Lupe looked at each other with amusement, and we went back to our breakfast. It was cold, but great ... especially now that our mood had changed for the better.

As the laughter faded and the tension of the morning gave way to a sense of hope, my thoughts turned to the next step. *All I need now is to get to a pay phone and call the number on my foot.* The anticipation of getting word to Angélica that I had escaped and that I was okay made me impatient.

"Brat," Aleida repeated. She gave me one of her mischievous grins from above her plate. It was a grin that I was getting to like. She laughed to herself before going back to her food.

"I'll see what I can pack for the two of you," Doña Lupe said. "I have a couple of backpacks that I can stuff with extra clothes." She moved about her small home pulling boxes out from everywhere.

"Did your friend tell you where we would be crossing?" I asked, taking my plate to the sink.

"No, but I know they always crossed around here into El Paso. Why?"

"I need to use a phone urgently to let my friends know that I'm okay and that I'll be crossing into El Paso."

I put all but one thousand pesos back in the waistline of my shorts and put them back on. I needed money to use the phone and whatever minor expenses we might have.

"Is there a phone close by that I can use?"

"Yes," Aleida said. "They have one at the grocery store where I went this morning. It's only a few blocks away."

"Rosa," Doña Lupe called from her small living room. "Come try on some of these clothes."

A few pieces of clothing that she wanted me to try sat folded on the armrest.

"Would it be okay if I go make my phone call first? I'd feel better trying on clothes without that worry on my mind."

She frowned, then placed a neatly folded pink blouse on the sofa's armrest.

I looked at her shyly.

"Hurry back. That uniform you're wearing looks like it's been through the Mexican Revolution."

Aleida and I giggled at Doña Lupe's sarcasm. Then, Aleida took my hand and led me out the front door and down the street. The sun stung my face with its healing rays. The sense of freedom seemed foreign to me, yet exciting. It took five minutes to walk to the store. The bottom half of its walls were painted a deep purple. The upper half was bone white. Paintings of groceries adorned the walls. The interior was crowded with inventory. A young man sat behind the counter reading a comic book. A loud fan blew behind him.

"Gustavo, we need to use your phone," Aleida said.

The young man looked up and smiled. "Sure, Aleida, anything for you. Local or to *Los* United?" He took a cordless phone from its place and handed it to her. Aleida took the phone and gave him a flirtatious smile.

"Why, to *Los* United, of course."

She took my hand and led me to a secluded aisle.

"That'll be ten pesos," Gustavo called.

Aleida rolled her eyes and made a goofy face. "Okay," she called back. "I have him wrapped around my finger," she whispered to me. Then, ready to dial, she asked, "What's the number?"

I removed my shoe and sock to show her my tattoo.

Aleida's eyes went wide. "That's a new one. I thought you had the number stashed in your sock, but a tattoo? You're like a holocaust survivor." She read the number and dialed. When it rang, she passed it to me.

The sound of it ringing filled my heart with excitement. "Please, someone answer," I whispered impatiently.

"Hello," a male voice said, "DEA."

"Uhm, yes. Hello?" I said nervously in what little English I knew.

"Can I help you?"

"I, eh, *necesito* ... need ... *hablar* Pablo *y* Angélica Reyna."

"Okay. What's your name?"

"Name? *Ah, nombre*. Rosa. Rosa de los Santos."

"Let me see."

I heard papers shuffle.

"Ah, yes. They've been expecting your call. Are you okay?"

"*Oquei*, yes, *oquei*. *Estoy en Juárez. Dígales que estoy en Juárez. Escapé del cartel.*"

"Got it, you escaped the cartel ...."

"Yes ... *y cruzo a El Paso esta noche* ... tonight cross *a* El Paso."

"Right. *Sí ... yo les hablo a Pablo* and *Angélica*. In Phoenix, Arizona. *Ellos* in Phoenix, Arizona. You *escribir* something, *sí?*"

"I need something to write with," I told Aleida.

She walked to the counter and got what I needed.

"*Oquei*, yes."

I wrote down Pablo's number as it was dictated to me in Spanish. The man knew numbers *en español!*

"Hurry up," called Gustavo. "My mom's coming."

"*Dígales que llamaré tan pronto cruce a El Paso.* I call *de* El Paso."

"*Cuidado. Peligroso. Hombres malos.*"

"*Sí, ya sé. Muchas gracias.*"

"Hurry," called Gustavo.

"Bye."

I handed the phone to Aleida. She hung up and rushed it back to the counter seconds before Gustavo's mother walked through the front door carrying large bags of supplies. She set the bags on the counter, purposely blocking her son. She gave Aleida and me a look of mistrust that said, "Buy something or leave."

We walked out of the store in a hurry. Aleida looked back at Gustavo, who peeked around the bags with a smile. She blew him a kiss behind his mother's back.

Holding hands, we ran off toward Doña Lupe's. Aleida giggled, towing me along, making me giggle too.

I felt an overdue happiness for the familiar sense of freedom. It overwhelmed me despite my injuries. We slowed to a walk. Aleida tore open a pack of gum, gave me a piece and took one for herself. The taste of grape exploded in my mouth. We were a block away when Aleida jerked me to a halt and pointed at the taco stand. López's gray car was parked beside it with its doors open. We retreated in fear, turned around and ran as fast as we could. We passed the store, heading toward the main street. My breathing was hard. I was confused. *How did they find me?*

Aleida waved down a taxi and pulled me into the back seat. "Take us downtown, quickly!" she told the driver.

The taxi drove off, blending in with the traffic. I spied out the back window, partially obstructed by a big black ribbon bow on the trunk. Aleida was bent forward with her face on her knees.

"Oh, God," she prayed. "Please don't let them hurt Doña Lupe."

Her prayer fueled my fear. Those men were at Doña Lupe's home. The thought of them hurting her for my sake filled me with guilt. Aleida pulled me to her. We were terrified thinking of what Doña Lupe was going through at that very moment.

"How did they find me? Why won't they leave me alone?"

She looked at me in confusion, trying to figure it out.

"Let's go, Aleida! Let's go to the river now!" My lips trembled with uncontrollable fear. "Please," I begged.

"We will," she whispered. "Let's just get away from them. We need to find some place safe.

The driver gave us concerned glances over the rearview mirror. He seemed to want to ask something.

"Right here's fine," Aleida told him.

He pulled over across from a small park. "That'll be a hundred and twenty pesos," the driver said, flipping his hand over his shoulder to get paid.

I dug into my pocket and pulled out two-hundred pesos and paid him.

After we got out of the taxi, it drove off, leaving us exposed on the sidewalk.

"Come on," Aleida said, towing me across the street to the park. "We have to call Amanda to let her know where we are."

She led me through moving traffic, lifting her palm to stop vehicles. A chorus of honking cars and trucks surrounded us, adding chaos to panic.

"Aleida, stop!" I said, once we were safely across.

"What?" she asked with forced patience.

"They're at Doña Lupe's!" I looked down. "I don't understand what these men want with me!"

"I don't know either, but you can't be seen in public. Come on, let's go!" She took my hand and towed me toward the phone booth. "Stand behind me. I'm sure all their lookouts are hunting you."

I stood behind her, hidden from street view, as she dialed a number. I couldn't stop shaking. I wanted to run, to hide where no one could find me.

Aleida hugged me closer. "Amanda? Change of plans. We'll be waiting at Sandra's. Please hurry. I'll explain when you get here."

She hung up the phone and led me to the center of the park with a garden of pink crosses. Businesses surrounded the small park with people coming and going. We sat on a cement bench.

"I think we're safe for now," Aleida said.

I was terrified that a cartel member would pop out of nowhere. The hair on the back of my neck was raised in fright. But I was able to calm down after a few minutes.

"Amanda said she would be here in twenty minutes," Aleida whispered. She caressed my head tenderly. "Come. I want you to meet someone." She took my hand and led me through the garden of pink crosses, each of which had a picture of a woman in its center.

"Who are they?"

"They're the three hundred missing women of Juárez that Doña Lupe told you about."

The sound of her name caused a lump in my throat. I looked around in disbelief at the multitude of crosses surrounding us. *So much death. So much needless pain.*

We walked carefully among the crosses until we reached one that brought Aleida to her knees. She stared at the picture in the center of the cross without speaking.

I looked down at the picture. It was the face of a young woman that looked a lot like Aleida.

"She was so beautiful," she said.

I nodded sadly.

She gave me a sad smile that triggered a thought deep within me. It hadn't occurred to me that she and I shared the same tragedies. Our lives were so much alike. We both had lost our elder sisters to vicious murderers. Yet destiny found a way to bring us together, as if to fill the empty slots in our lives. I finally understood why she called all the girls at the orphanage her sisters. We were sisters in pain, sisters in sorrow, sisters of misfortune.

"Her name was Sandra. Everyone called her Sandy." She looked beyond the cross. "After Mom died, Sandy quit school to work in a factory. Our father left to work in the US. He abandoned us. We didn't need him, or anybody else. She did okay supporting the two of us while I went to school. One day, she never came home. She worked the evening shift. Some of the workers said the last time she was seen was walking to the bus stop in the middle of the night. That's all I know."

She looked at the picture again. "I was declared a ward of the state and placed in the orphanage. All our stuff was looted from our apartment. My only belongings were the clothes I wore and two pictures. One of them is on this cross. The other is of my mom, Sandy and me. I keep it at Doña Lupe's."

Tears tainted by memories ran down her face, blackened by eyeliner and heartache. She touched the picture affectionately. "This is my new sister, Rosa. I really like her. We're going to cross into El Paso. Please watch over us." She kissed her fingertips and placed them on the picture. "I miss you, Sis."

"Aleida!" a female voice called. We looked around to see who it was.

"Over here," said a woman waving from the street. Behind her was a white VW Beetle.

Aleida pulled me toward the woman. When we reached her, they gave each other a peck on the cheek. I stood on the sidewalk, feeling vulnerable.

"Rosa, this is my sister, Amanda," Aleida said, happily.

"Amanda, meet the new sister I told you about. Her name is Rosa."

"Hola," I said, desperate to get off the street.

"Hola," she replied looking me up and down.

Amanda was pregnant, dressed in denim maternity clothes. She had a pudgy, pretty face.

"Wow, you're huge," Aleida said. "When are you due?"

"Some time next month," she said, rubbing her tummy. "I can't wait to have my baby. Alfredo's already bought lots of toys. Are you ready to go?"

"We're more than ready. We have all the money to pay for the crossing."

"What are we waiting for? Get in and let's get out of here." Her demeanor changed. She looked around suspiciously.

Aleida opened the passenger door and leaned the seat forward enough for me to get in. She sat in the front.

Amanda started the engine and, like a pro racer, put the stick shift in gear, and the VW lurched into congested traffic.

"The cartel's looking for Rosa," Aleida said. "They probably have my description. I doubt that Doña Lupe will give them anything, except poisoned tacos."

We drove the rest of the way in silence. Doña Lupe was clearly on our minds. Amanda pulled into the gravel driveway of a small home on the outskirts of Juárez. The home was made of cinder blocks with a flat concrete roof. Rebars stuck up from the four corners. Small trees and flower beds were planted around the home showing signs of a family in bloom.

"Come inside, and we'll see what Alfredo has in mind," Amanda said after turning off the engine.

We followed her into the small living room. Alfredo was sitting on the couch with his bare feet on the coffee table. He was watching television.

"Hola, Freddy," Aleida said. Her optimism gave me a sense of security.

He stood up to greet us.

Aleida went into his arms and kissed his cheek.

"Congrats on the new baby," Aleida said when she was back at my side.

"*Gracias*. How've you been?"

"Good." She hugged my shoulder. "This is my sister, Rosa."

"Hola, Rosa," Alfredo said.

I looked with fear into his eyes, thinking he might look familiar. He didn't. "Hola," I whispered.

Alfredo sensed my fear. "Amanda tells me you want to cross into *Los* United?"

"Yes," I almost shouted. "Can we go now?"

"I don't think so," Alfredo said. "We haven't been able to cross into El Paso in over a month. The river's hot on account of the missing women and the cartel wars."

"What?" My countenance fell. I looked at Aleida. "Where will we hide?"

"There's another way. It would require you walking across the Sonoran Desert and into Arizona. That's where everyone's crossing right now."

"How far is Arizona from Phoenix?" I asked, filled with new hope.

"Arizona's the state Phoenix belongs to," Aleida said.

"It's about a five-day walk, following a guide. It's the only way to get across right now." Alfredo said.

"The desert?" Aleida whispered. "How?"

"You'll be driven to the state of Sonora, where you'll meet up with other migrants in a town called Sonoyta. You'll have to carry your own water and enough food to make it across. I know the guide personally. They call him Prieto. The only people that he won't take are children, people with medical conditions and the elderly. He just takes ordinary, healthy people who are able to make the long walk."

Aleida and I stared at him, processing the information. She looked at me, most likely thinking of other options.

"I'm sorry. That's all I can offer now." He sat back on the couch and placed his feet back on the coffee table. "Your other option is to wait until I can get you across to El Paso. Just don't count on it being anytime soon. *La migra* is on high alert. If we try to cross, you'll probably be caught and put in jail until they send you back on foot across the international bridge. It's up to you."

"If we accept to cross through the desert, when can we leave?" I was more afraid of the cartel than walking across the desert.

"Prieto's got a van ready to go as we speak. If you miss this ride, you'll be stuck for another two weeks to a month until the next trip."

I needed to leave Juárez, no matter the risk. I had to put some distance between the cartel and myself. "If we cross through the desert, which is closer, Houston or Phoenix?" I asked.

"Phoenix is about an hour from where you'll be picked up by Prieto's people in Casa Grande."

"Okay, I'll do it."

"Rosa, are you sure?" Aleida asked. "It sounds dangerous."

"Yes."

Thoughts of a pink cross without a picture came to mind. *What was I thinking?* Nobody knew me. I wouldn't even get a pink cross.

"Can we go now? I need to get to the US."

"I'll go into town and talk to Prieto," Alfredo said and started putting on his boots. "What about you?" he asked Aleida.

Aleida thought for a moment, then gave me her mischievous grin. "I wouldn't miss this adventure for the world."

"Then it's settled," Alfredo said. He took the keys from Amanda and kissed her cheek. "I'll be back in a few minutes."

When Alfredo left, I sat wondering if I had it in me to make a journey that sounded so dangerous, but the more I thought about it, the more convinced I became that I had to do it. Staying in Juárez held a worse fate.

I'll make it into the US or die trying, I told myself.

Cuervo & López

After the tacos, López and Cuervo drove back to the orphanage. They parked far enough not to be noticed. López did not want to be close when the girl came up missing. Not that it mattered. Girls from Central America came in and out of the orphanage all the time. No one noticed any of them. No one cared.

Kidnappers, on the other hand, got an infinite fountain of youth.

The sun rose over Juárez as López and Cuervo waited in anticipation for Rosa to come out of the orphanage. By ten o'clock, only a few girls had emerged.

Cuervo grew impatient. "Why hasn't she come out? The place looks deserted."

"I don't know," López said. "They're usually all out by eight or nine."

Cuervo looked at his watch. It would soon be eleven.

"Look," López said. "They're starting to come out."

He put his car in gear and crept forward. Cuervo leaned into the windshield to look against the bright sun with sleepy eyes. He tried to get a good look at the girls coming out of the building.

"I don't see her," he growled.

"Find that damn girl," Cuervo ordered angrily.

"Be patient. I'll go ask one of those girls over there for her," López said, pointing.

"Do it now!" Cuervo snapped.

López parked the car in front of the orphanage and got out. He tried to look professional. A small girl stood in the shade playing with a naked doll. She looked at him innocently.

"Come here, little girl," López said.

The young girl shook her head.

López reached into his pocket for some change and offered it to her. "Do you want some money?"

The young girl came closer and picked the coins from his hand.

"I need you to do me a favor."

"What?" she asked.

Other girls gathered around her, hoping to receive some coins, too.

"I need you to go inside and call a girl for me. Her name is Rosa. She came in last night."

"She's not here anymore."

López's jaw dropped open. "Do you know where she went?"

"She left with Aleida to Doña Lupe's Tacos. They're going to cross the river."

López remembered the girl working the taco stand and how she tried to hide her nervousness through fake smiles. The more he thought about it, the more he remembered both women acting nervously. He walked back to the car and braced himself for Cuervo's reaction.

Cuervo impatiently spewed, "Well?"

"She's not here." He put the car in gear with the taco stand in mind.

Cuervo was furious. "Where the hell did she go?!" He looked directly at López, as if the wrong words were bullets to López's head.

López let out a deep breath. "To Doña Lupe's Tacos."

"Where is that?" The answer suddenly hit him. "Are you shitting me?"

"She ran off last night with another girl, probably before we got here."

"Damn, damn, damn!" He smashed his fist onto the dashboard after every curse, then glared at López. "You imbecile!"

"How was I supposed to know she would go there?"

"Get going to the taco stand. She could be anywhere by now." Cuervo laughed with rage.

"No wonder the two taco ladies were nervous last night."

"Who isn't nervous around you?"

Cuervo gave López a cold stare, then faced forward.

They arrived within minutes. López parked facing the front door of the home. Both men rushed out of the vehicle, leaving the doors open and the engine running.

Cuervo kicked in the front door with his gun in hand.

Doña Lupe looked up from the pile of beef she was preparing. She recognized them immediately. "What do a pair of demons from the pits of hell want here?"

"Where's the girl that came here last night?" Cuervo asked while López searched her home for clues and noticed the dirty dishes and the two backpacks.

"They're gone," Doña Lupe answered.

"Don't kill her until we know exactly where they went," López said.

"I don't have anything to say to you! Get out!"

She knew this day would be her last. She set down the butcher knife as Cuervo breathed on her neck.

"Tell me where they went, old woman." He brushed his lips over her ear. "Or I'll cut off your fingers one at a time with your own knife."

The repugnant breath sent chills through her body. She turned her head toward him, straining her eyes, grabbed the butcher knife and raised the sharp blade up to his face. Cuervo jumped back and grabbed his cheek, then let it go to look at his hand for blood. He felt a cool breeze come in through his cheek. The cut was worse than he thought. He tried to close his jaw, but it hung open. Fear crept through him, leaving him stunned. He closed his jaw with his left hand, holding the flaps together.

Doña Lupe's complexion never changed. He realized, too late, that her countenance was not of a helpless old woman but more of a quick-witted killer. She could have sliced his jugular, but she aimed for the corner of his mouth, slashing his face up to his ear.

"You fuhgen bith!" he slurred.

Just as she started to grin, he raised his gun and shot Doña Lupe in the face. She fell over the pile of beef. The knife clanked to the floor.

López rushed to look out the front door to see if anyone was coming. "Look what you've done! Let's get out of here."

"Fuhgen bith!" mumbled Cuervo, holding his jaws together. "Thake meh tho a dother!"

He grabbed a pink blouse resting on the couch on his way out and placed it on the side of his face. They got in the car and headed to the cartel's doctor.

"Shit!" López exclaimed, slamming his palms on the steering wheel. "I'm really going to miss them tacos."

Cuervo turned his head crookedly, straining his eyes to glare with contempt at López as he held his face together.

Pablo & Angélica

Plastic toys floated in the shallow pool where Wendy and Pablo Jr. played. They sat across from each other, splashing water and giggling, when the phone rang. Wendy jumped out of the pool and ran to the patio table to answer.

"Hello?"

"Hello there," a male voice said, recognizing the voice of a child.

"Is your daddy home?"

"Who's this?"

"Tell Daddy it's Joseph Richter ... DEA."

"Who is it, *m'ija*?" Pablo asked.

"It's Joseph somebody D-A."

"Rosa!" He let go of Angélica and went to take the phone from Wendy. "This is Pablo Reyna."

"Hi, Pablo, we heard from your girl .... Rosa de los Santos."

Angélica stood next to Pablo with Pablo Jr. wrapped in a towel. Wendy waited beside them, dripping wet, anticipating the good news.

"Did she make contact?" Pablo asked.

"She did. And she wanted me to let you know that she's fine. She said that she has escaped from the cartel and that she's hoping to cross into El Paso tonight."

Pablo related the message to his family.

"Thank God," Angélica said.

She hugged Wendy, who could not control her excitement.

"She seemed to be in a hurry. I managed to give her your number before she hung up. She said she would call you as soon as she was across."

"We appreciate the good news. Please let us know if she calls again."

"Will do," Joseph said and hung up.

Pablo discussed the good news with his family. Everyone was happy and excited that Rosa had somehow managed to escape. It was only a matter of time before they saw her again.

Angélica hugged Pablo with tears in her eyes. Wendy danced around the patio, making Pablo Jr. giggle in his mother's arms.

"Yay!" Wendy sang with enthusiasm. "Rosa's coming! Rosa's coming!"

"I better call the general in Honduras, so he can give the good news to Rosa's mother," Pablo said.

"The poor woman must be devastated. This bit of good news will give her some relief," Angélica said.

Pablo let go of his wife and dialed the general's number. They spoke for several minutes about different matters, mostly about Rosa.

That evening, the Reyna family ate dinner in silence as they waited for Rosa's call.

"As soon as she tells us that she's in El Paso, I'll call some of my contacts to pick her up and take care of her until we get there," Pablo said. "Then, we'll take her to her aunt in Houston."

Wendy ran from the dinner table to her room to get Rosa's backpack ready, along with her own. The thought of going on a trip to pick up Rosa filled her young heart with happiness.

Pablo and Angélica smiled, enjoying their daughter's good spirits.

"I'll call Jimmy to see if he can use his government contacts to get Rosa political asylum," Pablo said. "Get the children ready."

Angélica stood up from the dinner table and kissed her husband.

Pablo dialed Jimmy's number.

"What's up, Pablo?" Jimmy said, after looking at the caller ID.

"I've got great news."

"Tell me the kid got away." There was hope in his voice.

"She did. She called the hotline and left a message saying she got away from the cartel and that she's crossing into El Paso tonight."

"Did she leave a number to reach her?"

"No, only that she would call when she was stateside. My wife and I were hoping that you would use your influence to get her political asylum, like you did for us."

"I can do more than that. Our government will be really interested in knowing everything she heard the cartel boys talk about. Text me any information you have on her and a description of what she looks like. I'll forward it to my contacts at Customs. As soon as she calls, tell her to go straight to the international bridge. If she's still in Mexico, just have her walk across and tell the agents who she is. They'll process her and hold her until you get there."

"Really?" Pablo wished that he had called earlier. "It's that easy?"

Jimmy laughed. "You must not know who I am."

"This'll make the wife and kids really happy."

"All I can say is, you've earned the friendship of our government. By the way, how's the rental?"

"Rental's fine."

Both men said their goodbyes and hung up.

The family was ready to go within the hour. All they needed was to get the call from Rosa. They waited until midnight, but the phone never rang. The next morning came, and still no call. Rosa did not call as she had promised. Everyone feared the worst.

The Desert

Amanda, Aleida and I hardly spoke, as we worried about what lay ahead. The more we thought about it, the more we realized that it was going to be a difficult trip. The thoughts and questions that flooded our minds kept us in silent suspense. Yet staying in Juárez was out of the question.

Alfredo came in, relieving the tension. "Okay, here's the deal," he said. "The van's headed for Sonora in an hour. I was barely able to get you on, but we've gotta go now. You girls carrying any luggage?"

"No," we answered in unison.

"Just what we're wearing," Aleida said.

She gave me a questioning look, as if wondering if I really wanted to go through with this.

I looked from her to Alfredo. I was determined to go, with or without her.

"Good," he said. "You don't want to carry anything but the essentials. There's one minor detail."

"Detail?" I asked, fearing that I had been discovered. "What is it?"

"The fee. It's a bit steeper."

"What?" asked Aleida. "We agreed on fifteen hundred pesos apiece. That was our deal, remember?"

"Our deal ... but this is Prieto's deal. He wants two hundred and fifty dollars for each of you before you board the van. Otherwise, they leave without you."

Aleida looked disappointed by the change in price.

"I'm sorry, but it's the lowest he would go. He actually charges five hundred a head, but since he's ready to leave with two empty seats, I managed to bring him down to half price."

"That's okay," I said. "I have the money. Can I use your bathroom?"

Amanda pointed to the door at the end of the hall. I went in and took the money out of the waistline of my shorts. When I came out, I handed the money to Aleida. She counted the five hundred dollars into Alfredo's hand.

"*Vámonos*," he said.

We arrived at a shopping center on the west outskirts of Juárez. There, we would meet the van to take us on our long desert journey. I purchased two backpacks, toilet paper, four packs of flour tortillas, two kilos of dried beef, sweet bread, chocolates, eight gallons of water and rope. We sat in the food court and placed our supplies in the backpacks. Alfredo used the rope to tie the gallons of water to the shoulder straps of the backpacks. Two gallons hung in the front and two in the back. When we were done with the backpacks, Alfredo took them to the VW. We waited by the van for our ride.

After a while, a white, extended van with dark-tinted windows parked in front of the VW. A thin, dark-complexioned young man jumped out of the driver's side and walked toward us.

"*¿Qué tal*, Prieto?" Alfredo said as he greeted his associate with a handshake.

"You know me, working. Where are my *chivos*?"

"These two young ladies right here," Alfredo said, nodding toward Aleida and me.

"Oof," Prieto sighed with relief, "I thought you were giving me the big pregnant one." He looked at Amanda with a teasing grin.

"Whatever, Prieto," Amanda said, annoyed. "I'm not going anywhere with you."

Both men laughed at the thought of having to deal with a pregnant Amanda in the middle of the Sonoran Desert.

"Let's see the parrots," Prieto said.

"What parrots is he talking about?" I whispered over Aleida's shoulder.

"American dollars."

Alfredo handed the money to Prieto.

"Is it all here?" Prieto asked. He looked at Aleida and me with suspicion.

"Quit being an ass," Alfredo said. "It's all there in hundred dollar bills."

He put the money in his pocket, then turned to us and asked. "What're you carrying with you?"

"Just the supplies for the trip," Aleida said.

"Good. Most women think they can bring their entire wardrobe. Let's get going."

We followed Prieto to the van. He got in the driver's seat and turned the ignition on.

We walked between the two vehicles to open the VW's trunk and the van's back doors. The van was crammed with backpacks and supplies. Alfredo wedged in our belongings and closed the doors. He opened the sliding door to let us in. The inside was filled with men, women and more backpacks.

"There's two seats in the back row," Prieto said. "Get in and let's go."

Aleida and I squeezed through to the back seat and sat down. The safety of the van gave me a sense of relief to be leaving Juárez. Aleida leaned across me to wave goodbye to her friends. They waved back with a whispered *adiós*.

The van was soon speeding down the main highway. Prieto drove with easy calm. A large mirror had been added to the front, giving him a wide view of the interior.

"Listen up," he said. "We have six hours to Sonoyta. It's approximately two o'clock. Our first stop will be in Nogales, three hours from here. That's our half-way marker. We'll take a quick restroom break while I fuel the van. We should arrive no later than nine. I have more goats waiting there."

"Why does he call us *chivos*, goats?" I whispered.

"I don't know. Coyotes have always referred to immigrants as goats or *pollos*, chicks," Aleida whispered back.

Prieto gave us an angry look over the rearview mirror.

"You two have something more important to talk about?"

"My sister was asking why you refer to us as goats."

I elbowed her lightly.

"Because you are, okay? That's your answer. Now keep quiet. I don't need to explain myself to you unless you'd like to lead the walk across the desert."

"Sorry," Aleida said, feeling foolish.

A devilish grin drew across Prieto's face in the mirror. He looked ahead and continued with his announcement. "We'll be walking all night. We will take ten-minute breaks every hour on the hour. We'll sleep during the day. Our pickup will be in Casa Grande, Arizona. We'll have to walk ninety kilometers to get there. I've made the trip in five days with four gallons of water ... and as long as seven days with slow people holding me back. You people look healthy. We should make it in five days, or less. Any questions?"

"I have one," Aleida said, raising her hand.

"What?" Prieto asked, annoyed when he saw who it was.

"How far is Casa Grande from Phoenix?"

Prieto frowned. "A little under an hour."

"What are the dangers?" A young woman asked.

"Wild animals, dehydration, heat stroke, robbers."

"Robbers?" I blurted out. "Why would anyone care to rob a bunch of poor migrants?"

"There are gangs from the US who like to rob drug smugglers," Prieto said. "You don't have to worry about them. They're not interested in a bunch of broke goats. But, no worries. I always send a scout ahead to warn us of anything suspicious. That includes border patrol and minutemen."

Prieto turned on the radio. We listened to music until Aleida and I fell asleep on each other. Some of the others fell asleep as well.

We woke up to the movement of the van pulling into a gas station. It came to a stop next to the fuel pumps.

Prieto clapped his hands loudly. "Wake up, everyone. We're in Nogales. I'm going to fuel the van. Everybody, pee-pee poo-poo *y vámonos*," he chanted.

Aleida and I were the last ones out of the van. We followed everyone into the store, heading toward the restrooms.

"Wait," I said. I took her hand. "Let's buy some toothbrushes and toothpaste. I haven't brushed my teeth in days." We paid for our things, then headed to the ladies restroom.

When we came out, the van was waiting for us. Everyone was already inside. Prieto's frustration penetrated through the windshield. "Are you two ready to go, or would you like me to stop at a beauty salon as well?"

"Take it easy, Prieto," Aleida protested. "The place was crowded. We needed to brush our teeth and use the restroom. Who knows when we'll be able to use another decent restroom?"

"Get in and let's go," Prieto said.

The van sped down the highway. Everyone snacked, enjoying the views. Aleida and I chewed gum. We watched the evening turn into night. After that, there wasn't much to see through tinted windows, other than headlights coming at us like shooting stars.

Everyone seemed happy. I felt free and out of danger. I was surrounded by regular people and leaving the cartel behind.

Aleida and I remained awake for the rest of the trip. We talked about our families and how much we missed them. We made plans. The thought of the price we had to pay to have a future made tears well up in our eyes.

"I've never been to Houston, or Phoenix," Aleida said. "El Paso is really nice. The people are friendly. One time I was placed in county jail for a couple of days until I was deported. It was like a five-star hotel compared to the dog pound in Juárez. Food three times a day, sometimes with dessert."

Aleida could talk like a radio. Even when I didn't pay attention, she kept on thinking out loud. It was nice having a friend like her. She kept my mind from wandering into my nightmarish past. Before long, we pulled onto a dirt road that led to a skeletal, cinder-block house.

"Are we here?" the young woman asked.

"Yeah," Prieto answered.

He drove the van to the back of the house. Men and women waited behind a large cargo truck with a tan canopy. Chills ran from the back of my neck to my legs. I began to panic. My heartbeat accelerated as I looked for a way out. I could never forget that truck.

Prieto parked behind the truck and killed the engine. He sat back and waited. A young man came to his window. Everyone waited in silence. My heart drummed in my chest.

It wanted to burst out as much as I wanted off the van. No one moved.

"How we doing?" the young man asked Prieto.

"Good. I'm ready to hit the desert tonight."

Aleida noticed my state of panic. "Are you okay?"

"No." I was trying to remain calm until it was time to run. "I need to pee."

"Prieto," Aleida called.

He looked back through the mirror. "What do you want?"

"We need to use the restroom."

"Wait. The house is busy."

"I can go behind that truck." I blurted out.

"Damn it." He got out and opened the sliding door.

I hurried Aleida to get out, pushing her impatiently. We walked through a few migrants to the side of the cargo truck and stopped at the cab. I didn't know what to do, where we were or which way to run.

Aleida put her hand on my shoulder. "You don't really need to pee, do you?"

I turned around, panic-stricken.

"What's wrong?"

I didn't know if she would believe me. I let out a deep sigh and was about to explain, when we heard them come out of the house. We stepped backward into the dark brush and watched them head toward the van.

Aleida immediately recognized my dilemma and brought her finger to her lips. "Shush."

Goosebumps erupted from my skin when I recognized the driver and the gunman who had chased me. I gasped perhaps too loudly when I saw the four gunmen walk to the van and tell everyone to get out. The passengers did as they were told and unloaded all their supplies. The gunmen drove off leaving our two backpacks on the ground.

Prieto came looking for us. He peeked into the brush. "If you two weirdos are done, come pick up your backpacks, so we can get in the truck and go."

"We'll be right there," Aleida said and gave me a hug. "They're gone." She caressed the back of my head. "Let's go get our backpacks."

"What if one of them is still here and recognizes me?"

"Just come out to where Prieto can see you but stay in the shadows. I'll check if they're gone."

When she gave me the all-clear sign, I followed her to the crowd of immigrants. They waited for instructions from Prieto, while Aleida brought our backpacks over. Then she went to take a peek inside the house. I waited for her to return, fearing for her life. She came out looking normal.

"They're all gone," she whispered when she reached me.

"I need everyone to climb in the back of this truck," Prieto ordered. "It'll take us to the drop-off, where we'll begin our walk."

A tall young man carrying a lantern climbed into the back of the truck and motioned for everyone to follow. The women climbed in, unaware of its evil uses. They stepped around a large stain of dried blood on its wooden floor. Some frowned at it, as if wondering about someone's tragic end.

"Don't step on that blood," Aleida said as if it were someone's grave.

A tear full of awful memories rolled down my cheek. "It's mine."

"What?" she asked, fighting her disbelief.

"That's where I woke up. I was bleeding from my head." My voice went hoarse and weak.

Aleida didn't ask any more questions. She just hugged me from the side and led me to sit in the same place where I had sat with Jazmín the day before. I closed my eyes, overwhelmed by fear.

We waited until the men climbed aboard. Each carried a green military duffle bag. The thick aroma of fresh marijuana filled the truck. Another young man climbed in with Prieto.

"This is what we're going to do," Prieto announced. "Larry here," he pointed at the guy holding the lantern, "will drive us to the drop-off. Simón," he pointed at the other, "will be our scout. The guys carrying those duffel bags will fall away with him at a certain point. You already know what to do from there. We'll meet up in Casa Grande. Is everyone ready?"

"Yes," answered a chorus of enthusiasm.

Prieto turned to Larry. "*Vámonos.*"

The three men jumped out. We heard the cab doors close, followed by the familiar roar of the diesel engine coming to life, this time on a different mission.

A sour taste erupted from my throat, caused by my nervousness, warning me of the impending evil and making me feel like a lamb headed for the slaughterhouse. I let out a short breath and closed my eyes. The truck began to move. Everything about it was familiar to me, the vibration, the bumpy ride …. The truck traveled on a dark, lonely highway and then exited onto a dirt road. The driver turned off the headlights and crept slowly. The familiar brakes screeched to a stop, and I held my breath.

Prieto came to the back and opened the tarp. "We're here. Everyone come down," he whispered.

Aleida and I waited for everyone to get off. I was afraid, not knowing who or what to expect. She picked up her backpack with her left hand and pulled me to my feet with her right. I grabbed my backpack and followed her. She jumped out first. I handed her the backpacks and jumped off. I felt antsy, expecting the worst.

Larry came to the back with the lantern to make sure the cargo bed was empty. After a quick look, he climbed back into the driver's seat. The cargo truck crept away slowly with its lights off. It disappeared into the darkness.

"Everyone, put on your backpacks and follow me," Prieto whispered. "Try to stay quiet. Simón and I need to be able to listen to the desert."

We followed Prieto for an hour beneath a dim moon, then stopped for our first ten-minute break. The one-hour walk helped convince me that everything was going to be all right. It was a close call, but I managed to elude them.

"This isn't so bad," Aleida said. "I could've kept walking."

"And after a while, your body would've shut down," Prieto interrupted from behind. "Then, you wouldn't be able to walk at all. Out here, I've seen the strong fail and the weak survive. You wanna know why?"

"Sure," Aleida said with a sarcastic tone.

"First of all, they listened to me. Secondly, their hearts were filled with courage," he hit his chest twice, "like mine. And out here, that's what'll get you across the desert."

"Okay, Tarzan. We get it," Aleida said, smiling.

"Rest time's over," Prieto then announced. "Time to knock out another hour. Stay close together and don't wander off the trail."

He knew the path by heart. At times, he walked ahead. Others, he fell back to make sure that everyone was accounted for. We were weak and tired by daybreak. Prieto led us to a shrubbery patch where we could each find a little shade to sleep off the rest of the day.

Aleida and I drank over half a gallon of water each throughout the night. It made me wonder if we had enough water. We took our shoes and socks off and lay down next to each other using our backpacks for pillows. I stretched my feet and wiggled my toes, letting the morning breeze air them out. My feet felt relieved. Aleida did the same. We woke in time to see a beautiful sunset. I felt better. A sense of freedom overwhelmed me. It filled me with the courage to keep going.

"Everybody up?" Prieto asked. "I suggest you drink plenty of water and eat a little something. You did good last night. I don't expect any less of you tonight. We move out in fifteen minutes. Any questions?"

"Yeah," Aleida said, walking toward him.

"Why am I not surprised," Prieto said under his breath. "What?"

"Will you let us know when we're actually in the US?"

Everyone looked at Prieto for an answer.

"Congratulations. We crossed the border before daybreak," said Prieto.

"Oh, my God! I made it!" I looked at Aleida. "We made it." It was hard to control my excitement.

"Yeah, well, we still have a long way to go before you can do your victory dance," Prieto said. "Now, unless you two want to throw a party out here, I suggest we move it."

"We're here," I told Aleida, not caring if Prieto disliked my excitement. I was out of reach of the cartel and the Maras. "Now all we need is a payphone."

"Some of the bushes have payphones," Prieto said, laughing.

"I bet he can do this with his eyes closed," Aleida whispered.

Aleida and I walked happily ahead of the crowd until our next break.

"Drink some water and eat a snack. You need to keep up your energy," Prieto said.

We rested for about ten minutes and ate a bit, then Prieto jumped to his feet.

"Time to move. Everyone on your feet, let's get going."

At 7:00 a.m., we stopped again to sleep. This time, there were no trees to give us shade. Aleida and I lay against each other. We were so tired that we fell asleep instantly under the biting sun.

Prieto woke everyone at dusk. Aleida and I lazily put our shoes on and washed our faces, trying not to waste too much water.

At the 2:00 a.m. break, Prieto got everyone's attention. "We're making good time. We might make it in three more nights."

After his encouraging speech, we continued our journey. I grew to like his motivational speeches. He knew how to keep us going, always saying we were doing good and seeming to mean it. We met up with Simón at 3:30 a.m. The men with the military duffel bags said their goodbyes and followed him in another direction.

I was relieved to get away from them. The thought of dealing with anyone interested in their drugs terrified me. I was tired of running into evil men. There was no possible way that I could get away from anyone out here and survive. The desert would hand me over for sure.

At daybreak, we arrived at a sign that read "*Agua para tomar*," but someone had emptied the jugs of water next to it. Apparently, the water was put there by people who cared for human life, but only empty boxes and gutted plastic containers remained scattered on the ground.

Aleida and I looked through the debris, hoping to find a good gallon.

"Who would do such a thing?" I asked, looking around in the early morning light, wondering if the immoral being who did this was still around.

There was no doubt that good people had been there. Who else would go to all the trouble of bringing water all the way out in the desert to save someone's life? But more disturbing was the thought of someone coming all the way out to destroy the only thing that could save lives.

Aleida and I still had a gallon and a half each. We walked about fifty yards from the water sign and stopped to get some sleep under the pale shade of scattered shrubs. We took our shoes off and lay a few feet from Prieto. We were tired, malnourished and filthy. Dirt was encrusted in every wrinkle of our skin. The terrain was covered with sharp rocks that caused pain any way we tried to lie, making it hard to sleep.

I had grown used to the bugs crawling in my hair. I touched the wound on my head. It had turned into a thick, moist scab. I did not mess with it. "Ow," Aleida complained. "Something bit me behind my armpit."

"Let me see."

I lifted her sleeve. At the upper crease of her armpit was a fat tick. I pulled it from her skin and tossed it.

"Ow, what was it?"

"Just a bug."

The Arizona sun rose, taking its vicious toll on our bodies. Yet within seconds, we were fast asleep. That's when the robbers came.

The Robbers

It was very hot, and we could barely sleep on the uncomfortable desert ground. I was suddenly startled awake by someone shouting. I sprang to my feet and saw some of the women crying, begging on their knees not to be hurt.

"No one is going to get hurt," a gruff-looking man said. "I need all of you to gather 'round, so I can ask you a few questions."

Fear and adrenaline transmitted throughout my body.

Two other men walked slowly toward us. One of them—I heard someone call him Lobo—held a double-edged dagger. It was similar to the dagger that the Mara has used to kill Julia. I could not believe my eyes. After all this time and distance, the dagger had found me. I was more afraid of it than the gun the other man was holding. My eyes fixed on the shiny blade, the sun glinting off its surface, laughing at me, mocking me, telling me that this time I would not escape its fate.

I looked down at my shoes. There was no time to grab them. Aleida and I instinctively stepped back onto some sharp desert rocks that cut into our feet.

One of the men made a grab for Aleida's hair, but she quickly reacted with a knee to his crotch. He fell back with both hands between his legs.

We tried to run against the unbearable pain in the soles of our feet but only made it a few yards. Our feet left behind a bloody trail. We would have to face our oppressors.

Lobo came at us with the dagger gripped tightly. He pushed Aleida violently to the rocky ground. I left her there and tried to escape his reach, but then I felt a strong arm grab me from behind and trap my arms. I remembered the groin snatch. He moved away when I scratched his crotch. That's when this Mara, or whatever he was, froze.

Helicopter rotors thundered above, and the robbers quickly dispersed, their attempt to rob us had been foiled.

I waved my arms frantically, trying to get the attention of the helicopter. The rotors grew louder, and then there was action on the ground, all around us. Two border patrol agents were marching Lobo, handcuffed, in front of them. They were followed by two vehicles.

"Ralph," I heard an agent call to one of them and say something in English, like "Women ... smuggled."

I later learned his name was Rafael Martínez, and he spoke Spanish. He found all of us women hiding in the brush, and Aleida and me still on our knees. Other agents got out of their vehicles and brought us bottled water. There were other Border Patrol vehicles that drove up, and we were soon being transported away from the site of the assault.

The United States

"Oh my God! This cheeseburger is delicious," said a familiar voice. "The cheesecake ... awesome. It's so good."

I opened my eyes to look for person behind the familiar voice. Aleida came into view on the next bed. We were in a hospital, recovering from dehydration and some bruises. A tray of food sat on Julia's lap. Next to her bed stood Agent Ralph Martínez, enjoying her enthusiasm.

Aleida turned toward me. "Rosa! You're awake!"

I looked at her with a frown. She handed the tray to Agent Martínez and peeled the blanket from her legs. She swung her bandaged feet out and dropped clumsily onto the cold floor. Aleida winced and paused until the pain subsided.

Agent Martínez rushed to her side. "The doctor said you shouldn't be out of bed unless it's to use the restroom," he said. "And that's in a wheelchair."

He reached for the IV stand and brought it to her to use for support.

Aleida was determined to make her way to me. She hobbled over and shouted, "Oh, God," and hugged me tightly but carefully.

I couldn't help but cry and laugh from the pain and joy.

Angélica woke at the sound of our giggles. She stood up from the recliner where she napped. Pablo Jr. slept in his carrier next to her.

"How're you feeling, kiddo?"

Just one look at Angélica and tears burst from my eyes.

"Angélica," I cried with joy.

"The doctor said you're going to be fine." She looked at Aleida, then back at me. "You were both very lucky."

I found it hard to speak through tears and fear of bad news. "I thought I was going to die and never see you again. How did you find me?"

"Hola, Rosa," Agent Martínez said, from where he was standing next to Aleida. "I'm Agent Ralph Martínez with the Border Patrol."

"He's the hero who saved us," Aleida said.

Agent Martínez blushed. "I was just doing my job," he said. "It was the tattoo on your foot. The doctor called me to tell me about it. I called the number and gave them the code. They gave me your name and contacted the Reyna family." He waited a moment to let his words sink in.

My confusion began to clear up.

"I hear you're quite the fighter. Everyone's already given me their version of the story. I would like to hear yours, maybe ask you a few questions, whatever you can remember about the cartel."

I nodded.

"I'll show you some pictures to see if you recognize any of them. That will help our agents take them down, if they ever decide to cross the border." He smiled. "Would that be okay with you?"

I nodded again.

His smile was confident, assuring me that I would be safe from now on. "For the time being, you two will receive temporary visas during the processing of your petitions for political asylum. The prosecutor is willing to help in exchange for your testimony against Luis Mendoza, aka Lobo. Seems the guy tried to live up to his nickname."

I turned away with tears in my eyes, remembering the wickedness I had seen in him.

"You girls are safe now," he continued. "No one can hurt you here." He reached into his shirt pocket. "Here's my card. Call me anytime you remember anything. Things will come back to you slowly." He gave my hand a gentle squeeze and smiled. "I'll leave you all for now. I'm sure you have lots of catching up to do." A faint smile drew across his face as he was leaving "*Hasta pronto.*"

"*Ba-ay*," Aleida chanted, trying to speak English.

I couldn't help myself. I let out teary bursts of distressed laughter. "You're so goofy," I said, not knowing whether to cry or laugh.

Angélica and I giggled at Aleida.

"What?" She asked, baffled.

There was a knock at the door. "You girls decent?" We heard Pablo ask.

"Come on in," Angélica said.

Pablo and Wendy entered the room carrying a tray of food.

"Rosa!" Wendy exclaimed, running to my bedside. "Are you okay?"

"Yes," I whispered, choked by the sight of her. I was so happy to have found them all here, alive.

"Hola, Rosa," Pablo said. "*¿Cómo estás?*"

"Hola," I whispered with a broad smile on my face.

"Nice to have you back," he said, beaming. "How about some food? Anything in particular you'd like to eat?"

I looked at Angélica to order for me, but Aleida spoke first.

"Agent Martínez brought me a double cheeseburger with fries, a strawberry shake and a slice of cheesecake. Get her that," she said. She turned to me with her mischievous smile. "You're gonna love that cheeseburger and cheesecake ... 100% American!"

"Cheeseburger and cheesecake it is," Pablo said and left, closing the door behind him.

I was so happy that I almost thought it was worth all the trouble I went through to get there. I had experienced so much hate those last few days that I couldn't help but soak in all their love and recharge my inner being with the will to live.

"I have your backpack at home," Wendy said. "My mom didn't let me bring it."

I stretched my hand to hers. "Thank you for taking care of it for me."

Pablo Jr. giggled from his carrier.

"Look who's also up," Angélica said and lifted him to see me. Instant joy covered his small face. He gave me a slobbery smile.

My heart pounded with happiness to have all my new friends here with me.

Soon, Pablo returned with the food. It smelled delicious. After the first bite, I hungrily dug into my food. I took a drink from the shake and swallowed. A small burp escaped my lips. I covered my mouth, embarrassed by my bad manners.

Everyone stared at me with big smiles and burst into laughter, including the baby.

"You're such a pig," Aleida said.

I blushed with a shy smile.

"You know what?" Wendy asked me.

"What?" I asked, relieved that her question would divert the attention from me. "The doctor said that you can come home with us in two days."

I looked at Angélica.

She nodded with a smile.

"What about Aleida?" I asked.

I was concerned for my friend, who had called me her sister from the day we met. She had saved my life. We had so much in common, and I was ready to face the world again with her.

"Where will she go?" I looked at Wendy. "I'm sorry. I can't leave her."

"*Oh, Rosa*," Aleida said with an English accent, "we already got all that worked out way before you woke up." She raised her eyebrows a few times and smiled. "I'm coming with you."

I looked at Pablo. "Is this true?"

Standing next to his wife and children with his arms folded across his chest, he said, "Yup."

Wendy cheered and clapped her hands.

⇢⇢⇢

After two days of observation, the doctor cleared us to go home with Pablo and Angélica. Agent Martínez was there to help wheel us out of the hospital. The sun's rays hit my face, giving me a sense of overwhelming freedom.

As soon as we got to Pablo and Angélica's house, Pablo set up a conference call with General Garza. I was able to see Mamá and Juanito through a laptop. Juanito was so happy to see me.

Mamá looked worried. "When are you coming back?"

"I have to save money for the flight, then I have to ask for permission from the US government."

"Have you seen Aunt Teresa?" Juanito asked.

"Not yet. She's getting a room ready for when I arrive. I'm going to attend school there. And as soon as I finish with school, I will get a job and save money for an attorney to send for you."

"Rosa, come home," Mamá begged.

"I can't. I'm already here. We need to take advantage of my authorization to stay in the United States."

Mamá looked down, disappointed. She sounded different and looked tired, defeated. She was slow to answer my questions. Life had dealt her some severe blows. My only hope was for the three of us to be reunited in Houston with Aunt Teresa.

→→→

Aunt Teresa and I spoke on the phone every day until I was able to make the bus trip to Houston. Wendy was saddened by me leaving. All I could do was promise to keep in touch.

When I arrived at the Greyhound station in Houston, I recognized Aunt Teresa immediately. She was as beautiful as Mamá, only younger, healthier. She had a nicely furnished apartment in southeast Houston. It was a big change from the home I was brought up in. Aunt Teresa was happy to have me live with her.

The high school I enrolled in was a block away. I was determined to learn English and focused my attention on my English-as a-Second Language class. I even enrolled in summer school. I couldn't wait to graduate. I wanted a job to help Aunt Teresa gather goods to send to Mamá and Aunt Hilda.

I got excellent grades and did graduate. And then I got a job as a teacher's assistant in a pre-school. All my experience with Wendy came in handy. And that job allowed me to go to

Houston Community College and then the University of Houston, where I studied to become a teacher, what I had always dreamed of. Best of all, with the help of Agent Martínez, I was able to request asylum for Mamá and Juanito.

Agent Martínez and Aleida fell in love. How could they not? They were two orphans wanting to have a family. He was the son of immigrant parents. His father died trying to cross the desert with his pregnant wife. He was found dead in the desert next to his dehydrated wife. She died in the hospital giving birth. The doctors were able to save the baby boy, Agent Ralph Martínez, and he was adopted by a young couple. When Ralph was old enough, they told him the truth about his biological parents. He went on to become a border patrol agent because he wanted to help immigrants who, like his parents, were trying try to make the dreadful journey across the Arizona desert. He kept in touch with Aleida after our rescue and he eventually proposed, although I think she proposed to him first. It was a true love story of a hero saving a damsel in distress. They had a simple wedding with only a few friends and his parents. Her in-laws loved her. They were fascinated by her stories of survival in Juárez.

My family now extends to Arizona, where Aleida, Ralph, Angélica, Pablo, Wendy and Pablo Jr., have made a life. We keep in touch frequently, and I go to visit them during holidays. When I think of them, I think about the journey that led us here.

What I once thought was chance; I now understand was something else entirely—the strength I'd carried all along, and the kindness of people who chose to help a stranger find her way home. I used to think my life had been shaped by what I was running from. Now I know it's been shaped by what I was running toward—the chance to become who I was meant to be. Every choice I make now is my own. Every door

I open leads somewhere I've chosen to go. One day, I'll be a citizen of this country that gave me a second chance—not because luck finally found me, but because I never stopped reaching for it.